A BRIDGE OF MAGPIES

Struan Weddell, lotus-eating in the Aegean to forget the bitterness of a failed naval career, is suddenly called back to South Africa by the C-in-C, Cape Town. His mission: to guard a stretch of the mysterious, forbidden Sperrgebiet or Diamond Coast, while a team of experts search for the lost city of Doodenstadt.

He meets Jutta Walsh, a beautiful redhead, looking for a clue to her past. But the appearance of a strange Korean survey ship, followed by two brutal murders, catapults them into the present – a present filled with passion and violence and deadly danger . . .

GEOFFREY JENKINS

A Bridge of Magpies

FONTANA / Collins

First published in 1974 by William Collins Sons & Co Ltd
This Continental Edition first issued in Fontana Books 1975

© 1974 by Geoffrey Jenkins

Made and printed in Great Britain by
William Collins Sons & Co Ltd Glasgow

A man is exactly as great as
the tide surging beneath him
Bismarck

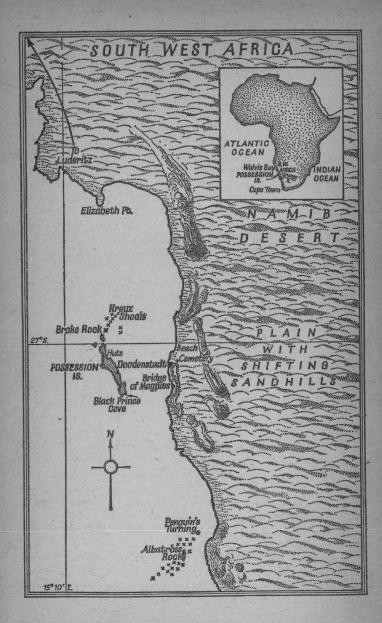

SOUTH WEST AFRICA

To
Luderitz

Elizabeth Pt.

NAMIB
DESERT

ATLANTIC
OCEAN

Walvis Bay
POSSESSION
IS.
Cape Town

S.W.
AFRICA

INDIAN
OCEAN

Kreuz
Shoals

Broke Rock

27°S.

Huts
Doodenstadt

Beach
Cemetery

POSSESSION
IS.

Bridge
of Magpies

PLAIN
WITH
SHIFTING
SANDHILLS

Black Prince
Cove

N

Penguin's
Turning

Albatross
Rock

15° 10' E.

PRELUDE: INTO WAR

26 February 1936
New York Times report: 'The Japanese army, led by revolutionary elements, has taken over the government of Japan. The situation is confused, and shooting is reported from the centre of Tokyo and around the Imperial Palace. Violence and assassination seem to have been directed principally at members of the Cabinet and holders of prominent offices of state close to the Emperor. Among those reported to have been marked out for elimination are the Lord Keeper of the Privy Seal; the Grand Chamberlain to the Emperor; the Emperor's closest adviser and Japan's most honoured elder statesman, Prince Kinmochi Saionji; as well as other traditional hereditary office-bearers, some of whose titles date back many centuries . . .'

27 February 1936
Red Army Fourth Bureau, Intelligence, Moscow. Receipt of urgent dispatch from Head, Far East spy ring, Tokyo: 'Sorge to Fourth Bureau. Motivations for the 2/26 Incident are complex and the murder of hereditary office-bearers close to the Emperor requires careful study. Only one person was observed by agents to have passed through the army cordons surrounding the Imperial Palace during the first twenty-four hours of the coup. He was a young naval ensign in full uniform. He was seen to be carrying a small, well-wrapped parcel and was admitted – apparently by prior arrangement – at a small secret side door of the Palace. Because of a snowstorm, identification was impossible. He re-emerged a short time afterwards still carrying the same parcel. It is not known what his purpose was in visiting the Palace and it seems unlikely that such a junior officer would be admitted to audience with the Emperor.

'The ensign successfully re-negotiated the cordons – probably due to his uniform – and was traced to a small central Tokyo hotel. He came away from it dressed in civilian clothes, then made his way to the docks. Here he boarded a cargo ship, the *Brazil-maru*, due to sail on the next tide for Cape Town, South Africa. The significance of this incident is obscure, but, because of its link with the Imperial Palace, is given in some detail.'

1 June 1943
Signal intercepted by code-breakers at United States Combat Intelligence HQ, Pearl Harbour: 'Japanese Fleet HQ to *Befehlshaber der Unterseebote* (C-in-C U-boats). *U-160*, now refitting Japanese base at Penang, Malaya, assigned to carry out pick-up mission at Bridge of Magpies, South West Africa. Your agent code-named Swakop will be landed and our man Tsushima will be brought off. Suggest active operations by *U-160* against Allied shipping be banned in view of importance of mission.'

2 June 1943
BdU to Japanese Fleet HQ: 'Mission agreed. *Kapitan zur See* Schlebusch to command. Schlebusch experienced in Cape waters, served in wolf-packs *Gruppe Eisbar* and *Seehund*. Cannot agree to restriction hostile operations. *U-160* will, however, confine attacks to unescorted ships out of convoy; or warships.'

7 July 1943
Signal received by escort commander of convoy bound from Walvis Bay to Cape Town: 'Most immediate. C-in-C South Atlantic to commodore convoy WV.5BX. Strong enemy D/F bearings reported Possession Island area. Probably U-boat.'

Commodore WV.5BX to C-in-C South Atlantic: 'Convoy turned away 240 degrees. Sound heavy guns down-horizon vicinity Possession. Proceeding utmost dispatch in frigate *Gousblom* to investigate.'

Liner *City of Baroda* to C-in-C: 'SSSS . . . SSSS . . . am being attacked by U-boat . . . Possession Island area . . . SSSS . . .'

20.15 hours
U-160 to BdU: 'British liner *City of Baroda* 8,000 tons, hit by two of quadruple spread torpedoes position Grid Merten P6 Lat. 27° oo'S., Long. 15° 11'E. Possession Channel.'

20.30 hours
Frigate *Gousblom* to C-in-C: 'Strong U-boat contact Possession Channel. Eight depth charges dropped. Continuing attack. *City of Baroda* seriously damaged, attempting to beach.'

20.40 hours
C-in-C to Convoy WV.5BX: 'Corvettes *Vygie* and *Aandblom* to proceed maximum speed to assist *Gousblom*.'

21.15 hours
U-160 to BdU: 'Attacked by frigate Flower class. Blew up following two hits ex stern tubes. *U-160*'s main ballast pumps damaged by attack, unable to dive. Jettisoned eight mines. Proceeding seawards partly submerged. Will signal position 06.00 hours dawn tomorrow.'

22.15 hours
Corvette *Vygie* to C-in-C: 'Unable to enter Possession Channel due to presence drifting mines and rising gale. No U-boat contact but sighted oil slick. *City of Baroda* ashore at Bridge of Magpies. *Gousblom* presumed sunk.'

8 July 1943
06.30 hours
BdU to *U-160*: 'Report your position immediately.'

10.00 hours
BdU to *U-160*: 'Report your position immediately. Repeat, report your position immediately. Repeat, report your position immediately . . .'

CHAPTER ONE

'Master of the Equinoxes, Lord of the Solstice.' The splendid-sounding title is engraved on one face of the blade of a knife which lies on my desk as I write. It is dark and discoloured. It is an unusual weapon: a thin, pointed blade, widening abruptly at the hilt, which is very flat and hammered out of copper. A design has been tooled into the metal: a seascape about three inches long and half an inch broad, showing a setting sun, and ships sinking after battle. On the reverse side of the blade are scribbled the last words the Master wrote with the lead tip of a Taisho pistol bullet, using it like a pencil, after he had plucked the knife from his side – 'Mei fa tzu!' – 'it is fate!' These words underwrite not only his own fate, but add a strange and awesome new dimension to two of the great decisive naval victories of the twentieth century: Pearl Harbour and Tsushima.

Looking back on it, the Greek island of Santorin, on the Mediterranean tourist cruise belt about sixty miles north of Crete, was an improbable curtain-raiser for the desperate events half a world away on the Sperrgebiet, or forbidden diamond coast of South West Africa, which ended the Master's eight-hundred-year-old reign of influence. Had I been able even to guess at them I would have dismissed them as being as unreal as a nightmare, that soft late afternoon when I sailed my boat into Santorin's great lagoon in the sunset and headed towards the landing-place at Thera.

The town's whitewashed houses on the cliff-top were still brilliantly spotlighted by the sun although the bay nearly a thousand feet below was darkening and taking on those unbelievable sapphires, blues, reds and golds which drive tourists and artists ecstatic. I had really meant to tie up off the villa of Oia situated at the northern tip of the thirty-seven-mile crescent which constitutes the spectacular bay of Santorin. Thera is another three miles away; if I had carried out my first intention the odds are that I would never have received the summons which was waiting for me or, by the time I had, it would have been too out of date to be acted upon.

What really switched me on to sail those extra miles was the prospect of a bottle of Thera's subtly sweet wine, because I'd had a blistering hot sail from Athens to Santorin on the *meltemi* or prevailing north wind. There is a bar on Thera's jetty, too, within easy reach of a mooring shelf of rock, compared with the mere offshore buoy at Oia. There is no regular steamer service to Santorin, only an intermittent cruise liner. Its berth was unoccupied on this occasion, which meant I'd have the bar virtually to myself. These were the small things which decided me in favour of Thera.

Clad in my old jeans I splashed up to the knees in the warm Mediterranean water to make the *Orga* fast, while the sun projected its last theatrical effects on to the knife-edged cliffs soaring to the white town perched high above. I waded ashore to the jetty. The bar was built out of wine barrels, the lower ones full and the top ones empty, with a canvas awning for a roof and a bright blue curtain across the back. The barrels creaked like a ship from the lift of the floating jetty. It was a good place to rinse from one's mouth, with wine, the salt of a hard sail, and to have the sea and your boat right there at your back, a spit away, if you got drunk.

'A bottle of Merovigli, Gigi.'

'My name's Annette, not Gigi.'

'You look like Gigi to me, Annette.'

'You get stoned again tonight, mister?'

'This is plain honest thirst, Gigi. It was bloody hot coming from Athens.'

She was dark, pretty, half Greek and half Alexandrian French. At twenty she could have been ravishing, properly made up; at forty she would be a hag. Her untidy blouse was too tight, and showed a tantalizing curve of white breast in the half-dark of the bar. Like me, she was barefoot.

She placed the bottle of wine in front of me. The first taste made that extra sail across the bay worthwhile.

'Does Professor Cacouris know you drink so much, mister?'

'What the hell's eating you tonight, Gigi?'

'I just wonder whether the professor knows, that's all. All those precious vases and things he gives you to take to Athens in your boat.'

'The best stuff doesn't go with me. I carry only the second-raters.'

'That's not what I hear, mister.'

'Call me Struan.'

'I can't say it. It's a horrid name.'

'Good Scots.'

'It's horrid because she must have used it.'

'Who's she?'

'The girl you ran away from. To Santorin.'

'For crying out! You're letting your imagination run away with you. Okay, then, if you're going to be unfriendly, stick to Mister Weddell.'

She leaned over the plank bar top. 'I'm not unfriendly; I'm only concerned.'

'Good. Then you're falling in love.'

'I would like to, but there's too much going on inside you. You would like me only for a little while in your bed. Then you'd be tired of me and I would be unhappy.'

'Let's stick to ancient vases and the prof's excavations. That way there'll be no emotional spin-off.'

'You don't want to talk about yourself, mister. You want the wine to talk.'

'In that case you'd better bring another bottle. Skaros, this time. Good, strong rough Skaros.'

'Your hair is much too long. It is long and blonde like a woman's.'

'There's no one to see it at sea.'

'You need a shave. Your shirt is dirty.'

'For Crissake, Gigi, put a sock in it!'

'A woman would be good for you, mister.'

'When I want a woman I know where I can get one.'

'It's not that sort of woman you want. You want – a real woman.'

'Listen, Gigi, I could have stopped off at Oia if I'd wanted. I came here for a friendly bottle of wine, not a load of bitching.'

'You came because you're frightened of being alone, mister. You could just as well have gone on to the excavation site.'

'Barbed wire, pumice dust, a spooky old place which blew up and killed everyone 3,500 years ago! No thanks!'

She was right, of course. Professor Cacouris was busy excavating an ancient Minoan city, on the southern horn of Santorin's bay, which was destroyed in one of the great natural disasters of antiquity. It ranks as one of the archaeological finds of the century. The principal treasures have been the superb frescoes which surpass any found elsewhere in the Mediterranean, including the famous ones from Knossos. There were also hundreds of pots, amphorae and vases; these provided me with profitable cargoes for the Archaeological Museum in Athens. The site was so valuable that it had been strongly fenced.

'I hear you are very good now with the old vases and things. One of these days Professor Cacouris will let you help with the frescos.'

'You hear a lot, Gigi.'

'It is a bar. People talk.'

'It's pretty empty tonight.'

'Don't you want to be alone with me?'

'Not in your present mood.'

'I am a woman.'

'You're needling me into getting drunk.'

'You could have done that on your boat.'

'I never drink at sea.'

'You drink on land, though.'

'Sweet Jesus! Can't you stop bitching and leave me to drink in peace?'

'It's not peace you're after – it's passing out.'

'Then you can put the body aboard the *Orga*.'

'Another horrid name.'

'When I get bored by my lady tourists I call her the *Orgasm*. Scares 'em off or lures 'em on. Depends. Actually it's the name of the village in Cyprus where she was built.'

'Cyprus! Who's taking my homeland's name in vain?'

Relieved to get away from Gigi's needling, I swung round on my stool to greet the newcomer. Byron, the Greek – a needle-sharp, devious, sophisticated ex-tanker officer who (if you believed his stories) had been washed by many waters, from the Persian Gulf to Piraeus. His long coal-black hair and lush sideburns against a tanned skin (also visible past swelling chest-muscles nearly to navel level through an open mauve shirt) would have made him the envy of any male model. And he knew it. Women couldn't stay away from him: he knew that, too, and bore the burden stoically. He sailed a bigger boat than mine. What his cargoes were was anyone's guess. Mine was that they were arms and ammunition. He had a *pied-à-terre* – the uncharitable would have called it a

14

funkhole – in the town of Thera, eight hundred steps up the cliff from the bar. We often drank together. He was witty and entertaining; the most delightful liar I've met.

'Byron! Come and help me get the taste of Gigi out of my mouth.'

He grinned and said something to her in Greek which sent her sulking to the far end of the bar.

'I thought Gigi's was the most likely place to find you.' He splashed himself a liberal dose of the Skaros. 'There are three people in Thera looking for you tonight.'

'Three?'

'Myself, Ari, and the postmaster, old Tsaras. He'd fall apart at the seams if he tried the steps.'

'You've found me.'

'But Ari has the telegram. He talked Tsaras into letting him deliver it to you at the excavation site.'

'Ari knew damn well I was away in Athens.'

Ari was an urchin, about ten years old, who attached himself to me whenever I came ashore. He was an orphan and lived in a hovel in Thera. Perhaps the strength of the proprietary feeling about me was in direct proportion to my liberal tips.

'Knowing Ari I'd say he was touching some sucker of a tourist for the fare to the site, and then hoping to double up by what you gave him.'

I laughed. 'You bloody Greeks are all the same at heart – from the cradle onwards.'

'Aren't you interested in the telegram?'

'Why should I be?'

'The typical beach-comber syndrome.'

'Where'd you learn that fine phrase, Byron? It sounds like the exit line of one of your women.'

He grinned. 'She was American. We met on an intellectual level.'

I looked him over. 'And you couldn't bear all that beautiful body going to waste.'

'The telegram is something special. Old Tsaras was all steamed up about it.'

Gigi came over and joined us. 'Maybe it's from Athens, about the vases you took.'

'Never. Athens wouldn't bother about me. They'd get in touch direct with the Prof.'

Byron spreading his hands in the deprecating, sympathetic way that only a Greek can, asked, 'Home?'

'No one gives a damn.'

'Old Tsaras said something about its being long-distance.'

I refilled our glasses. 'Long may the home fires burn. And burn. And burn.'

Byron gave me a penetrating glance and said something to Gigi.

She replied in English. 'He's been in this mood all evening.'

'Listen, you two,' I said. 'I don't want any sympathy and I don't want any tears; I don't need 'em. Santarin's my life. I'm here by my own choice and I like it the way it is.'

'That's why you're not interested in your telegram – maybe from the Cape?'

'Who said the Cape?'

'No one. But that's where you're from.'

'Know the Cape, Byron?'

'I've sailed round it times enough.'

'Fine. Then you'll understand what I'm going to tell you, being a tanker man yourself. Ever hear of the *Walewska*?'

'What tanker man hasn't? Ripped herself open on a reef off South West Africa, carrying a full load of 150,000 tons. In these days of shortages! Then some trigger-happy sonofabitch commanding a frigate sent her to the bottom without even waiting to see . . .'

'I didn't send her to the bottom. I blew her sky-high.'

A charge of plastic explosive under the seat of his pants couldn't have lifted him quicker off his stool.

'Christ! You! *You*?'

'Yes. Me. *Me*!'

Without being able to shift his eyes from me, he said to Gigi, 'Get me some of that whisky you keep stashed away for Americans.'

She gave us both a startled glance and scuttled away.

Byron said slowly, holding out his right hand, 'I want to shake the hand that threw away a million dollars in a flash of flame – poof! Like that.'

'Cut it out,' I replied. 'Don't get melodramatic. I had enough drama from the Press at the official inquiry into the sinking. From everyone, in fact. That's why I'm here.'

'You were kicked out – cashiered?' Byron's voice was full of awe and admiration.

Gigi came back with the whisky and a light which she placed on the bar counter.

'No I wasn't. I quit. Of my own free will. The Navy was on my side. All the way. But there was a king-sized ruckus over the *Walewska*. The tanker company sued the Government for millions. The court hearing went on for months and I was target number one. By the time it was finished I'd had the lot of them. Sure, I would have got another ship but I didn't intend to be strung along for the rest of my life at the end of a radio asking, "Please sir, may I do this, please sir, may I do that?" I was the captain of the frigate and I made the decision. I stand by it.'

'Fit for independent command,' murmured Byron.

'You're stuffed full of other people's cast-off phrases.'

He shrugged. 'If the cap fits . . . So, because you don't like other people's querying your actions and decisions, you pulled up stakes and quit – to Santorin? An ex-Navy captain sailing aimlessly from nowhere to nowhere?'

'Just that. I was fed to the back teeth with the whole bunch of them: inquiry, Navy, lawyers, the lot. Anyway, who the hell are you to tell me what I should or shouldn't do?'

He touched my hand wonderingly. 'A million dollars up the spout!'

'If you go on fiddling with my hand I'll begin to think I'm Lady Macbeth or you're a lady-boy.'

'Not in front of Gigi, please Struan!'

The wine – it had that fire which seems to be at the heart of all wines from volcanic soils – started to give me a warm feeling about Gigi; and I was wondering how to get rid of Byron, who was concentrating on the whisky, when Gigi exclaimed:

'Here's Ari now!'

'Telegram for you, Boss. You must hurry.' He was puffing and grinning as if he'd run all the way down Thera's eight hundred steps. He clutched a buff envelope. Only drachmas would loosen his grip.

'How'd you know, you little bastard? – you can't read.'

'Mister Tsaras said hurry. It's from overseas.' He offered the envelope. 'Money in advance, Boss.'

'Cape,' said Byron. 'I'll bet on it.'

He was right. Although I was half ready to accept that it might be, I nevertheless felt an odd contraction in my stomach when I saw that the office of origin was Cape Town.

It had been sent two days previously and read: *'Your mother critically ill. Imperative you come at once. Groot Schuur hospital.'*

'It's my mother,' I told them. 'It says, come at once.'

'Where is she, Boss?' asked Ari.

'Cape Town. It's five thousand miles away. I can get a plane direct from Athens.'

'Is she bad, Struan?'

I caught myself staring at Gigi's breast and wondering when I'd see her again. For a beach-comber Santorin hadn't been a bad bit of beach.

'Critical. That was two days ago.'

Byron said. 'First you've got to get to Athens. It's 150 miles. It'll be a hell of a beat right into the teeth of the *meltemi*. My boat's got an engine and I'd take you except I've got an appointment on the Turkish coast . . .'

'Thanks all the same, Byron. I'll make out under sail. Pity Santorin doesn't run to a steamer service.'

'Does it say what's wrong with your mother?' Gigi persisted.

'No. I'd guess a stroke, at her age.'

'The other brothers and sisters can be with her . . . in case. You needn't go.'

'There aren't any other brothers and sisters. I'm the only son.'

'And your father?'

'Killed in the war.'

'I'll come and help you sail the *Orga,* Boss,' Ari chipped in. 'Free. No charge.'

I looked at the pinched, pert face, surprised and touched at the generous gesture. He'd miss me – for a day or two.

'Thanks, no, Ari. You'd be left stranded in Athens after I'd gone. I can't tell how long I'll be away.'

Byron assessed the sky. 'You'll have to make a long haul towards Therasia before you'll weather the entrance to the bay, Struan.'

'Yes, the sooner I get cracking, the better. Right now . . . there's nothing to keep me.'

Gigi turned the light away so that I couldn't read her eyes.

'No, there is nothing to keep you.' She went on, speaking almost to herself, 'I wish you'd been drunk tonight then you couldn't have gone. Tomorrow, when you surfaced again, it would have been too late.'

'I'll come back, Gigi. The Cape doesn't hold anything for me any more.'

But she wouldn't reply: just went and prepared some food for my trip to Athens.

Gigi, Byron and Ari waded into the warm sea and pushed the *Orga* clear of the flange of rock which made the easy mooring. Ari chattered excitedly, while Byron passed on some local sailing lore; but Gigi simply stood there with the water swishing round her bare legs. When I brought the stern round and called goodbye she didn't wave or say anything. The *meltemi* was ripping directly into the great bay and I set out, as Byron had indicated, on the long pull towards Therasia island in order to strike through the bay's entrance to the open sea. The business of getting sail on the clumsy old caïque took time and when I looked back all I could see were the lights of Gigi's bar shining against the backdrop of the great cliff.

I set course for Athens – and the Cape.

CHAPTER TWO

The Boeing jumbo jet banked for the landing at Cape Town and I had a glimpse of Table Mountain through the overcast. A fine, cold rain was blowing off the ocean on a south-westerly gale – a typical, miserable Cape winter's day. The sight of the great mountain pitched a load of associations at me and made me depressed. The long tiring air journey – Athens, Lisbon, Las Palmas, the Bulge of Africa, Angola – added its own quota of discouragement. I wondered if I should have come: I would probably arrive too late to find my mother alive. The rain splashed against the plane's windows, a reminder of days at sea on the bridge. I made a derisive comparison between that Cape of Storms sea – a cold, grey, wicked mass, throwing a punch of three thousand miles of open water behind it – and the Aegean. The *meltemi* was a woman's wind compared with a Cape buster, and the tideless waves breaking on the picture-postcard islands had no more guts than a junkie.

Maybe my contempt for the classic sea had showed itself by the way I had hurled my old caïque into the *meltemi* after I'd left Santorin; I used a dozen seaman's dodges to avoid the deadly tack and tack-about into the teeth of the same wind which once had blown the Greek heroes from Troy. I had finally reached Athens only a few hours before a Cape flight was due to leave. In the rush I hadn't managed to have my one thin tropical suit smartened up, and it sat crumpled and untidy on me. I hadn't a tie but had bought a black string bootlace thing off a plane steward. The other passengers' eyes told me I looked like a kinky beach-boy.

After the landing, I was checking through the usual formalities. The sluicing rain on the way across the tarmac from the plane to the terminal building hadn't acted as the best of valet services to my suit and hair. They were soaked. I stood by while an immigration official examined my passport. He gave me a considering look, reverted to my photograph, regarded me again, then went off to an inner office.

Another official appeared and also considered me. Both disappeared for some time and returned with a third man wearing a cap and plastic raincoat over his uniform.

'*Wat is die Moeilikheid* – what's the trouble?' I asked.

'No problem,' answered the desk official. The raincoated man eyed me.

'You are Mr Struan Weddell?'

'Yes. It's all there, in the passport.'

'It's hard to tell from the photograph. The hair and the beard are new.'

'It was taken two years ago when I left South Africa.'

He stamped the passport and handed it to me.

'This gentleman would like a word with you.'

I then noticed the third man's cap under its plastic covering. He was a naval officer. He grinned at my surprise.

'Captain Weddell?'

'Yes.'

'Compliments of the C-in-C, sir. We've been waiting hours for the jet: she's late. Transport is laid on for you.'

'How did the C-in-C know I was coming?'

'I don't ask questions, sir. I was detailed to meet you and fly you to the hospital.'

'Fly?'

'Helicopter, sir. She's out on the apron.'

'Hold it. You mean to say the C-in-C actually . . .?'

'You must ask the C-in-C why, sir. I don't know. My orders were to meet the Athens flight and fly you to the hospital.'

I was touched. He'd no call to be generous after the way I'd thrown his job in his teeth as a result of the *Walewska* business. As I told Byron, the tanker tore out her bottom on a reef off South West Africa and I sank her. Her skipper was trying to cut corners when making a landfall at Panther head, which is the main landfall for ships heading up the Sperrgebiet, or forbidden diamond coast. The land looks like an old bone that's been gnawed and thrown away. It is desert and has the world's richest diamond fields. That is why it's forbidden territory – all eight hundred miles of it. I'd commanded a fisheries patrol frigate, and part of my job was to police the Sperrgebiet from the sea. On land there are motorized patrols and helicopters. The other part of my job was to keep an eye on the trawlers of all nations which frequent the coast. The Atlantic here matches the land for riches. Even the Grand Banks can't beat the fishing. There is a third source of riches on this God-forsaken shore: a string of rocky little inshore islands coated in bird guano – white gold, they call it. The *Walewska*'s oil would have killed off the bird and marine life of these islands if I'd allowed her to stay afloat. So I'd blown her up with special charges so that the oil was destroyed – rather than send her to the bottom and risk seepage from the wreck. The danger was compounded by a strong current which flows through the guano isles. I'd acted fast, and on my own initiative.

I meant what I said: 'Thanks. Thanks for coming.'

His grin behind the beard made him look ridiculously young.

'Let's go,' I said.

'First, I'll go and borrow you a coat from the chopper. You'll get soaked.'

'It doesn't matter.'

'It was told to look after you. You must be bloody cold, if I may say so, sir.'

'I hadn't noticed – not after the Navy's warm reception.'

He smiled, then strode out to the helicopter and brought me back a weatherproof. I felt good. I hadn't been looking forward to the cheerless process of landing unmet and making my way to a deathbed. We fell into step and made for the machine.

I broke the companionable silence.

'Is my mother still alive, Lieutenant?'

A flicker passed across his face. His reply was neutral.

'I don't know, sir. I've told you what my orders are.'

'She must be, otherwise all this wouldn't have been laid on.'

'I suppose so, sir.'

'Thank the C-in-C when you report, will you? I'll also call later and thank him personally.'

He didn't answer as he held open the door of the Wasp.

'Here we are, sir.'

A thick-set petty officer gave me a hand up and took my case. The pilot nodded. There were the usual clattering preliminaries and then we were airborne.

The international airport lies about fifteen miles out of Cape Town. Facing it, the city is on your right and a chain of suburbs and resorts stretches to the left as far as the naval base at Simonstown.

We lifted. Thin rain cloud drifted past the Perspex. I settled back and wondered whether the helicopter would land at the hospital – they must have built a heliport there while I'd been away. The craft clattered and banged onwards; after a while we changed direction and altitude. We'd dropped below the main body of the overcast, but it was still very thick. Then, through a gap, I spotted a big Old Cape Dutch style farmhouse and vineyards. I couldn't recall vineyards near the hospital.

Now I sat up with a jerk. I was sure I'd spotted a famous pass called Constantia Nek. If so, we weren't within a dozen miles of the hospital, but nearer the naval base.

It was useless trying to question my guide, because of the earphone muffs we wore as protection against the machine's racket. I tapped him on the shoulder and gestured at the landmark, but all I got back was a thumb's-up signal.

We sank lower and there were vineyards again. Then trees appeared below, together with a concrete landing-pad, a black-top road and security gates. Flanking the landing place were anti-aircraft batteries. Wetness streamed down the black barrels as they tracked the helicopter down.

I waited until the rotors' clatter cut off.

'What the hell gives, Lieutenant?'

Armed Navy guards in wet oilskins opened the Wasp's door.

'There's a security check. This place is banned to civilians.'

'But . . .'

'This way, if you please, sir.'

Near the guns was a sort of concrete cupola which housed a lift.

'See here, Lieutenant, this is no more a hospital than . . .'

'The lift, sir.'

The doors clashed shut and we dropped to ground level. They reopened to reveal a pair of massive steel sliding doors, about twice the height of a man and four times as broad, set into bunker-type concrete. My guide nodded to a guard, who used a red telephone standing in a niche. After a few words from him the big doors slid open as if operated by some hidden agency.

'Inside, if you please, sir.'

'I don't see why . . .'

But I was already in; the doors thumped shut and we were in a bare brightly lit concrete chamber. Another pair of steel doors lay ahead. We might have been on a Mars science-fiction set, except for a Navy guard sitting facing us behind a bullet-proof window. His telephone was yellow.

'The doors ahead can't open before those behind are closed,' said my guide conversationally. 'And that can't be done without that bloke's say-so. Security's a hundred per cent. Those doors can also take a direct hit from a 500-kilo bomb, without a blink. This space becomes an airlock in the event of a nuclear attack.'

'If you tell me this is Hitler's bunker and you're Eva Braun, I'll believe you.'

'No dolls here, more's the pity. Males, rugged as they come. Hand-picked. Zip-lips.'

'Listen! Before I move another bloody step . . ?'

'You'll have to now, sir. Can't stop here.'

The huge doors rumbled open on their runners. Several concrete passages radiated on the far side. I was propelled into one of them and my escort fell into step with me.

'Silvermine,' he said. 'It's called Silvermine. They found the metal here in 1687, I think it was.'

'I hear your words but I don't know what the devil you're talking about! Silvermine! Nuclear attack! Airlock!'

'It's new since your day, sir. It's the Navy's operational headquarters. It's sunk into the side of the mountain, storeys deep . . ?'

'The hospital, man! My mother's dying!'

'The C-in-C will tell you about that, sir. We're almost at his office.'

We turned into a side tunnel; a small pair of doors, now open, could seal off the passage. Nevertheless, we faced the same elaborate security paraphernalia. When finally we were admitted to an ante-room it looked less like outer space: I saw an ordinary office desk, a typewriter, filing cabinets and wall-to-wall carpeting.

'Hello, Godfrey,' said my escort. 'Well, here he is.'

'Welcome to Silvermine, Captain Weddell,' replied the aide. 'The C-in-C's expecting you.' Inevitably he checked on the telephone before taking me in.

The admiral sat at an outsize desk – the same tough, wiry little man with the boxer's broken nose and lopsided grin.

His eyes were welcoming now but I'd seen them on occasion shuttered and opaque. That was the time strong men ran.

He rose, hand outstretched. 'Good to see you, Struan.'

'I half expected to find a little green man in a space suit.'

'You get used to it pretty soon.'

'It isn't a hospital, though.'

'No, it isn't a hospital.'

'Look, sir, I appreciate what you did in sending a chopper to the airport for me. I don't know how you knew about my mother. But there's been a snarl-up somewhere: the lines must have got crossed. I've been brought here instead of to the hospital. I've got to get there – quick. Every hour may be vital.'

'Nothing got snarled up. She's alive. Relax. Have a cigarette.'

But I remained standing. He eyed me through the smoke.

'You've put on weight, Struan.'

'For God's sake! I didn't come here to talk about my weight. My mother . . .'

He nodded towards a cluster of three coloured telephones.

'Use the blue one. You'll find her at home. There's nothing wrong with her.'

The friendly eyes were starting to cloud up. But I told myself angrily I wasn't one of his subordinates any longer.

'The hospital sent me a cable to Santorin . . .'

'I sent it. Your mother knows.'

'*You* sent it! For crying in a bucket! You mean to say you bluffed me into rushing back to South Africa – what the devil for?'

'Sit down. Listen. I've a lot to say to you.'

'I'll stand. I'm going soon.'

He was leaning back in his swing chair, looking at me with a kind of amused contempt which needled me further.

'This outfit is called Silvermine . . .'

'I've already heard.'

'. . . It's probably the most modern naval operational headquarters in the world. Just behind me, through there –' he gestured – 'is the operations room. Top secret. Utmost top secret, in fact. So is this office. The whole place is bugged, monitored, lousy with devices, hidden beams and so on.'

'I didn't come here to listen to all this bull.'

He let go the chair and it came forward with a bump

against the desk.

'You didn't come here: you were brought. But you're an unauthorized civilian on top secret premises for which you can be locked away for a long, long time, simply at my say-so.'

He grinned and I didn't care for it.

'You couldn't go, even if you wanted to. Now shut up and sit down and listen to me.'

I sat down. I also took a cigarette.

'I had you shanghaied at the airport. I sent you the faked cable to bring you to Cape Town—with your mother's consent, I might add.'

'Why the devil couldn't you leave me alone?'

'See here. A couple of months ago one of my officers was on holiday in Santorin.'

'If I'd known I'd have given him a sail for old times' sake.'

'Spare the sarcasm. He was a junior in your day. You did meet him but you were too drunk to recognize him.'

'It has happened.'

'It did happen, and pretty often, I'm told.'

'Why kidnap me to Naval Headquarters? Alcoholics Anonymous is the place you want.'

'Don't over-dramatize. Snap that defence mechanism of yours out of top gear. Drinking may be a part of your *luilekkerlewe* (sweet life) but you're not a drunk.'

'Thanks for those few kind words.'

'My man overheard you using an Afrikaans expression in some dive on a jetty. That put him on to you.'

'It's a bar, not a dive. There's no entertainment except Gigi.'

'I was told there was a Greek tart there.'

'Gigi's a bit flashy but she's not a tart.'

'The long and the short of it was that what he took to be a bum in a bar turned out to be Captain Struan Weddell. Ex-Navy.'

'Emphasis on the ex.'

'I told you not to be a bloody fool and quit because of the *Walewska* affair. But you wouldn't listen. You gave me the V-sign and vanished.'

'I can look after myself. If this is your idea of putting me on the carpet, I don't buy it. The hell with it! The hell with you too!'

'Stop getting up! You've stretched your craving for being

a loner just about to the limit at Santorin. There aren't such things in this modern world as blissful isles of escape. Once I'd located you I had a check made. Soft, boozy, aimless. Women. Just enough to live on. Toying with archaeology. That sort of crap.'

'Your dossier's spot-on.'

'A purposeless layabout.'

'So what? It's my life.'

He spoke into a pale pink intercom.

'Has he arrived?'

He nodded at the answer, apparently satisfied.

'As you rightly say, so what? I knew I'd be wasting my time if I cabled asking you to come back. I had to winkle you out of Santorin – and I've done it.'

He eyed me through the cigarette smoke like a strategist who's pulled off a clever trick against the enemy.

'Again, so what?'

I'd got all set to take a dim view of another penny-lecture broadside from him when he said in a completely changed voice, 'I brought you here because I want your help with a problem, Struan.'

'You must be joking! Me!'

'You. You were meant for a somebody, not a bum.'

His eyes were distant and only half friendly.

My retort didn't have the range. 'The moral cat-o'-nine-tails again.'

He ignored the crack. 'I know you're screwed up still about the *Walewska* business. You don't have to be. You never had to be, from where I sit.'

'I haven't heard your problem.'

'Don't blow your nut and don't interrupt. You're well acquainted with the Sperrgebiet so that part of it doesn't need explaining.'

I thought of that grim coast and its grim grey islands, and the *meltemi* and the Greek isles stuck in my craw. You'll find Sperrgebiet names on old whalermen's graves in New England . . . a sailor's boast to be remembered by.

'I said, I don't know your problem.'

'What d'ye know about Possession Island?'

'Heard of it, of course. Never been there. The navigation's tricky. Not the place for a big ship like my frigate.'

'It's the largest of the guano isles, and that isn't saying

much. Any idea how wide that channel is between it and the mainland?'

'I'd guess about two miles.'

'You know Doodenstadt?'

'It's only a name.'

'On the mainland opposite Possession is Doodenstadt – the Town of the Dead.'

'A bit fanciful for a coast which doesn't have a human, let alone a town, for hundreds of miles.'

'It's really only a big group of rocks sticking out from the desert into the sea. The rocks are big and square like houses and there are lanes resembling streets. Hence the name. It's all very realistic, they tell me. It's half under water most of the time. What's Santorin like, Struan?'

'Real houses. Three storeys, some of them. Real streets. Fine carvings, superb frescos. The dry volcanic ash has preserved them, even the colours.'

'Would it surprise you to hear that a fresco has been found at Doodenstadt?'

There wasn't any sound except the air-conditioning; there were no residual noises in the flat silence after our voices stopped.

I said at length: 'I can ride with Santorin but not Doodenstadt. The place has been known for at least a century. If there'd been frescos, someone would have discovered them long before now.'

'Doodenstadt turns out to be not merely a figure of speech. It's real, it's a town. A lost city.'

'And Atlantis lies under Table Bay. I never thought I'd live to see the high office of Commander-in-Chief knocked by fantasy.'

'I almost said the same thing myself at first.'

'I've seen the way the egg-heads' minds go into orbit over Santorin. They steam themselves up into all sorts of improbable conclusions – it's Plato's drowned paradise, God knows what else. I'll bet it's the same about Doodenstadt.'

For an answer he rummaged in a drawer and produced a volume book-marked with newspaper cuttings.

'Ever heard of Farini?'

'No.'

'Farini was an American traveller who claimed to have

28

camped at a lost city in the Kalahari desert in . . . let me see
. . . 1885.'

'The Kalahari isn't the Sperrgebiet. Moreover, it's half-way
across the sub-continent from Doodenstadt.'

'I'm not suggesting a connection. Only it's interesting that
Farini found an ancient ruined city covered by sand.'

'Says who – Farini?'

'He wrote a book about it.'

'I'll bet he did.'

'I value your scepticism, Struan. Farini's discovery has
been kicked about by everybody. The weight of the evidence
is that he *did* finds ruins and that probably they've since
been covered over again by sand. His son even took a photograph of the place. Scores of expeditions in modern times
have searched for Farini's lost city – without success.'

I helped myself to another cigarette.

'The Navy's become a fun outfit since my time. We never
thought much beyond ships and the sea. Lost cities didn't
figure.'

'You've seen Santorin. There could be a parallel.'

'Look, I'm not an expert. I'm the dimmest sort of amateur
when it comes to this sort of thing. I've seen some of
Santorin's frescos – they're much too valuable for a duffer
like me to touch. My boat provided cheap transport for
some second- and third-rate stuff.'

'We don't lack experts. In fact, you're going to meet cne
of them pretty soon. He's sitting right outside waiting for
me to ring. Dr Hellmut Koch. He discovered Doodenstadt's
fresco.'

'Then why bring me here? – and with all that elaborate
cloak-and-dagger?'

'Think, man. For more than a century the Sperrgebiet's been
the mysterious, out-of-reach, get-rich-quick mecca of every
crook who could get himself a ship to sail in. First it was
for the "white gold" guano. Then diamonds. Now Doodenstadt could be stage three, sparking off a big-scale treasure-
hunt. I couldn't give a damn whether Doodenstadt is Atlantis
or a link in Farini's chain of cities under the sand. What I
am concerned about is that a lot of hoodlums could invade
the Forbidden Coast.'

'Not for the sake of a fresco or two.'

'That won't be the way the treasure-hounds will view Doodenstadt. That fresco will be an arrow pointing straight at buried treasure unlimited. Gold, ancient jewels, all the never-never stuff. Soon they'll be saying Captain Kidd's treasure is peanuts beside what lies under Doodenstadt. That's the way a treasure legend snowballs and there are always suckers to believe it. No-good suckers. When they don't find treasure they'll turn to a spot of illicit diamond running as a backstop against their costs. And ships willing to do that sort of thing cost plenty.'

'This is a job for the diamond police, not the Navy.'

'You're wrong. There are hundreds of foreign trawlers on the fishing grounds. If word leaked out about a lost city at Doodenstadt, the Navy's life wouldn't be worth living. And one thing's sure: the diamond police won't play ball over this hot potato. They argue, rightly, that the land security's as tight as all get-out but that it's wide wide open from the sea. And the sea is the Navy's responsibility.'

'Station a frigate at Possession. That would plug the gap.'

'How long do you think Doodenstadt's secret would stay a secret if I did that? Every trawler and every island headman would start asking, 'What's new? What's a frigate up to? Another big diamond strike to protect?" The buzz would spread like a veld fire. No, a warship would be the surest way to advertise a lost city. Besides, how effective would it be? You know that bloody Sperrgebiet weather – a gale twenty days a month. And the fog: every day there's that damn fog. Every day there's half an extra smuggler's night thrown in gratis. You can't win. You know yourself you can't operate a big ship like a frigate round Possession. There's no sea room and the reefs are thicker than pock-marks on a Hottentot's face.'

'A brace of fast patrol boats would do the trick.'

'Logistically sound; but, economically and ecologically, crap. Possession's one of the most important guano islands. Disturb the birds with high-powered boats' engines and they'll push off. No guano, no white gold.'

'We're playing verbal skittles. I put 'em up, you knock 'em down.'

'You're the only skittle that can't be knocked down.'

'What the hell do you mean?'

'The "lost city" game must be played cards close to the

chest. There must be security until Koch has time to sort out what really gives. But security with a difference: it mustn't seem to *be* security. What's needed is a one-man outfit – you.'

'*Me?*'

For reply, he spoke into the intercom. 'Send in Dr Koch.'

Koch was a tall, rangy Austrian with slicked-back hair and a pair of humorous grey eyes behind horn-rimmed glasses. He didn't look much older than me.

'This is our man, Koch.'

'Hotfoot from Circe and her wine, eh?' (It was the first flash of a sense of fun I came to know well; that, and his total dedication to his work: the investigation of sea-shore middens belonging to *Strandlopers* – 'Seashore Walkers' – who were a vanished Stone Age race of Sperrgebiet nomads.)

The way he said it turned me on. 'Gigi,' I corrected. 'Her name was Gigi.'

'The memory of sweet days ferments inside me,' he sighed. 'I remember once, in Athens, a bottle from Santorin . . . slightly sweet, but it had a fire . . .'

'You can swop boozy reminiscences later,' snapped the C-in-C. 'He hasn't accepted yet, Koch. Tell him about the fresco.'

'The admiral's put you in the picture about Doodenstadt?'

'Aye.'

'Here's the set-up: there are these enormous blocks of rock half-in and half-out of the breakers. There's the old wreck of a big liner lying on top of them. I was snuffling about there for middens one exceptionally low tide – a rare good chance for me: you don't often see the water as low as that. Or so calm, also a rarity in those parts. A large cave, originally a fault in the rock strata, had been opened up and formed by wave action. I went in. At its landward end the cleft led to a regular-shaped rock tunnel which ran clean under the desert. This tunnel was higher than the sea cave and out of reach of the water, and so quite dry. I went in only a little way, as I was scared of being trapped by the tide returning. But I spotted this with my torch and got a shot of it.'

He tossed me a photographic colour slide. I held it up to the light.

It might have been a duplicate – with variations – of one of the most precious finds to come out of Santorin: it was a small fresco showing two *gemsbok*, or oryx, cavorting, tails swishing, heads held high. Certainly the artists' treatment – light and graceful – was uncannily similar in the two cases. The Santorin scene had presented the pundits with an inexplicable enigma: had oryx (in modern times found only in the Middle East and Africa) once inhabited the Aegean islands? Or had there been a land link, now submerged by the ocean?

'I'll be damned!' . . . I elaborated on the Santorin discovery.

Koch was afire when I'd finished. The C-in-C sat back with the air of a magician who has produced rabbit quintuplets out of a hat when he'd expected one.

Koch's words tumbled over one another. 'If Struan's right we may be on to something much bigger than we imagined! If Doodenstadt's tied up in some way with the Middle East or a vanished Minoan civilization . . .'

His use of my Christian name was a tacit assumption that I was going along with the lost city idea. The C-in-C assumed that, too.

'It'll be a one-man assignment, Struan. And, let me warn you, no bed of roses. Also it's winter, and the island may be pretty miserable: there's no one else there, so you'll be secure, with a capital S. I've fixed a ship for you to use, a fishing cutter. She's there at Possession now. Koch wants at least a couple of months to explore. You'll assist, of course. We'll give you headman status. You'll relieve the present zombie, who has started mainlining. You'll go there in the usual manner of a new headman taking over – in the island relief coaster. You'll wear a headman's uniform. Nothing to arouse anyone's suspicions. Questions?'

Steady, Weddell, steady, I told myself. They're rushing fences. A nasty little voice at the back of my brain whispered: *you're being taken for a ride, a very clever shop-window to hide the true nature of the goods on offer. The soft sell, Sperrgebiet-style.*

Something of this must have been noticeable in my tone because the C-in-C glanced sharply at me as I asked, 'Communications? How do I contact you?'

'I've got a special transceiver – voice radio – laid on. RCA Navy job. Enough frequencies to chat to the moon. But that doesn't mean you're going to use it like a telephone.

Minimal use means maximum security. In the islands they gossip over the air like housewives in a supermarket. It's their main form of relaxation. Remember, anything you say will be public property within hours. Play any situation by ear. Don't come running to me.'

I leant forward and ground out my cigarette in his ashtray. He frowned.

I said deliberately, 'I hope this conversation is being bugged, because if you have any doubts about what I say you can make a playback. You needn't worry about that radio because I won't be using it – ever. I know a rehabilitation package when I see one, even when it's wrapped up in lovely romantic ribbons like these.' I indicated the colour slide. 'Next time, find someone stupider. If that's African then Siberia is Atlantis. I don't intend to be tricked into being landed on some remote bloody guano island five hundred miles up the most God-forsaken coast in the world, with no chance of a drink or a woman, because of your do-gooder inclinations. Thanks for the ride. It was nice seeing your superstar headquarters. In short, you can put your lost city up your admiral's jersey!'

He made a sound deep in his throat; half rose; and plucked away a switch and broken length of wire from his desk.

'We aren't bugged any longer: what I've got to say is for your ears alone. That slide is the real McCoy . . . but the hell with that. What is important is guts, and when I wanted someone with guts for a special job my first thought was of one man – Struan Weddell. Why d'ye think I went to all this trouble if I didn't believe you have what it takes? Seems I was wrong, dead wrong. Possession takes guts: I saw it at work there during the war and I'll never forget it. Convoy WV.5BX. I was in one of the escorts, a corvette. The escort leader was a frigate called *Gousblom*. Off Possession we heard the sound of heavy guns: a raider or a pocket battleship, we thought. That didn't stop *Gousblom*. That pipsqueak of a ship went off at full speed to fight. It was straight suicide, and she knew it. But she'd rather have thrown herself away than let the enemy get at the convoy she'd been entrusted with. Then a U-boat bagged *Gousblom*, right in the Possession channel. Her magazine went up. The U-boat had just torpedoed a big liner . . .'

'The *City of Baroda*,' added Koch. His manner, too, was

hostile now. '. . . the one I was telling you about, lying on top of Doodenstadt's rocks.'

It wasn't the barb or the C-in-C's taunt but the sincerity behind it which altered my decision. It *was* the job which was his objective, not me. I believed him now, believed Koch too. If I accepted the Possession assignment I'd have a ship of sorts, because they still run the guano islands as ships, and I'd be her captain. Independent command, I grinned to myself. Maybe too bloody independent; with only birds for a crew and bird-shit for a deck. But it might turn out to be fun, and deep-down I knew that a spell away from bottles and women wouldn't do me any harm. Weddell the Happy Hairshirt Hermit . . . I felt happier than I'd been in years . . .

'. . . we never found out what those heavy guns were that *Gousblom* heard,' the C-in-C was rasping with his eyes stabbing me like a laser beam. 'There was no big stuff, either ours or the Germans', about. But that's beside the point. It's a question of guts. If you chicken out . . .' He made a pansy's wrist-flapping, hand-on-hip gesture which would have won him a music-hall encore and would have been utterly ridiculous if it hadn't been part of his anger. He tugged at the bit of wire and glared at me.

I gave him a moment or two to run down. 'I've changed my mind. I'll go.'

If my turnabout had any effect upon him, he didn't show it. Maybe he claimed all the credit for himself. The frost didn't leave his eyes.

'You're under my orders from now on. No signals, except in emergency. Clear? Koch will fly back to Luderitz the day after tomorrow. All the paperwork is jacked up already. You'll sleep here. Silvermine has plenty of accommodation – part of the nuclear preparedness game. Go and apologize to your mother from me. You will not discuss Doodenstadt with anyone – understood?'

'Understood – sir.'

'Any . . . ah, attachments at Santorin?'

'Gigi? Give me some credit!'

'Good. That's all.'

Koch took my arm in a friendly gesture as we made for the door.

'Now what in hell do you think a Minoan *gemsbok* is doing on the Sperrgebiet?'

34

CHAPTER THREE

Panther Head is the gateway to the Sperrgebiet. Crooks and
'cruisers', gun-runners and guano dopes, New Bedford whalers and pirates – Captain Kidd included – have homed in on
this dirty grey chunk of eroded desert, sticking out into the
sea about sixty miles north of the Orange River; taken
sights on the triple peaks of the *Buchu Berge*; and set course
for sinister destinations among the fourteen fog-shrouded,
guano-stained islands skirting the coast.

The name itself stirs up the mud of history: *Panther* was
a well-armed thousand-tonner of the German Navy that kept
order on the coast in the first mad days of the diamond strikes.
She sailed into notoriety and history before World War I
by trying to seize the Moroccan port of Agadir for the
Kaiser. Her action almost put forward the world cataclysm
by a couple of years.

My pulses quickened when, from the deck of the coaster
Buffel taking me to Possession, I caught sight of those triple
peaks, and the mirror-like flash of a late sun reflected by
the innumerable salt pans backing the landfall. It is not until
about twenty-five miles north of the Orange River that the
first break in the monotony of the shoreline occurs, and one
begins to sense the mystery and lure of the Diamond Coast.
This feeling grows progressively as one approaches Panther
Head. The duplicity which seems to have soaked into the
Sperrgebiet is also at work on the coastline. Captains don't
trust what their eyes see here: if they do, it could cost
them their ships and their lives.

The stubby coaster plugged on with a head-down, sham-
bling gait which suited her name, *Buffel* – Buffalo. The wind
was fresh and sharp. The sky was full of small white clouds
as if a squadron of gannet, dive-bombing fish, had left their
feathers behind after peeling off for the attack.

I was *Buffel*'s only passenger. She was to bring off the
islands' last officials before they stopped work for several
months, until the laying and hatching season was over. One
of the men she was to pick up was Possession's headman,

whose place I would take.

I drank in the cold air eagerly. It was ten days since my encounter with the C-in-C. I had seen a lot of Koch before he flew to Luderitz some days before my own departure. I wondered what the C-in-C's reaction would have been to the sight of the irrepressible Austrian performing the sword dance in a sailors' waterfront dive! I had stayed on at Silvermine to enjoy a crash get-fit course; had visited my mother, a somewhat embarrassed collaborator of the C-in-C; had been made headman of Possession, officially, in Cape Town . . . and now I was here wearing the regulation corduroy clothes and a peaked cap decorated with the badge of office!

Panther Head came closer and a view of Chamois Bay beyond opened up. Four groups of reefs bunker the place about in a rough circle of about six miles. We had to negotiate the southernmost gap between them to enter the bay. Whitecaps creamed on the jagged fangs and threw up a drifting haze of spray. However, the coaster was safe enough. I was tense for a different reason: I was reliving my *Walewska* nightmare. It was here that the tanker had torn out her bottom and made a break for the high seas. I had been about fifty miles away when I'd received her distress signal. I reached her to find a big slick already streaming away to the north-west in the direction of the guano islands. Her load of 150,000 tons was enough to wipe out most of the wild life population of the islands – birds, seals, penguins. The *Walewska's* captain reckoned he could save the ship if he dumped her cargo.

I was caught in a double hammerlock quandary: if I allowed him to jettison the oil where he was he'd destroy the islands; if I permitted him to make for the open sea and dump there, he'd do the same thing for the fish life which thrives so abundantly round the great Benguela current. The Benguela flows to the Sperrgebiet all the way from the Antarctic. It is one of the world's major currents and transports vast quantities of plankton, the fishes' food.

There was a third reason for my decision to destroy not only the tanker but also her oil: the sea was in the grip of what is known scientifically as an upwell cell. Once every winter a very powerful, special wind is generated on the Sperrgebiet. It lasts only a few days. It is hot and blows from the desert out to sea. I'd seen sand columns, hundreds of feet high, miles offshore. This wind is so strong that it pushes the surface water bodily out to sea. In turn it is replaced by other water from deep down and far out – icy Benguela water. It's like some gigantic ball-valve mechanism going into operation. It is called an upwell cell because the sea does just that: it wells up on the coast. It hits maximum strength at a spot a little north of where the tanker struck, and consequently produces a strong current which flows up the Sperrgebiet. There was really only one solution. I took the decision off my own bat. Fast, too, because of the danger: I removed the *Walewska*'s crew and fixed delayed-action demolition charges in her holds so that we could get well clear before she blew up. It was a good thing I did. Ships sixty miles away felt that explosion.

I looked now for the *Walewska*'s stern section, which had been brought back by the current, and spotted it lying on the rocks which flanked the north-western entrance to the bay, white water shooting high up the side of its rusty hulk. The *Walewska* had become something super-heated inside my brain; I cursed the ugly bitch of a thing with a sailor's oath and felt better. The long light made a savage magic out of the desert, the coastal pans and low-rise sandhills. Experts say it hasn't changed a feature in a million years.

Captain Murray, a dour Scots-Afrikaner, anchored for the night inside the bay, keeping the coaster's head to the boisterous wind and strong in-shore current. The seas became steep and vicious as they hit the shallow water round Panther Head. It was as comfortable as sleeping on a pogo stick. The fog came down; the bay was full of unidentifiable noises. After an uneasy stay we set off next morning and picked our way past the *Walewska*'s hulk, unnaturally large and ghost-like in the thinning fog, en route for the first group of God-forsaken islands, as individual as their names – Little Roast-beef, Sparrowhawk, Sinclair, Black Sophie and Plumpudding.

It took most of the day to thump our way up the coast, calling in for brief intervals to take off an odd man here and there, until we reached Possession in the late afternoon.

Captain Murray spat nicotine and phlegm over the side of the bridge. 'Possession. Which being interpreted is, shit.'

It was quite a speech, for him. There'd been little more than grunts out of him the whole way up from the Cape.

'Shut up in that hole, I'd start to talk to the penguins.

Maybe you will before you're through.'

'Perhaps I'll quit by the end of the winter. I don't know. Depends.'

'On what?'

'I dunno. Depends.'

'You're a bit fancy for a headman.'

'It takes all types.'

'You ain't brought along any *dop-en-dum,* I see.'

'No alcohol allowed.'

'Headman, yes. The rest, no.'

'Well, I didn't.'

'So that's it, eh?'

'What's what?'

'That's what you're running away from.'

'I'm not running away from anything.'

'Weddell . . . Somewhere I know that name . . . Can't think where.'

I didn't enlighten him. I was busy watching a boat putting off from the island. *Buffel* had come the safe way through the channel's southern entrance to fetch up at the anchorage opposite a group of prefab huts ashore. Possession is about two miles long, a half broad, and seventy feet above the sea at its highest point; and shaped rather like a stretched-out version of a human foetus, a bit at the south resembling a head and neck. Submerged continuations of the island's northern extremity form the Kreuz shoals lying between it and the mainland at Elizabeth Bay, about four miles distant. The shoals make the northern channel very dicey unless the weather is dead calm – which is almost never.

Captain Murray seemed nervous. I reckoned he was talking in order to hear the sound of his own voice. Possession was as inviting as a seal rookery – and as smelly.

'Weddell . . . it'll come back.'

'Let me know when it does.'

'My next call is in three months' time. Maybe by then you'll be like that poor bugger coming off now in the boat. Started smoking grass. Grew the stuff with tender, loving care in a potty in his cottage, they tell me. If he'd tried outside, the wind would have finished the plants off in a day He's on to mainline stuff now.'

'Where does he get it from, here?'

'Where do any of them get it from?'

'Look at his eyes when he arrives. What made you take this job?'

'Interest.'

'Jesus!'

He slipped the pipe from his mouth and gestured with the stem at the coastline.

The channel was about two miles wide on a west-east axis and slightly longer from south to north. Then, about another four miles from Possession's northern tip, the mainland changed direction sharply and jutted westwards into the ocean, abruptly terminating the channel's south-north direction. A promontory called Elizabeth Point completed the U-shaped loop of the shoreline. Near it was a cluster of ruins, the site of an abandoned diamond ghost town.

The setting sun that still came over the shoulder of the island picked out the landmarks ashore, through a haze of spray. One dominated all the rest – a gigantic arch of rock opposite Possession, nearly two hundred feet high, whose centre had been completely carried away by the sea, leaving only about twenty feet remaining at either end. One leg of the arch was on land, the other in the breakers. The rock, glinting as though polished, looked like a black rainbow, fantastically plucked out of the sky and dumped on the coast – the Bridge of Magpies.

The shoreline round about it was composed of slabs of dark and variegated rock which had kept their surprising geometrical square shapes despite the continual scouring of the wind and waves. Doodenstadt. The Town of the Dead.

Behind Doodenstadt the desert began again in a series of low, light grey-brown sandhills which rose steeply from the sea, but nowhere reached a height of more than three hundred feet.

The Bridge of Magpies was the eye-catcher, but almost rivalling it in the field of the fantastic was the object perched on top of Doodenstadt. Like a great wounded animal, a big two-stack liner sat upright on the rocks, outwardly apparently undamaged.

Captain Murray's pipe-stem fixed on it. 'The *City of Baroda*. Torpedoed in the war and beached. She's out of reach of the waves, else she'd have disappeared long ago.'

He clamped his teeth back on to his pipe and exclaimed, 'Why can't that bloody boat hurry up from the island? That wreck gives me the willies. It shows what can happen around here.'

'Aren't you staying tonight?'

'*Nooit nie!* – never! I'm pulling out as soon as you're on your way ashore. That dump also gives me the creeps. I see they've got the ghost light going already and the sun's not even down.'

A point of light showed in one of the panes of a prefab. It resembled a chance reflection of the sunset.

'It burns all night, every night. No *gamat* would stay otherwise.'

Gamat is an affectionate term for the fine half-caste Malay fishermen of the Cape and South East Africa. Their Far Eastern origin – the first were brought as slaves in the seventeenth century – endows their rites and religion with a touch of the supernatural. Like all other sailors, they are deeply superstitious.

Captain Murray measured the distance of the approaching boat.

'If you get a sight of it from the sea through the fog it looks like a damn ghost itself.'

'Whose ghost is it supposed to be?'

'A woman's. She was drowned in an old windjammer called the *Auckland* over on the island's west side. A shark took her legs. They say she haunts the place searching for them with two huge hounds for company. They were with her in the *Auckland*.'

'Nice neighbours I'll be having!'

'It sounds like a *vaaljapie* (brandy) yarn to me, but once you've lived on Possession for a while you'll believe anything. If you want an example, take a gander at that lot!'

'*Buffel,* ahoy!'

The cry came from a *gamat* standing in the stern of the approaching island boat, and using a steering oar with great skill. The boat's design was new to me – some whaling ancestry somewhere.

'He's the laziest bastard in the isles – Breekbout.'

'Breekbout! You must be joking! That's not a name!'

'He got it because he split his arse in half from sitting on it too much: Breek-bout.'

'It doesn't affect the way he handles that boat.'

'No, he's good. First-class. But look at that sonofabitch

ruin with him.'

He was the headman I'd come to relief, Van Rensburg. They threw a mooring line from the *Buffel*. It hit him but he didn't make a move to make it fast. He was hipped in his own twilight world.

'For crying out loud!'

'Maybe Breekhout's sense of humour will save you from going the same way. It's pretty way out, but anything's better than nothing on Possession. Take my tip though – get to know that *gamat* over there.'

He pointed with his pipe at a fishing cutter riding at anchor at the head of the channel, close to the dangerous shoals.

'Kaptein Denny. Damn fine sailor. He's one off for a *gamat*. Keeps to himself. If my ship was in trouble I'd like him around.'

He broke off abruptly. They'd tied up the whaleboat while he'd been talking and now Van Rensburg came up the bridge ladder to join us. He might have been one of Possession's strolling ghosts – the stiff way he walked, like a marionette.

I decided to leave, quick.

'*Totsiens* (goodbye) Captain. Thanks for the ride.'

I tried to edge past but Van Rensburg blocked my way. His eyes were shuttered and remote.

'Good luck, Captain Weddell. You need good luck on Possession.'

His form of address caught me off balance for a moment. It had slipped my mind that I was, in the ship tradition of the isles, Possession's new captain. It flashed through my mind that there'd been some leak of the C-in-C's secret when he called me by my naval title. So I didn't answer.

He said in a thin, venomous, unnatural voice. 'A high-hat and a shit, eh? Possession'll cut you down to size damn quick.'

I stopped with one foot on the ladder.

'We'll see.'

His laugh was as bad as his voice, mainly because it left his face completely blank, and his eyes, too.

'We'll see! Possession's a prison-house, didn't you know. No escape. Anywhere. Anyhow. Good luck, Captain-stuff-you-Weddell!'

I went quickly overside. A couple of the crew passed down my kit, which I'd had ready on deck. The transceiver from

Silvermine I carried, myself, in a battered old leather suitcase which we had specially chosen to hide its contents. Captain Murray began to shout sailing orders.

My first close-up view of Possession turned me off as quick as it apparently did Captain Murray, who was high-tailing to sea by the time the whaleboat reached the island's concrete jetty. He was right about the stink. The wind, blowing directly off the guano rocks, was pissy and ammoniacal as a shebeen urinal.

Another impression struck me forcibly. I hung for a moment on the rusty iron ladder leading from the water to the top of the jetty and looked down at Breekbout.

'There aren't any birds, man!'

'Gone. Fly away April. Back in July. Same every year.' I liked his grin.

Away from the jetty the birds' breeding-flats were walled off from a group of stores, barracks and the headman's cottage. Everything was smeared a dirty unpleasant grey by the guano.

'*As jy daar loop, dan val jy in die nat op jou gat* – if you walk there when it's wet you'll fall on your backside,' Breekbout went on. '*Dis waarom ek altyd sit* – that's why I always sit.'

'*Jou skelm!* – you bastard!'

His cheerfulness was a buffer against the grim, depressing, graveyard air of the place. The first wisps of fog were drifting in from the sea and the grey coastline was becoming greyer. The only man-made object in sight was the cutter, which was named *Gaok*. Her deck was deserted.

'What's she doing here?' I asked Breekbout.

'Fish.'

'Fishing's banned inside the twelve-mile limit.'

'Kaptein Denny always fishes here.'

'We'll see about that tomorrow.'

'Kaptein Denny is a very good sailor.'

'So I hear. But that doesn't give him the right to fish where he shouldn't. Any self-respecting fisherman would be snug at home on a night like this.'

'Kaptein Denny has no wife, no girl. Maybe his prick's too small. *Gaok* is his home.'

'*Gaok* – what the devil does that mean?'

'Ask Kaptein Denny. He knows everything.'

'He's quite a boy, it seems.'

'Very strong. Very tough. Speaks German too.'

'How old?'

'Fifty, fifty-five maybe. He'll live to be a hundred. No women, no *brannewyn*.'

'We'll pay him a visit tomorrow.'

He couldn't be doing much out of line, whatever it was, in the Force 5 wind which was kicking up sharp seas in the channel and whistling down the grotesquely-shaped rocks of my new home. Breekbout showed me over Van Rensburg's cottage. Most of the furniture was gone and it shared an air of forsakenness with the empty barracks where the labourers slept during the guano scraping season. Breekbout had a corner in the barn-like place. I plumped for company rather than comfort and found myself a bunk. There wasn't even the scratting of a mouse to give life to the shadows where the lantern didn't reach. The atmosphere was as relaxing as a blow to the Adam's apple. I would have put two ghost lights in the window. I slept badly.

In the morning Breekbout turned out, from the ship-type galley, a slovenly breakfast of half-burnt mealie-meal porridge and boiled penguin eggs. We ate the mess by lantern light, as the island was still shrouded in impenetrable fog. It dripped in outsized drops off everything. A complex of gutters from the roofs channelled the precious water into big concrete storage tanks. Baths were out.

I wanted to get up and go and explore Doodenstadt but the fog made it impossible. So I killed time by setting up the transceiver. The gleaming set had everything that opened and shut. My code call-sign was wv.5bx, the C-in-C's choice. The instrument fascinated Breekbout, so I taught him how to operate it. Transmissions, however, were out because of the C-in-C's ban; but I rang the reception changes from long- to short-wave, as well as VHF. There was enough island and ship gossip on the air to give us plenty of practice.

When I could make out the breakers on the mainland under the haze I decided to set off in the whaleboat. It was about mid-morning. Wisps of fog still clung round the island's stark topography; shorewards it was lighter. *Gaok* remained hidden in the curtain to the north-east. The previous day's southerly blow had backed into a light north-wester.

Breekbout propelled the boat by means of an odd and seemingly unworkable rowing action with one oar in a stern rowlock. Once clear of the jetty the murk was still thick on the water and I was lost; but he seemed to know where he was all the time.

Gaok showed up unexpectedly. She was a typical sturdy, bluff-bowed job, beautifully built by Fritz Nieswandt's yard in Luderitz. She was about seventy feet long, powered by both sail and diesel. The enclosed deckhouse was aft, and the mainsail boom swung clear above it. Scores of similar vessels I had seen in the fishing grounds had all had a typical blunt stem but this one had a kind of carved whalebone figurehead added.

'*Gaok!* Ahoy!'

The deckhouse door opened and a short stocky figure dressed in a sun-faded fisherman's jersey and thick corduroy pants emerged. His head was round and set close on his shoulders and there were a few grey streaks in his otherwise very black hair, not short and curly as a *gamat's* usually is, but straight and rather long. His face was weatherbeaten, more tawny than copper, and strangely smooth. It had the typical high cheekbones and Oriental appearance of the Malay. He made us fast with large, strong hands.

I jumped aboard. My first impression was of his rather dignified aloofness – something natural in his bearing, perhaps – because he was quite friendly.

'Kaptein Denny?'

'*Dis my –* that's me.'

'Weddell. The new headman of Possession.'

'So?'

'I've arrived.'

'I saw.'

He inclined his head towards the long-boat, switching into English. Some of his vowels had unusual values.

'You're out early, Captain Weddell. With a rifle, too.'

'Your English is pretty good.'

'I thank the Sonop School in Cape Town. I like to give it a workout when I can. I don't get much chance. There's not much need for that rifle around here, Captain.'

'It's a standard headman issue.'

'Van Rensburg used his a lot on the seals.'

'I'm not Van Rensburg. It's my job to protect them. And the fish – inside the twelve-mile limit.'

'That's a new duty for a headman. I hadn't heard about it.'

'Every fisherman knows it's illegal to fish inside the twelve-mile limit, Kaptein Denny.'

'Not all fish, Captain.'

'All fish.'

'It's cold up here on deck. Come below.'

He led me to a day cabin under the wheelhouse; a second smaller one led off it. Both were much better fitted out than the spartan accommodation I had seen in other cutters.

He fiddled at a small mahogany bar. 'Something to keep out the cold – a *dop-en-dum* (brandy and water)?'

'The sun's not over the yardarm yet.'

He smiled fleetingly. 'We'll call it night because of the fog. That makes it all right.'

'A small one then.'

He turned to fix the drinks and I almost sat on a cushion which had been crushed down hurriedly on the locker. It half concealed a woman's handbag and a white silk scarf. I supposed the woman was hidden away somewhere below. We must have disturbed them by coming unexpectedly out of the fog. It blew Kaptein Denny's image which Breekbout had given me. Yet it was nothing to do with me if he brought his goodies along to enjoy in the solitude of the Sperrgebiet.

He must have noticed the crumpled cushion when he handed me my brandy but gave no sign. He drank orange juice: Breekbout was correct about him there.

'I can't drink alone,' I said.

'It's against my religion – sorry.'

'Don't be sorry. You a Mohammedan?'

'No. Malay. My sect forbids it.'

'*Gesondheid!*'

'Good health.'

He sat down and stared at me with curious, unreadable eyes. I felt awkward drinking his liquor and pulling my authority while doing it.

'I don't want to crack down on you about this fishing business. It'll be okay if you just clear out. Say it's a friendly warning.'

'I've been coming here every winter for . . . over thirty years, it must be. It gives me a sort of squatter's right.'

An unexpected remark from a fisherman, but it gave me a clue to why he had taken over leadership of the Luderitz *gamat* community.

'In court that would be called argument by false analogy.'

His eyes remained expressionless. He just sat passively regarding me. I felt uncomfortable.

'Look, I don't want to play rough and start acting like a new broom. But you know it's against the regulations.'

'I come only in winter.'

'Why?'

'It's the sort of fish. In the summer the current's wrong for them.'

'It could be as you say.'

'I know this coast very well, Captain Weddell. There are some very strange things.'

Strange as hell! Right under his keel was the strangest of all: a lost city. I told myself I mustn't make an overkill of the fishing issue or else he might suspect something. On the other hand I didn't want him hanging around and watching, once Koch arrived. That could be any time.

I downed the brandy. 'Thanks for the drink. It's my first day and I'm taking a look-see at my kingdom. I'm on my way for a run ashore.'

'I wouldn't go, Captain Weddell. There's a big blow coming up. You could be trapped.'

'We had a gale, yesterday.'

'Come up on deck and I'll show you what I mean.'

The fog had lifted and visibility was a couple of miles. On the seaward horizon, however, lay a thick bank of it still. It was unusual because between it and the sky was a clear-cut seam of the horizon.

'That means a buster. It'll be here before you've had your run ashore.'

'I've also sailed this coast. That's simply a hangover from the morning fog. It'll be gone in an hour.'

'It means trouble – here, close inshore. A few miles out it's different. There's one weather on the coast and another at sea.'

He was too concerned about my welfare and it made me suspicious. I must have shown my scepticism.

'It can be blowing only a moderate breeze out to sea when a full gale tears up the channel. You won't like it if you're caught ashore. There isn't any water. You'll be stuck there until the wind drops. Besides, it's almost a full moon.'

'What's that got to do with it?'

'It always blows hardest at Possession at the full and change of the moon.'

'I'm learning.'

'There are always things to learn on the Sperrgebiet, Captain Weddell.'

The odd way he said it clinched my decision to ignore his advice.

'I'll take my chance. Thanks all the same . . . Breekbout!'

'Aye, aye sir?'

'Doodenstadt. Make it snappy.'

Kaptein Denny said. 'You can't land on the rocks. The best spot is to the north . . . there's a bit of a beach . . .'

I decided to ignore that too. Nor did I ask Kaptein Denny how he came to know where the best landing-place was on a shore where landing was prohibited.

Doodenstadt, when I got close enough, hadn't a chance of convincing me it was a lost city. No way. It was little else – outwardly at least – than an outcrop of formidable rocks of unusual shape; the 'streets' a series of gullies possibly resulting from the erosion of a thousand storms. Of course Koch's fresco was away out of sight, but I was thoroughly disenchanted.

'Keep clear!' I snapped at Breekbout. 'Do you want us to finish up alongside that other bloody wreck?'

'Kaptein Denny was right: no landing here,' he mumbled truculently. When I still hesitated about giving in, he added, 'Kaptein Denny always right.'

'Okay, blast you. Back to the beach. I want to check the liner.'

Breekbout stayed with the boat at the little beach while I plunged through a tangle of alleys between the sandhills, in the general direction of the *City of Baroda*. The going opened up farther on when I struck a wide sandy watershed leading towards it. I followed this. It effectively masked my approach to the bow section of the wreck.

Then there were men's voices ahead. There was plenty of cover, and whoever was speaking couldn't see me coming. I crawled forward, making sure my rifle didn't make a giveaway clink. The sound gave me a clear bearing all the time but the nearer I approached the more strident the voices became – distorted, almost mechanical.

They *were* mechanical!

The gully narrowed and kinked and ended against a platform of rock.

Sitting on this in the lee of the wreck, her back to me, was a girl. Next to her was a tape-recorder – whence the voices I'd homed in on!

CHAPTER FOUR

She seemed to be having trouble with the machine, which gave out a jumble of Donald Duck noises. Maybe the distortion was caused by the tape snagging in the wind. Whatever the cause, it gave me a chance to observe without being observed. She stood up and busied herself rewinding the spool with one finger, doing it very carefully as if she didn't want to entrust the task to the recorder's own automatic device.

The rock on which she stood was at my eye-level. Her back remained towards me, so I couldn't see much of her face: indeed, even when she half-turned, the wind blew her hair from under her beret, masking her face. The hair itself was enough to stare at, though – red-gold, as if she'd been caught in a desert sunset. What little I did glimpse of her features made me certain she hadn't been out in the wind and Sperrgebiet sun for long. She was wearing a crumpled loose hip-length suède jacket, darker than the sand, and slacks, also crumpled.

I laid the rifle silently on a ledge of rock above my head, intending vaulting up after it. I paused, however, when I caught sight of various objects the girl had spread about: several very large maps weighted down with stones, a small pile of notebooks and some printed books, one of which bore a remarkable resemblance to the Admiralty *Pilot* for the Sperrgebiet. There was also a compass on top of the books which had been lined up on the wreck: I could tell this because it was one of those instruments with a mirror case, in which I spotted the reflection of the needle. A man found on the Sperrgebiet with so compromising a load would have to do a lot of fast talking to a diamond patrol. As for a woman . . . I couldn't begin to guess.

She turned suddenly, and I ducked out of sight. At the same moment the tape started up again. She'd been so near to spotting me that I didn't try to retrieve my rifle, for fear of making a noise. It looked safe enough, however, because the ledge it was on was out of her sight, slightly below the level of her rock.

What the tape said killed my previous intention of getting up there and and demanding what she was up to. It was German. I understand it though my spoken attempts wouldn't win me any language awards.

'Come in, Swakop,' it said. '*U-160* to dinghy. Come in! Testing, testing, testing. D'ye hear me? Answer. Over.'

I slid down into a sitting position against the wall of the gully, hunching myself up in defence against the sand blowing in from above.

'Dinghy to *U-160*: Swakop speaking. Receiving you loud and clear. Do you hear me?'

'Okay, Swakop. Loud and clear. Captain asks, do you sight shore party?'

'Not yet, *U-160*. Beach not visible. Hidden by big rocks.'

'How far to go?'

'Quarter-of-a-mile, maybe. Breakers and rocks to starboard. Can see the Bridge of Magpies . . . *Achtung!*'

'What is it, Swakop?'

'Beach comes in sight. Recognition flashes. One white, two red, three green. Correct. It's all clear.'

'Captain says pull finger out then. Those flashes can be spotted miles out to sea. This place is a trap. No sea room, no depth of water.'

'Swakop to *U-160*. Answered code signal. Correctly acknowledged.'

'Sure?'

'Sure.'

'Captain says tell those men with you to keep their eyes skinned and guns ready. It could be an ambush.'

'Coming close in now, *U-160*. See a man standing on the beach.'

'Captain says, re-check that it's Tsushima. Use the code.'

'Swakop to *U-160*. It's Tsushima all right. I'm going ashore now. Wading. I'll keep in touch.'

'Are you ashore yet, Swakop?'

'No. Still in the breakers. It's bloody cold. Our own Jap is kicking up rough about something. Protocol, I think. The man on the beach must be a big shot. Lots of fuss and bowing. Our man's taking a parcel from him now.'

'Where are you now, Swakop? On the beach?'

'No. Behind it. On a sandhill.'

'Captain says, what the hell's the delay? Why don't those goddamned Japs get aboard the dinghy?'

'Our Jap's wading out first with the parcel. Looks as if he's going to go back for Tsushima – maybe he's too important to get his feet wet.'

'By God he is! Captain says – *Gott in Himmel!* There's a ship and it's firing at us . . .!'

'Hydrophone operator to Captain: HE bearing red o-five-o! Propeller noises!'

'Periscope lookout to Captain: Distant mastheads bearing red o-five-o!'

'Number One to Captain: Captain on the bridge, sir! A big ship entering the channel from the north-west!'

'Captain here. Lookout, what sort of ship? Warship? I can't make her out from down here on the bridge.'

'*Ja*. Armed merchant cruiser. A big one, *Herr Oberleutnant!*'

'Number One, get that periscope down with the bo'sun's chair and the look out! Quick!'

'Aye aye sir!'

'Captain to hydrophone operator: enemy's course, speed, distance?'

'Steering 120 degrees, sir, south-east by east – Sir! AMC is coming round on to a new course . . . one-one-o degrees . . . coming round still . . . o-nine-o, steady on o-nine-o, now heading due east, across our bows . . .'

'Speed? *Schnell*, man!'

'Twelve knots – speeding up.'

'She'll run herself ashore if she holds that course, Number One. Do you see her yet?'

'No, sir.'

'Damn this night sight! It's no bloody use at all!'

'I'd say she's manoeuvring for the mouth of the channel over towards Elizabeth Bay, sir. There's about four miles between us. When she picks up the ten-fathom line, I reckon she'll turn and steer right down the middle.'

'And slap into us! Stand by! Action stations!'

'Aye aye sir! She's starting to come round again . . . turning . . . turning . . . steady on course one-eight-o true . . . increasing speed . . . fourteen knots now . . .'

'Distance?'

'Three and a half miles, sir'

'Captain to control room: Group down, slow ahead together, port fifteen!'

'Control room to Captain: Port fifteen it is, sir. Slow ahead together.'

'Helm steady amidships, sir!'

'Stand by to clear the bridge – what is it, Number One?'

'Shore party dinghy right astern, sir.'

'Belay that order. Stand by. Get those men aboard. Captain to control room: Stop engines! Slow astern both! Are all the men there, Number One?'

'All ours, sir. There's only one Jap though. Swakop got ashore all right.'

'Get 'em aboard, quick! This is going to be a bloody difficult shot. I can't let her come too close or we'll blow ourselves up at the same time. I want the conning-tower just awash – understood? Just deep enough to be out of sight. Channel's too shallow for a submerged attack. Clear the bridge! Clear the casing!'

'Aye aye, sir!'

'Captain speaking from control-room now. Conning-tower clear, Number One?'

'Conning-tower clear, sir. Hatch secured.'

'Good. Start the attack. Who's that talking? Silence!'

'It's the Jap, sir. He's pretty upset about something. Can't understand what he's saying.'

'Tell him to shut up. We're in action.'

'Very good, sir.'

'Enemy masts in sight now.'

'Up periscope a bit more, sir?'

'No. Hold it. We mustn't be spotted. Their bloody radar's like magic. She's a big one, every bit of ten thousand tons. She's taking a hell of a chance in this shallow channel. What's her speed, Number One?'

'Plot reports fifteen knots, sir.'

'Stand by, torpedo tubes!'

'All tubes ready, sir.'

'Fire on HE bearings, sir?'

'No. Visual. Port five. Easy now. What's her DA angle?'

'Very fine, sir. Very tricky shot.'

'A quadruple spread should fix her. Flood tubes, open bow doors!'

'Tubes flooded, bow doors open, sir!'

'Permission to fire, sir?'

'No. Hold it. When she comes opposite the settlement, that's the best place. Slow ahead, Chief, SLOW! Don't let her go! Target's only thirteen hundred metres!'

'Fire now, sir?'

'Hold it, hold it!'

'Now, sir? Fire?'

'NOW!'

'Tube One, fire!'

'Tube Two, fire!'

'*Rohr drei, llosss!*'

'*Rohr vier, llosss!*'

'All torpedoes running, sir!'

'Coxswain, the time please!'

'Zero minus three, sir!'

'All torpedoes running, sir!'

'Six, seven, eight, nine, ten! . . .'

'Coxswain?'

'Any moment now, sir . . .'

'Torpedoes running . . .'

'Christ, one and two have missed!'

'Hydrophone operator reports three and four still running, sir . . .'

'*Donnerwetter!* Hear that, Number One! A hit! *Gut!*'

'Hydrophone operator reports two torpedo explosions . . .'

'Got her, Number One! Two – right between the tits!'

'Breaking-up noises from AMC, sir. HE bearing . . .'

'She's coming straight for us, sir!'

'Down periscope. Engines full ahead together, port fifteen, steer two-nine-o. She's trying to ram us!'

'No, sir! She's running ashore!'

'We'll have to cut right across her bows – on the surface, too. God, for some bloody deep water! What's the depth now?'

'Eleven fathoms, shallowing, sir!'

'Sir, sir! Hydrophone operator here! New propeller noises. Outer channel. Green o-three-o. Closing fast. Warship!'

'Where the devil's he sprung from, Number One?'

'Coming into the main channel, sir, between Possession and the Kreuz shoals.'

'There's barely four to six fathoms there! He must be mad!'

'Or very brave.'

'Range, speed, operator?'

'Mile and a half, sir. Twenty-two knots.'

'Give me a bearing for the AMC now, too. I want to see what she's up to.'

'Close, sir. Maybe half a mile. Slowing all the time.'

'So would anyone be with two torpedoes in their guts.'

'She's still holding to the channel, sir. But coming at us.'

'Up periscope! Destroyer fires a starshell. No, she's a frigate, Number One. She's made it, too, through that short cut! Into the channel now.'

'Orders, sir?'

'Stand by, stern torpedo tubes!'

'*Achtung!*'

'Set 'em both very shallow – twelve to fifteen feet. Bring the stern to bear, Number One.'

'Aye aye, sir.'

'Hydrophone operator to Captain: two groups of propeller noises merging. Confused echoes, sir.'

'Damn! The closer they get the tougher our problem becomes. Down periscope a shade! The AMC's blocking our shot at the frigate, Number One! I can't fire like this. Damn and blast! Hold it! Hold the attack!'

'They sound right on top of us, sir.'

'That's the AMC. I could spit on board. If she rolls over now, we've had it.'

'Hydrophone operator to Captain: Sir, warship's screws close! Dead astern!'

'Here she comes! I can't shoot like this! Sweet Jesus, give me a firing angle! *Stand by, all! Hang on! Stand by for depth charge attack!*'

'Sir . . .'

'*Gott in Himmel!* What hit us?'

'You okay, sir?'

'All right, all right, Number One. Got chucked against the eyepiece, that's all. Eight bloody depth charges!'

'You're bleeding, sir . . .'

'It's nothing, Number One. He'll come back! Damage reports – quick!'

'All compartments report damage, sir. But still in action.'

'Give me a look! She's coming about! This is our chance! Stand by! Stand by! Continuous reading! Flood tubes, open doors!'

'Flood tubes, open doors it is, sir!'

'Bring her round, *bring her round,* Number One!'

'Fire both stern tubes!'

'Fire!'

'Torpedoes running, sir!'

'Time, coxswain?'

'Zero minus three, four, five, six, seven, eight . . . nineteen, twenty . . .'

'Jesus! *Her magazine's gone up!* That's knocked the bugger off, all right!'

'Two right up her jack, sir!'

'Christ! For Chrissake, Number One, what hit us then?'

'Dunno, sir. Right on top of the conning-tower. Must be something big blown off the frigate.'

'Big as a bloody locomotive! Maybe one of her own gun turrets! Damage party! Here! At the double!'

'It's slipping clear whatever it is, sir – listen, scraping the casing – there! It's gone!'

'Periscope?'

'Out of action, sir.'

'Stand by, the bridge party!'

'It's no good, sir. The hatch is jammed fast. Can't move it!'

'We must get the hell out of here – quick, Number One! They'll have seen that explosion fifty miles away! Damage reports – *schnell!* Is she making water?'

'All valves on the outer hull reported loose in their seatings, sir. Main ballast pumps out of action. Angle gauge wrecked. Telemotor and gyro compass systems out of action.'

'Those depth charges couldn't have come closer! Engine-room, what does the Chief say?'

'Plenty, sir. Starboard diesel ripped off its bed, camshaft snapped . . .'

'The port engine – is it okay?'

'Okay. Electrics okay too.'

'*Gut!* Group up, half ahead, together. Steer three-four-o.'

'She's badly down by the head, sir. With the gauge gone, we'll have to trip her by guesswork. The change-over valve's jammed open. I guess it's smashed too.'

'We can't see and we can just about move, Number One. But we've got to get out of here: this channel's a death-trap. Silence, that man!'

'It's the Jap again, sir. He's protesting. Says we're ratting on the mission. The important guy got left behind when the dinghy chased after us.'

'Tell him to save his breath and the oxygen! He can't get out of this boat now – no one can. Where's the AMC?'

'Must have fetched up ashore by now, sir. That magazine blast killed the sound of everything else.'

'Poor bastards! It might have been us.'

'It might still be, sir.'

'Keep your voice down, Number One! I want an immediate signal sent to BdU – is the radio still working?'

'Yes, sir. About the only thing left that is.'

'Say, "*U-160* to BdU. Attacked by frigate. Flower class, which blew up following two hits ex stern tubes. *U-160*'s main ballast pumps damaged, unable to dive. Jettisoned eight mines. Proceeding seawards partly submerged. Will signal position and damage assessment 06.00 hours dawn tomorrow." Well, Number One, what is it?'

'Sir! Radio operator reports ship-to-shore voice radio has been transmitting to Swakop throughout the attack! In the panic somebody forgot to switch it off!'

'I'll have his guts for that! What a giveaway! No wonder the frigate came right at us – he must have heard every word inside the sub and homed in on our signals! Switch the damn thing off – *now!*'

CHAPTER FIVE

As if on cue, the recording cut out.

I opened my eyes. The girl was kneeling on the rock platform above, holding my rifle. She handled it as though it might bite her. Her hands were all in the wrong places and the muzzle pointed at the sky: at least it wasn't trained on me. Our eyes met across the blue-black line of the barrel. She eyed me with the intense fascinated compulsion you reserve for a dangerous snake emerging from its hole, when you don't know whether it or the weapon in your hand is worse.

I took all this in as I got to my feet. 'The iron gun in the iron hand,' I mocked.

She seemed to find it hard to speak properly because her lip muscles were out of control.

'What do you want? Why are you spying on me?'

'Not spying; just investigating.'

Her face closed up in blankness. 'I didn't say that. I . . .'

'Yes?'

'I spotted you in the compass mirror, peering over the edge of the rock,' she jerked out. 'Your hair was blowing all over the place . . .'

'I must remember to have my barber fix it before I set out on my next spying mission.'

'I'm serious.'

The barrier of tension between us was as real as an electric fence. I felt it was time I got my gun out of those inexpert hands. It was loaded, but the safety catch was on. I was quite sure she didn't mean to threaten me with it: she'd only grabbed it because it was there. Anyway, the time for finesse was past.

I vaulted up alongside her and took the weapon away. She didn't resist. I think she was glad to be rid of it.

'It's always better to be the shooter than the shootee,' I quipped.

'Who are you?'

'That can wait. The question is, who are you? What sort

of sound-track is that you've got there – radio? Television?'

She stared back, uncomprehending. She was operating on quite another wavelength from me. She blinked rapidly. Her right eye seemed to have some grains of sand in one corner and there were traces of face-powder stuck in her polo-neck sweater. After her hair her eyes were her best feature, sea-green with flecks of light in them. She seemed younger than I, about thirty.

'This place is off limits,' I said. 'Diamond territory. *Verboten*. That covers stunt recorders as well.'

I asserted it emphatically but in my own mind that didn't quite include the maps and other things I'd seen.

She wasn't with me yet: she was still living with something in the recording.

'Stunt? That's when I was born,' she replied.

'If that's so, all I can say is that the language of maternity wards has caught up with the permissive age.'

She made a stagey, throwaway gesture at the tape-recorder that underlined the first conclusion I'd jumped to.

'I mean – born. When the liner was hit.'

'You artistes live out your scripts, don't you? But don't get too carried away. When you come back to earth you'll discover that the bit of Sperrgebiet you're standing on is very expensive. It could cost you a thousand-dollar fine or a year in jail.'

She remained tense and uptight. 'My name's Jutta Walsh. I was born thirty-one years ago today in a boat which rescued the liner's passengers. Here, at the Bridge of Magpies. No one ever found out who the rescuer was because he disappeared next day. My mother died. That liner's a part of me! Nothing's going to stop me going aboard her. That includes you!'

'My name's Santa Claus – alias Struan Weddell. I'm headman of that island over there. It's Christmas Day today.'

The touch of colour that came into her cheeks wasn't from windburn. My sarcasm, however, didn't break down her defiant attitude. She regarded me in silence, with cool hostility.

'I know how you got here: Kaptein Denny,' I went on. 'There's no debate about this territory. It's Sperrgebiet, and on the Sperrgebiet you're guilty until you can prove yourself innocent. What I'm trying to say is that I don't have to listen to your reasons in order to clobber you. Being here is enough in itself, but I realize show-biz is a hell of a razzmatazz and you've got to have local colour to pay off. The sound effects on your tape are good – very good.'

'Listen to me clearly! I tell you I *was* born here! The *City of Baroda* was carrying women and children to the Cape. My mother was pregnant . . .'

'Babies *are* born that way.'

'The shock of the U-boat attack brought on labour. I was a month premature.'

'Congratulations on your script. That sort of soap opera should be a wow over the air. But here you've no audience to cry over it. Even the birds have gone. You'll have to get out.'

She remained strained and intent. 'You've got it all wrong. Believe me – what you overheard on the tape *happened* in real life, a long time back. What you call sound effects are actual battle noises radioed from inside a U-boat which was in action and fighting for its life. Those men – all of them – died later. '

'And I'm U-boat Admiral Dönitz in person.'

'You stupid thick-headed clot!' she blazed. 'You're plain bloody-minded and stubborn.'

'Cops usually are.'

'You're a cop?'

'Sort of.'

'Blinded by your job.'

'I'm new. Now get your things together and march! Back to my boat! I'll see you aboard *Gaok*.'

'First I'm going aboard that liner.'

'Says who?'

'I've come a long way and I've waited a long time. I'm going aboard.'

'The hell you are!'

She tried to push past but I grabbed her. The force of her rush took us among her books and maps. I knocked over the compass and trod on a chart.

The damn-you expression went from her eyes in a split second; just as Sperrgebiet fog changes the colour of the light. In it's place was genuine appeal and a touch of desperation that wasn't play-acting. I knew then that I'd misjudged her: I found myself believing her story.

'Please!' she burst out. 'Please – those are priceless!'

She didn't put her hands above her head to signal surrender but the way she picked up one of the books and held it out to me said the same thing. It was titled *Nuremberg Trials, Vol. XIII*. There were a couple of other similar ones. She also handed me a paper with neat hand-written columns of figures, dates and names. It was headed, 'U-boats which operated in South African waters 1939-1945'. There was another, 'U-boat types, class, tonnage, speed, armament, range' – and a sheaf of other papers, including photocopies and official-looking letters. The map I'd trodden on turned out to be a naval chart of the Possession channel, annotated in German.

We became intensely conscious of one another.

'Your work?'

'Yes.'

'The illusion of war.'

'You could call it that.'

'It's more than that, though.'

'It's more than that.'

I made a sweeping gesture which took in the collection and tape recorder. 'In old cathedrals people listen to tape explaining the architecture and art they're looking at, but I wouldn't have thought the Sperrgebiet qualified for the same treatment.'

She stayed silent for a few moments. Maybe, I thought, she was weighing my remark as a good let-out. However, I discounted my suspicions about that the moment she replied. Her voice was warm, and revealed how grateful she was I'd accepted her story as 24-carat.

'I hadn't thought of it in those terms but mine's the same sort of idea – if you put the site of a naval battle in place of a cathedral. The lecture was going fine – until you showed up.'

'I was – am – trying to head you away from trouble.'

'Thanks. There wasn't anyone around. I thought I'd get away with it.'

'You have.'

'What do you mean?'

'If I accompany you it's okay. This shoreline's part of my pad. Possession's my ship: I'm a sort of re-tread captain. Let's go and look at the wreck together.'

'I can't begin to thank you . . .'

'Call me Struan: that'll be thanks enough.'

'Struan.'

'Is this a pilgrimage or a picnic, Jutta?'

'Something of both, I guess.'

She didn't go into that. Nor did she explain further her sight-and-sound set-up when we collected the documents and books and put heavy stones on top of them to keep them from blowing while we were away at the wreck. They made a formidable, and interesting, pile of documentation.

'You've done a lot of homework, Jutta.'

'Yes. It took years.'

Again, no more. She smiled, though, and I was pleased to see the pinched look go from her face. I left the explanations for later.

We traversed the dome of rock which comprises Dooden-stadt, winding and back-tracking through the 'streets' to get to our objective. The strange geological formation projected into the sea on one hand and into the desert on the other. At shoe-leather distance the lost city impressed me still less. We couldn't board the liner from the landward side. You could have driven a train through the torpedo holes in her. It was a miracle she'd stayed afloat long enough to be beached. Also, it must have been a spring tide that put her high up where she was.

We stood and looked at her rusty plating. Jutta's interest took the chill off the sense of static disaster which the years hadn't softened.

She said unexpectedly, 'Sorry I was like that back there, Struan.'

'Forget it. We're here now.'

'It's just that it meant – means – so much.'

I was on the point of asking for the explanation which I felt was becoming overdue; but I decided to play it gently for the moment.

'You a historian, Jutta?'

'Sort of.'

She didn't seem inclined to elaborate. It was faith, not fact, which had made me trust her in the first place. But patience isn't one of my strong suits. She intrigued me.

I said, 'The South African sun didn't give you that complexion.'

She flushed, which made it better still. 'No. London. I flew here, only a couple of days ago.'

'That's a very long way to come for a view of a rotting old hulk. Especially one that's out of bounds.'

'I told you, you could almost call it my cradle.'

'A small reason for a big journey.'

'Maybe. Don't come the cop again, Struan. You're nicer without.'

'Let's try the other side of the wreck.'

We caught the force of the wind there because the hulk had acted as a windbreak before. Now the spray came in jets when the breakers burst against the rocks. I found the wreck's air of desolation total and depressing. The weather side was red with rust. Crabs scuffled up and down the rotting plates and there was a population of tide-things a man's height up from the keel. Some smashed remains of lifeboats hung from perished falls.

'*Jut* means davit in Danish,' Jutta said.

'You're all sea.'

'Maybe too much so, Struan.'

I waited for the follow-up to this cryptic remark but it didn't come. Instead, she occupied herself with studying the ship's side, trying to find a way in. Finally we located one and slipped and scrambled up on to the deck. It was a grim spectacle. Looters and strippers had picked the place clean. Green slime clung to a lot of the metal 'tween-decks and the stairways were dangerous.

'What are you searching for, Jutta?'

'My mother's cabin.'

'Number?'

'I don't know. The most I could discover was that it was among the single accommodation on the starboard side.'

'Single? How's that?'

'She wasn't married.'

'I see.'

'You don't. But you're too polite to pry.'

'It was wartime.'

'Wartime.' Her voice took on an edge. 'If you only knew how that fogs everything! That simple question you asked about her cabin – you can't begin to guess the involvements it took to get the simple answer.'

'Jutta, what do you hope to find in your mother's cabin?'

She side-stepped my question. Instead she said, 'There's a passageway. It might lead to the cabins.'

It did, but it was wet and half-dark. The liner had taken the torpedoes on her port side and probably all the passengers on the opposite side, where we now were, had got away safely. If they'd left anything behind in their flight, the looters had taken it. Every cabin was a bare steel shell. Coffin seemed a better description.

I sniffed. 'Seals! Whew!'

We explored until it was impossible to go farther because the 'tween-decks had collapsed. Jutta was very withdrawn when we found nothing.

We retraced our steps to the bridge. It had shared the fate of the cabins. All the instruments, even the wheel, were missing. We had a wonderful view of the Bridge of Magpies, which seemed close enough to reach out and touch. The pillars on which the twin legs of the arch rested were striated by the weather – like the engine of a giant motor-cycle. At its highest point the structure narrowed to a mere couple of feet thick, which gave the whole thing an airy lightness.

We shared the scene and the silence. It was companionable and felt good. Maybe what we were sharing was something more indefinable, more basic.

'Why magpies?' I asked.

'Not a clue. The name had the American code-breakers stumped, too.'

'Please, teacher!'

We laughed at and with one another.

'Do I sound as bad as that?'

'Professor!'

'It's all back there amongst my things: everything about U-160's mission.'

'Mission?'

'You heard the tape. It wasn't an operational cruise.'

'There was enough shooting.'

'Nevertheless, it wasn't. The first buzz of it emerged when Pearl Harbour intercepted a Japanese Fleet message to U-boat Headquarters. Those code-breaker boys were hot stuff, real super-stars at their job, but the name Bridge of Magpies had them beat. As a result the signal got shelved. It should have been passed on to the British because these waters were in the Royal Navy's sphere of operations; but it never was.'

'What's at the back of all this sleuthing of yours, Jutta?'

You could almost hear the barrier clang down between us! I wasn't so far along with her as I'd imagined.

She said shortly, 'To do with – my mother.'

'Whom you never knew. That's a load of filial piety, Jutta.'

'Please don't needle me, Struan. You've been very sweet and considerate bringing me here. Don't spoil it now.'

'Would it spoil it to tell you I've suddenly thought of something?'

'About my mother?'

'It's what you want, isn't it?'

'Yes . . . no.' Her eyes – sea-green as deep water – had been on my face, but now she looked away. 'Tell me. The moment's gone, anyway.'

I put my hand on her shoulder. Irrelevantly, I thought: Gigi must just be about opening the jetty bar now. That careless bit of breast that always showed. I wondered what Jutta's breasts were like. There was almost no shape to her because of the suède jacket.

'Breekbout – that's my Man Friday – told me yesterday that there's an old graveyard back of the beach in the sand-hills. Maybe your mother's buried there.'

Her reaction wasn't what I'd expected. She certainly wasn't suffering from an overdose of mother-fixation. She put her hand on mine and said coolly, matter-of-factly, 'Let's go and look.'

We left the wreck, collected her paraphernalia, and hiked away into the wind-carved sandhills, which followed the coast's indentation like a half-cupped hand. Farther inland was a plain with shifting, smaller sandhills and beyond them showed the dark line of a range of fretted, rocky outcrops. We made brand new footsteps in the wind-scoured surface. The dusty smell of the desert was still damped by a sprinkling of dew. The sun shone but the wind was cold.

We stopped for a breather. Her gear was more cumbersome than heavy.

'What was "the sound of guns" mentioned on the tape, Jutta?'

I was watching her closely, waiting for the shut-down in her eyes that had followed my earlier questioning and had made them seem to be looking at me from another place,

But it didn't happen this time.

'I don't know what you're talking about.'

Nor did she: but she was fascinated by what I had to tell her about Convoy WV.5BX and why *Gousblom* had broken away from it into the channel. I left the C-in-C out of it, of course.

When I'd finished she said speculatively, 'Seems I'm not the only one who's done homework. You're pretty well informed for a headman.'

'It was Possession's main event for a century. The story gets passed on from mouth to mouth.'

'I wonder.'

I kept wondering, too – about her. I decided to risk my sixty-four dollar question.

'I'd like to go over all this material of yours about Possession.'

Her eyes disappeared into another time-track.

'It's copyright. Mine.'

'Does that mean no?'

'I said, it's mine.'

'Let's get on,' I snapped.

The anger lay between us and soured the rest of the hike. Her brush-off burned me up because now I reckoned she'd turned on the charm to get her way with me about the wreck and play me for a sucker. I swore to myself that once we'd seen over the graveyard I'd have an ironclad reason out of her for being on the Sperrgebiet. Or else.

We negotiated the corner of the last dune blocking off the graveyard. I was in the lead.

I caught sight of a cluster of mounds and some derelict crosses. I also spotted something else.

I pulled Jutta back into the angle of the dune; then unslung my binoculars and brought the graves into sharp definition.

A man was kneeling at one of them, his hands busy in the sand.

'Was your mother's name Joyce?' I whispered.

She nodded.

'Then Kaptein Denny is either robbing her grave or caching something in it.'

'Is that it?'

'The cross is pretty crude – looks like a piece of wreckage.'

I read, ' "Joyce Walsh . . ." Come back, you little idiot!'

She'd jumped up and sprinted towards the kneeling figure. I snicked back the rifle bolt, made sure it was loaded, and ran after her. Because of the wind, Kaptein Denny didn't hear her coming until she was very close. When he did, he threw us a startled glance, leapt up and scuffed the mound with his foot so that a scatter of things – some of them bright seashells – went flying.

I was up to him in a moment. I slipped the rifle's safety catch. He had a knife in one hand and in the other some rings and jewellery, and what appeared to be a rather time-worn passport. Jutta was confronting him as if she couldn't believe her eyes.

'You bastard!' I exclaimed. 'Fishing . . . balls! You bloody grave-robbing bastard!'

His face was a mask; he didn't retaliate; just came towards me holding out the battered passport. I wasn't dumb enough to fall for that one.

I kept the gun steady on him. 'The knife – drop it! At my feet!'

He hesitated, unflappable and therefore dangerous. But he saw I'd blast him if he tried any tricks. He gave a slight shrug and threw it open.

'Now the passport!'

It joined the knife.

'Hold out your hand!'

There were a couple of rings and some trinkets in his palm.

I risked a glance at the things he'd kicked away: a tiny coloured porcelain figurine and some smashed painted shells which had been stuck together to imitate flowers.

'Now get off that grave!' I ordered. 'You're under arrest. Where'd you get that loot from?'

He indicated the mound. The wind had long ago blown the shabby cross askew – by contrast, most of the other graves were unmarked – and the sand had filed away the lettering, which appeared to have been burned in with a hot iron. It read, 'Joyce Walsh. Died in childbirth, July 1943. R.I.P.'

Jutta's thoughts were a millisecond ahead of mine. She snatched up the passport, flicked it open, paged through it rapidly, concentrating on the wording and franking-stamps. Before she'd reached the last page her eagerness seemed to have evaporated.

Her voice was dry and level as if she'd experienced some big let-down.

'My mother's.'

'Yes,' said Kaptein Denny. 'The rings – I took them from her fingers myself.'

'Christ, you're a cool one!' I exploded.

Jutta said in the same level, unemotional voice, 'If that's true, you didn't do it just now. That grave's not been disturbed.'

She was right. It certainly hadn't been dug up and unless the body lay six inches deep he couldn't have got at it.

Kaptein Denny left me out of what he had to say next. 'I made that cross. The liner captain gave me your mother's passport so I'd get the name right. I took the jewellery. I've kept them all . . . it's a long time now.'

'*You were there!*'

'I was there. These things belong to you now, Miss Jutta.'

'Jutta!' I echoed. 'You're mighty quick off the mark for a charter skipper.'

'I've known Miss Jutta a long time. From the moment of birth, in fact.'

'Rescue!' Jutta exclaimed. 'It was *you*! *Kaptein Denny!*'

He remained unruffled. 'I rescued a lot of people that night. Your mother among them. You were born in my boat.'

'Don't play the fool with me,' I snapped at him. I put up the gun but kept my foot on the knife. 'Let's have your story straight – and quick.'

'I was in the Possession channel that night *U-160* sank the *City of Baroda* . . .'

'Doing what?'

'Fishing.'

It was too pat. Fishing nets a multitude of sins.

'In wartime? With enemy subs around?'

'I was fishing.'

I let it go.

'I saw the liner beached. It was a wild, stormy night. The passengers wouldn't have stood a chance in the seas that were breaking over the rocks. I took off a lot of them – including Miss Jutta's mother, as I said.'

Jutta fiddled with the rings. She was clearly lining up on his side. Maybe she'd never left it. Maybe that's why both of them were ashore the same day . . .

'You must have known all along who I was when I came to you in Luderitz for a boat – why didn't you say?'

'The time wasn't then.'

'You vanished before the survivors from the *City of Baroda* could even say thank you. No one was ever able to identify their rescuer.'

'It's the way I'm made.'

I said, 'It takes a power of modesty to dodge a couple of warships out hunting a U-boat. Yet you succeeded.'

'They concentrated on the mouth of the channel near the Kreuz shoals where the oil slick was. I took my boat round the other way.'

'Okay,' I said. 'You were super-modest. It's all in the past and it doesn't matter a damn to me whether you wanted modesty or a medal. What concerns me is the present . . .'

'It's Miss Jutta's birthday,' he interrupted. 'It's also a death-day. I'm a Malay. That was a rite for her mother's spirit you interrupted.'

Jutta gathered up the figurine and the broken seashells.

'Fine,' I said to Denny. 'You've done your stuff, both temporally and spiritually. I couldn't care less. What I care about is that both of you are defying the law. *This is Sperr-gebiet!* Get going!'

'You can't – not now!' Jutta was incredulous.

'Now's just the time.'

'Not when everything's going my way . . .'

'What way is that?'

She didn't answer. What had been brewing inside me, ever since our breather-stop, lashed back at me. I went on, 'You had a lot of show-me wishes. I obliged. The party's over.'

'Struan!'

There was more than disappointment and anger in that one word – it could have been hurt. I bulldozed it aside.

'This shore isn't a free-for-all. You both seem to have for-gotten that. Now let's get moving to the boat.'

'And then?' All feeling had left her voice.

'Luderitz. Kaptein Denny will take you back.'

'That "will" sounds exactly like a re-tread captain's order.'

'Re-tread or not, it's an order. I'm also confiscating all

this stuff until I can go through it.'

'I'm staying! That's flat!'

'What have you got to say, Kaptein Denny?'

'I agree to return to *Gaok*. There's no law against a man sitting in his boat in the channel. Merely sitting.'

He was right, of course, Essentially, he was saying the same thing as Jutta, but more cleverly.

I was saved by the bell from further argument. I heard Koch's Land-Rover before they did, because I was expecting him. It was grinding through an outcrop barrier behind the sandhills, and trailing a long plume of dust.

I pointed it out to them; and tried bluffing, because I didn't want Koch to come and find me unable to shift a girl and a fisherman from the beach.

'That's probably a diamond patrol. You're in a hot seat. You can save yourselves trouble by coming to the boat right away.'

'I'll give you my word not to come ashore,' said Kaptein Denny.

'And you, Jutta?'

'No.'

There was a tight silence. Then she exclaimed. 'You don't . . . can't . . . understand! It would take hours to explain. You've been wonderful – and beastly – today.'

'The boat.'

'Oh, damn and blast you!'

Kaptein Denny said, 'That's not a police patrol. Their vehicles are painted bright orange so they can be spotted from their air if they're in trouble.'

Koch broke it up by coming round the sandhills in a tearaway slide. He'd clearly sighted our group. There wasn't much of his Austrian charisma in evidence when he finally pulled up hard and covered us in dust.

'What the devil goes on here, Struan? Showing tourists around?'

'Keep your cool. We were just sorting things out.'

'A woman too!'

He'd had a rough ride over the desert, judging from his red, hollow eyes and dust-covered face. His cheeks were stubble-shadowed; and dust made a tracery in the lines about his nose, making him look angry and older. A roof tarpaulin covering his gear and extra jerricans of petrol had blown loose and flapped in the wind, drawing attention to the load.

Koch saw that Kaptein Denny was eyeing it and snapped, 'Get in. I want a word with you.'

'To the boat,' I ordered the other two; but they just went on standing there. Koch slammed in the gears and we drove up a dune, out of earshot.

I got in first. 'Now . . .' I gave him a quick rundown of the situation and why Jutta was there.

'Be your age, man!' he retorted. 'Women in these days don't dare deserts simply in order to brood over sites of minor naval actions and placate ancestral spirits! Lady Hester Stanhope's dead!'

'Maybe she's different.'

'They all are – to start with. To the birds today the male is simply a gun loaded with chauvinism and sperm. Get that straight and you'll be a happy man.'

'Her story sounded okay – at least part of it.'

'*Vive la différence!* Nor did I like the look of that bugger with her.'

'Maybe he's at the bottom of it all. I don't know yet.'

'Letting her down lightly again, Struan? You were given a job to do here – remember? The Sperrgebiet isn't Santorin, all lesbians and love-ins.'

'I like your language when you're drunk. It's even better when you're mad. What do you want me to do?'

'Arrest them both. Throw them out.'

'Kaptein Denny's given his parole – well, sort of. Isn't interested in coming ashore. This once was an exception.'

'And she?'

'Refuses to budge.'

'You've got a lock-up on Possession.'

'You can't throw a woman into a place like that.'

'I can. You will.'

'Let's see if we can't talk some sense into her.'

But we couldn't, and she even held out her wrists and mocked me to clap handcuffs on her. Without a boat Possession is as good as a prison anyway. Those two or three miles of white-capped channel water between the island and the mainland would, if a man were stuck there, lengthen to two thousand. The island looked like a nicked knife blade lying in the sea, one of those curved things that have a thick back. The craggy bits, where the zombies hadn't managed to clear the guano, were still white, and the rest was grey where they had. Parts of the island were so low against the water that they looked like three or four islets loosely linked together.

Finally, under pressure and protest, Jutta agreed to accompany us. She remained adamant in her refusal to return to Luderitz.

The four of us, plus Breekbout, piled into the two boats and we crossed to the island.

CHAPTER SIX

'Welcome to the commune.'

Jutta eyed the guano-splashed prefabs, and didn't answer for a moment. The pissy wind came cascading over the rocks, and bits of feathers and nests made unerringly for one's eyes and nostrils. It was about mid-afternoon. In an hour or two the fog would start coming in. When it did, the wind would fall. The huts were sited under the lee of the island's northernmost high point, which – instead of giving shelter – acted more as a booster to jack up the force of the wind, breaking it up into eddies which searched out every nook and cranny and brought a continual avalanche of debris. You couldn't escape, whichever way you faced.

We were all standing on the concrete apron near the jetty.

'Which is the jail?' Jutta demanded.

'The whole place is a jail,' Koch retorted. 'You've got an exercise yard over two miles long and half a mile broad. But don't get ideas. The most level bit is what you're standing on.'

I added, 'Careful over the rocks. They get very slippery because of the guano and the fog. They're like ice every morning.'

'*Every* morning? You've only been here . . .'

Breekbout muttered something and he and Kaptein Denny grinned.

I translated the patois, as it was obvious the crack was directed at her.

'He says, please stay the winter and you'll grow webs on your feet like the birds, from climbing the rocks. He's never seen a woman with webbed feet . . .'

'Save it!' It made her angrier.

Koch, too, was becoming more irritated. He pulled me away from the others to the headman's cottage where they couldn't overhear us.

'What sort of white-shoe captain are you?' he demanded.

'Don't blow your bilges. What the hell do you expect me to do with her?'

'Spell it out. Spell it out to both of them that they aren't staying. Throw 'em out.'

'They've heard that already. She won't budge. I can't stop Kaptein Denny anchoring his boat and just sitting.'

'That bastard has a racket. I don't buy that yarn of his. He isn't at Doodenstadt for a full frontal view of the scenery.'

'Don't get your knickers in a twist. I can't touch him; not legally anyway.'

'Find a reason; invent one if you must. If he gets back to Luderitz he'll spread the rumour.'

'Well, *do* something, for crying in a bucket! I'm not going to start operations with Kaptein Denny watching every move I make. Get rid of him!'

'I believe the girl's story – the part of it she told me. She wasn't acting for my benefit. But it wasn't the whole story, I'm certain. Whatever Kaptein Denny's racket is, he's using her as a front for it.'

'Your concern for her is so touching. You make me want to cry! Listen, man! There's a lost city under these rocks. Treasure, probably. If Denny gets back to Luderitz the whole security screen is blown. Sky-high. He'll manufacture just the situation the C-in-C is trying to avoid. We'll have a queue of bums, no-goods, wide boys – they'll be here like flies. Trump up a reason to hold him.'

'For how long? Months?'

'Get on the blower to the C-in-C if you feel you can't cope.'

'First day in command and I can't solve my own problems without running to the boss! Never!'

'Here's a way, Struan. Take the girl to Luderitz in your official boat. You can make it in less than a day. Dump her. Make a few discreet inquiries; try to get some dirt on Denny. It can be done: the top brass there has been ordered to feather-bed you.'

'She'll kick up hellish rough.'

'The scratching and kicking won't last more than a day. Then you can push the cat over the side and have done with it.'

'And leave Kaptein Denny to go scot-free while I'm away?'

'No. I'll stay, right here on Possession. I'll answer for him until you get back. Breekbout can stand turns on guard with me.'

'I suppose it's okay. However, he did promise he wouldn't go ashore.'

'Not while we watch, he won't. But half the bloody day and all the night there's fog. You won't ever know where he is. There's a lot of craftiness there, boy, make no mistake.'

'Kaptein Denny . . .'

'You always give him his title, I notice.'

'There's something about him. Something out of the ordinary. Don't ask me what: all I know, it's there.'

'That makes him dangerous. We've got to break up this lost city party of theirs, Struan.'

'You're sending flowers before the funeral.'

'Maybe. I like flowers better than funerals.'

'Funerals . . .' I told him about the graveyard. 'I've never known Malays use sea shell ornaments before.'

'It's just one more sound reason why we should lock him up. It could have something to do with his racket.'

'What do you think that is, Hellmut?'

'My guess is that he's got a lead on the lost city and is playing the zip-lip with his dumb fisherman act.'

'Brace yourself; let's go and tell 'em our verdict.'

Jutta, Kaptein Denny and Breekbout were hunkered down, drinking coffee in the cheerless bunkroom in front of a small cast-iron stove. There wasn't any proper furniture. A few boxes and packing cases served as chairs and tables. There was a big stove in the galley to meet the needs of scores of guano workers but it was too much trouble for Breekbout.

I helped myself to a pint-sized chipped mug and a biscuit. We'd missed our lunch ashore. I moistened my throat with a couple of sips and told them what I intended. I didn't beat about the bush. Jutta took it quietly, eyeing me as she remained squatting, cup in hand. But I saw the tension in her eyes: I wondered how much pressure she would stand.

Kaptein Denny remarked in a neutral kind of way, 'I gave you my parole I wouldn't go ashore.'

'Bull!'

Koch laughed derisively before I cut him short.

'Will your boat be safe where she lies? I won't be away

more than a couple of days.'

He shot me a glance of appreciation. 'The holding ground is good where she is. Mud and shell in five fathoms. Just outside the line of the main channel. There's a rock which I use as a sort of *ansteuringstonne.*'

He used the word quite naturally but it brought me a fresh rush of suspicion regarding the seamy-faced skipper. *Ansteuringstonne* means an approach buoy. But it's U-boat jargon.

Jutta said, 'I'd like to collect my things from Kaptein Denny's boat.'

I was relieved to be able to break up the tight group.

'Is there anything you want, Kaptein Denny?'

'Not immediately.'

Jutta and I used the whaleboat to cross to the cutter. I was equally relieved to exchange the ammoniacal stink of Possession for the varnished smell of *Gaok*'s mahogany cabin. Jutta spoke only once on the trip across. She'd been viewing the old liner and the shoreline as though to photograph them in her memory.

'Will I see this tomorrow before we leave?'

'Maybe. Depends on the fog.'

She bit her lips. I had the impression I'd pumped the tension a little nearer exploding-point.

While she collected her things from the inner cabin I made a quick check of the anchor cables and then the bridge. *Gaok* was a honey and I'd have loved to have owned her.

I finally went below into the main cabin and opened the mahogany bar.

Jutta came into the doorway.

'What are you doing?'

'Brandy,' I said. 'The Possession party may need a bit of livening up this evening.'

'Do you always help yourself to whatever you want aboard somebody else's ship?'

'Always. It's in the blood. I come from a long line of wreckers.'

She opened her mouth, then bit back whatever she'd meant to say.

I added, 'I also intend to make a thorough search.'

'You've no right!' she flared. 'You're abusing your position. Me first, then him – I mean, his ship – when he isn't here to defend himself . . .'

I put down my drink and faced her, both of us strained and hostile.

'You've taken a hit over this thing, Jutta. I tried to make it easy for you there on shore. I showed you what you asked to see. I believed – believe – your story. As much as you told me. Thousands wouldn't. I've got a job to do: don't get in the way.'

She was distant and ungiving. 'You showed me round: the benevolent grandstanding gesture! At the point of a rifle! Watching every move!'

'You didn't come clean with me. So you got hurt.'

'Hurt! I could howl!' She stood for a long moment getting her face under control, then came up to me at the bar.

'I want to stay. Get that clear. More than anything else, I want to stay. But I'm not going to throw you a load of four-letter bitchery to try and get my way. I could also try a spot of instant sex. It would be easy now we're alone. The situation's tailor-made. Suppose I took off my clothes?'

I saw, now that she was so near, that the little spot in the corner of her eye which I thought was sand wasn't sand at all but a swollen tear-duct.

'If you talk about it, it isn't instant.'

'There's a saying that nice girls always finish last.'

'I wouldn't know, in the Sperrgebiet stakes. You're at the short end of things because whatever you're after is too way-out. Likewise, Kaptein Denny is after something, to, though I don't know what it is – not yet.'

'So you're planning a sneak search of his ship?'

'Not any more. I've changed my mind.'

'Don't let's elbow one another aside in the rush for the boat, then.'

I poured myself another slug and allowed it to coast over my tongue.

'Join me?'

'No.'

'I'm a good listener. Pull out the bung. Get it off your chest. Four-letter words, if it helps.'

'There's nothing more. Except . . .'

'Except.'

She picked up the cheap case containing her things.

'You're going to dump me on the quayside at Luderitz and

say, the hell with you, Jutta.'

'The quay, yes. The rest wasn't in my mind.'

'I've got a one-way air ticket from London. There's nothing left to pay for the return.'

'Get a refund from Kaptein Denny. It'll help.'

She looked away and I knew that he hadn't charged her for the charter of his boat. My suspicion that they might be working in tandem blew up afresh.

'Too bad. If he won't, you can always run home to Daddy.'

If I'd slapped her face the reaction couldn't have been greater.

'You bastard! You unspeakable bastard, for saying that!'

'That's as good an exit line as any. Let's go.'

If she could have moved any farther away from me in the boat she would have. But we were obliged to face one another, I rowing and she sitting in the stern. The sunset was a napalm burst on the clouds out to sea. Its flares caught Jutta's hair and made it more incandescent than gold. She'd got rid of the beret and the wind blew her long hair this way and that, changing the lights in it as it blew. It gave her something to do to fuss with it rather than endure the tight silence. I for my part was grateful for being occupied rowing. It took a long time to reach the island because the run of the sea was against us and I hadn't Breekbout's skill with the heavy craft. By the time we arrived at the jetty the sunset was gone and the sea was bleak and cold. The fog bank loomed close, which made for a shut-off feeling, as if Possession and the two-stack wreck were the only things left in the world.

Koch and I hosted a dismal dinner. We tried to make a party of it by selecting tinned specialities from the abundant store room, and he dressed them up skilfully over the stove. However, our attempt at a semi-festive air, helped by a couple of brandies from *Gaok*'s bottle, exploded when I pitched into Jutta as soon as she appeared. She'd changed into tawny-coloured pants and a green sweater which offset her hair and made it look lovely in the dicky light.

It was her first words which blew the powder-keg.

'It was a wonderful bath, even if it was cold.'

'You – had – a – bath?'

The term was unknown to Breekbout. The others gaped.

'What's wrong with that?'

'Don't you realize that every drop of water on this island is for drinking and drinking alone? That it all comes by ship from Cape Town or from the sun condensers on the roof?'

'Pulling rank again!' she blazed back. 'For every petty thing you have a "do this, do that" . . .'

'My dear girl . . .'

'I'm not your bloody "dear girl"! Nobody said anything about not bathing! It's a good thing I'm leaving: I couldn't stomach much more!'

I thought of the next day's journey. A small boat isn't the place for two people to be at one another's throats. I smothered my retort.

Koch also tried to be placatory during the meal, which was probably the most sumptuous Possession had ever seen; but it didn't come off: for most of the time she was irritable and silent.

It was Kaptein Denny who put the party into neutral gear.

'What's your route to Luderitz, Captain Weddell?' he asked.

'A broad sweep out to sea to the north-west first. Then I head back to the land and make port.'

'Keep away from the deep sea. Use the in-shore route.'

His opinion was worth respecting. After all, he'd used Sperrgebiet waters all his life.

'In-shore? Never heard of it.'

'Between the reefs and the shore.'

'It sounds crazy.'

'Maybe. But it's July and the signs are there. The fog's thicker. The sea's sulky. There's heavy weather coming: a big blow.'

It flashed through my mind that a soft sell about the weather could be an easy way to liquidate me. Lost at sea. No trace. No comeback.

'It isn't what the radio weather forecast says.'

He pulled something from his pocket and handed it to me. It was like a square bit of chamois leather. It had claws.

'Dried albatross foot. Feel it. When it's soft like now it means something special is blowing up. Normally it's hard.'

I showed it to Koch. He by-passed Jutta, who sat silent.

Kaptein Denny went on, speaking with authority, 'You'll be caught, for sure. You're using a boat you don't know.

I don't expect Van Rensburg kept her up to scratch.'

I began to believe him.

Jutta interjected, 'It won't help either of us if we're drowned.'

'Go my way and you won't be.'

He smiled and I found myself warming to him. He'd been the skipper Captain Murray said he'd like around if his ship was in trouble.

'Make a good offing to the north-west once you get clear of Possession,' he went on. 'It's going to be squally from the north-west and west, to start with. You don't want to be close to the land then. Later, head back shorewards and keep inside the shoal plateau all the way up the coast.'

'You talk as if I meant to sail. I'll use the engine, of course.'

'In your place I'd sail. After the squalls you'll find the wind will hang in the west and then back strongly to the south-west. If you stick inshore you'll make most of the passage with a free wind. But if it gets too bad – and I think it will – you can hole up in Alabama Cove. Perfect shelter. But you won't make the cove if you head out to sea.'

Maybe the brandy had stoked Koch up more than he showed because àt the mention of the name Alabama he suddenly burst into the song which is as traditional to South Africans as 'Waltzing Matilda' is to Australians:

Here comes the Alabama, the Alabama comes o'er the sea,
Here comes the Alabama, the Alabama comes o'er the
    sea . . .

Breekbout grabbed a tin dish and started to thump out the catchy rythmical beat. All of us except Jutta joined in the rest of the song.

Girl, girl, the reed-bed girl, the reed-bed is made up for
    me,
On which I can sleep.
Girl, girl, the reed-bed girl, the reed-bed is made up for
    me,
On which I can sleep.

The *Alabama* was a famous Confederate raider which harassed

Yankee shipping off the Cape during the American Civil War. She was joined by a consort, the *Tuscaloosa*. The *Alabama*'s exploits won the hearts of South Africans and were commemorated by the strolling Malay singers for whom Cape Town is famous.

Our nonsense seemed to snap Jutta out of her fit of the blues, especially when the four of us stomped out a kind of war dance. Perhaps that is how the ditty was born in the first place.

I said to Kaptein Denny when I'd sat down and got my breath back, 'I knew the *Alabama* had a base somewhere on the Sperrgebiet but I didn't know where.'

'You'll see Alabama Cove and Tuscaloosa Rock for yourselves if it turns out to be the breed of buster I think's coming,' he replied. 'You'll bless them before you're through, too. When do you leave tomorrow?'

'As soon as the fog starts to lift.'

'It'll be a hairy trip, very hairy.'

'Where's this cove place?'

'About half-way to Luderitz.'

Breekbout broke in unexpectedly on our conversation. 'Give me another shot of brandy, skipper – the ghosts are coming in with the fog tonight.'

Kaptein Denny added, '*She's* coming!'

I explained to Jutta. 'Possession's favourite apparition: a lady without legs. A couple of dogs, too, beside which the Hounds of the Baskervilles looks like a pup.'

I tried to keep it light but she shivered and shed the cheerfulness she'd had during the song.

I tried to jolly her further. 'You have the distinction of being the most tangible female ever to have set foot on Possession.' But she didn't respond.

Breekbout threw back his brandy at a gulp. '*Sy slinger soon 'n piss-pikkewyn.*'

'She staggers like a sozzled penguin,' I translated for her benefit, but even Breekbout's unique gift of articulate speech failed to cheer her. Perhaps it was untranslatable anyhow.

I tried to shut him up but he went on, with a kind of lugubrious, serio-comic deadpan humour, 'I'm now going to put another light in the window so that the ghost can see her way properly.'

'He talks of her as if she were real!' exclaimed Jutta.

Kaptein Denny said, 'On Possession ghosts are as real as . . .'

I don't know what made me say it or why. I didn't intend to kill the party stone dead but I did. There was too much going on below the surface – and the lost city was just below the surface.

'As Swakop or the *City of Baroda* or *U-160*.'

'*Who* did you say?' The legless ghost might have confronted Kaptein Denny, the way he looked.

'Swakop.'

He appeared to need both the ghost lights and the brandy. I intended to string him along because of my suspicions, but Jutta spilt it about the tape recording before I could stop her. The fact that he didn't know about it was a point in her favour. The tape wasn't the sort of thing partners would have kept from one another.

Her explanation gave him time to hang on to the ropes and get his breath back. I watched him all the way. So did Koch.

'Is that all?' he asked.

'Isn't it enough?' I countered.

'Nothing . . . about . . .?' He let the question hang.

Jutta's voice was stony with resentment. 'I'd gladly play it over to you but the strong arm of the law has taken it away from me.'

I'd locked away her tape-recorder and documents in a steel cupboard. This was in the headman's cottage, which I'd allocated to her, while the men shared the bunkhouse. I'd begun to feel better disposed towards her after finding out that Kaptein Denny didn't know about the tape; moreover, I'd been so struck by the evidence of the feeling which Jutta's mention of it had aroused in him that I reckoned a full playback might bring out other interesting things as well.

'Why not?' I asked; and Jutta looked surprised. 'We're becoming involved with one bit of Possession's spooky past, so why not some of it that's for real? That tape's history wired for sound. I'll go and get it.'

Outside, the fog was so thick it was like custard, and my torch didn't penetrate, just threw back a yellow blob of light. If it hadn't been for the concrete path I would have strayed. The smell of the sea was everywhere. It was quite still, and I had my doubts about Kaptein Denny's gale forecast.

I collected the tape from the grim, cold cottage and returned thankfully to the bunkhouse fire.

But my moment had passed as far as Kaptein Denny was concerned. He sat poker-faced and listened with an impenetrable, impassive air while Jutta re-ran the recording. Even the final drama failed to send him, although it had Koch chain-smoking and made me forget to ask him whether the U-boat's two torpedoes which missed the liner had exploded against Possession's cliffs. Even Breekbout, who didn't understand most of it, was infected to the extent of helping himself, unasked, to a few more drinks.

When it ended we waited for Kaptein Denny's reaction.

He said in a strained, tired voice, 'That was like a conversation with a voice from the grave.'

I said, 'You must have seen what happened to *U-160*! You were there!'

'My activities really began in a big way where it leaves off. The liner ran ashore: I went to help, as you know.'

'You and the U-boat must have passed smack next to each other, on opposite courses in the channel.'

'Maybe.'

'Surely you spotted her!'

'It was foggy. Very thick. A wild night. The liner was my only concern.'

'The explosion of *Gousblom*'s magazine must have lit up the whole channel.'

'It did – for a moment.'

'Yet, you never spotted *U-160*?'

'No. I sighted a lot of oil later.'

'The oil was in the north. You took the southern exit. You said so yourself.'

'I went backward and forward all night to the *City of Baroda*. The sea was breaking right across her. The passengers jumped form the stern to reach my boat. She was still among the breakers and not far up on the rocks, like now. When I left next day I could see the oil – and the warships waiting.'

I couldn't fault him and he wouldn't be drawn, so I dropped questioning him further. But his attitude served only to keep the finger on him as far as Koch and I were concerned. Jutta didn't mention what I'd told her about the underlying reason for *Gousblom's* sortie into the channel. Nor did I . . . at least, not until the early hours of the following morning.

She'd stayed by the fire for a long time and I had finally seen her back to the cheerless cottage. I didn't blame her for not wanting to be there, especially alone. The fog was thicker than ever.

I slept fitfully, and so much on a hair-trigger, that I was already awake at some other noise before a violent knocking at the bunkhouse door had me on my feet and racing for it. Kaptein Denny leapt up at the same instant.

It was Jutta. She was shoeless and had been sleeping in her old shore clothes.

I didn't have to ask what it was when I wrenched open the door. I felt the sound in my belly. It wasn't the sharp retching crack of small-arms, but a flight of deep decibels through the darkness which socked one below the diaphragm.

She might have been Possession's lady ghost herself, she was so white.

' "The sound of guns",' she whispered.

CHAPTER SEVEN

It wasn't guns, of course. But what was it?

Kaptein Denny and I ran outside, but Jutta kept to the doorway. Denny stood listening and swinging his head about like a radar scanner. The fog was warmer and clammier.

The past was unwinding and rewinding like Jutta's tape machine. It underscored *Gousblom*'s act of blind courage.

I said in a murmur to Jutta, as if a human voice could possibly have erased the mysterious sound, 'In the Royal Navy it is a captain's prerogative to steer for the sound of guns – Nelson started it.'

'What . . . what . . .?' she began, but Koch yelled from his bunk, 'Struan – what the hell gives?'

I shut him up. It was only nerves, because you couldn't miss that deep horizon-thudding sound again.

We waited. We strained our ears. It didn't come again.

Then Kaptein Denny asked, as softly as a hoarse whisper could be soft, 'What did you say about guns?'

I ga e him a collapsed version of the Convoy WV.5BX affair . . . 'Here!' I exclaimed, 'why am I telling you this? You were at Possession that night! If *Gousblom* heard gunfire, you must have, too.'

Perhaps it was the distorting effect of the fog, but there seemed to be a dead-fish gleam in his eyes which I couldn't get past. He'd got control of his voice since his tension-shot whisper earlier: it was dry and flat now.

'I heard it.'

'Go on, man!'

'It was heavy gunfire . . . somewhere south of the island. The sound was carried on the wind. It was very loud – louder than tonight – and frightening.'

'Did you see the gun flashes?' asked Jutta.

'No. It was a dark, stormy night.'

I said, 'It might have been guns in wartime but it couldn't be guns tonight.'

'It couldn't be guns tonight,' he echoed.

'Don't stand there repeating what I say,' I snapped. 'It

could have been some side-kick to the main event – then. What is it *now*?'

'I don't know.'

'You've been fishing here for thirty years and you don't know . . .?'

He remained silent under my stare. Breekbout and Koch joined us.

Breekbout said, 'It's that ghost leaping up out of hell. It happens when *she* comes.'

'*Bly stil* – pipe down!' ordered Koch. 'What are you talking about guns for? All that's over – years ago.'

I went closer to Kaptein Denny, as if that way I might get at what he knew . . . if he knew. There were new dark stains under his eyes, which were as unreadable as fog-clouded lenses.

'Let's have it!'

'I've heard it now and I heard it then. I don't know what it is any more than you do.'

It was impossible to get anything more out of him. I didn't believe him. The man's duplicity underlined my belief that the decision to break up the Jutta-Denny party the next day was a right one.

We all stood around near the door in uncomfortable silence, until it became too cold. There was no repetition of the sound. I told myself there must be some explanation for it – but what? Sonic boom? Not in the pre-jet era of 1943. Thunder? It never rains on the Sperrgebiet. Man-made? If so, how? After all, you don't mock up a 16-inch broadside on an uninhabited coast just in order to entertain the birds and seals. They'd never heard of Nelson.

Finally we all went inside and had coffee. At 1.30 a.m. the human brain is supposed to be at its lowest ebb and I couldn't get anything out of mine to make sense out of my suspicions about Kaptein Denny, though I was broad awake and on edge. We all were. Jutta decided to come to the bunk-house for what remained of the night, and I fetched her blankets and shoes from the cottage. We kept a light going. Even indoors the condensation dripped from the lamp-glass and made a mini-sound which jarred in the silence. None of us slept much.

It wasn't much of a way to start our passage to Luderitz next day. Kaptein Denny remained uncommunicative and dampened any breakfast sparkle Koch or Breekbout might have been capable of. Jutta and I said perfunctory goodbyes to the others. Breekbout ferried us out to my official boat, the cutter *Ichabo*. The anchorage was blotted with fog and layers of cloud lay low down on the south-western horizon. A slight northerly breeze rippled the channel. The *Ichabo* was a sharp contrast to Kaptein Denny's boat. She was spartan, neglected and dirty. The diesel hadn't been cared for and it sounded pretty rough after I'd battled to start it.

I headed for the gap between the Kreuz shoals and Possession's northern tip: *Gousblom*'s short cut to get at *U-160*. Making it dangerous was Broke Rock, an evil fang which stuck like a bone in the throat of the passage. Jutta was distant and unco-operative. She stood on deck all the time I was busy with the preliminaries of getting under way; staring at what she could make out of the liner wreck and shore, with the intentness of a lovesick teenager.

I was working my way past the reefs before standing off the coast to avoid squalls as Kaptein Denny had advised, when the engine died.

'Jutta!' My temper was shot to hell – by the danger combined with her attitude.

'Forget that view: lend a hand here with the wheel while I fix the engine.'

'I don't know the first thing about steering.'

'You don't have to. Hold it steady, that's all. And keep your eyes skinned, straight in front of you.'

She did as I said, reluctantly. I went below; I tinkered with this and tinkered with that but the diesel wouldn't fire. After a while I put my head out of the box which was the engine room and took a look at the sea. *Ichabo* was being carried towards Broke Rock by the seaward set of a fairly strong current that was pushing northwards up the channel at a couple of knots.

'The bloody thing won't start,' I told Jutta. 'It's in a shocking state.'

'That means we'll have to go back?'

The relief in her voice needled me. I wasn't going to have my plans wrecked at the outset. My irritation laid my decision slap on the line.

'No. We sail.'

'You never give up, do you?'

'No.'

I'd begun to sound a bit tough, even to myself. I softened the come-back. 'No, Jutta. Especially not when I've got a thing like that –' I gestured at the Broke, which was now not more than a couple of cables' lengths away to starboard – 'almost under my keel.'

The northerly wind was backing and becoming flukier: I'd have to make a couple of sharp tacks to get clear. The sea was changing, losing its green and becoming greyer. I didn't like the look of that cloud-bank either. But there was no turning back now: I was committed.

'Steer . . .' I gave her some elementary helm orders while I made sail. The big high boom – the height of a man by the mast gooseneck – was designed to swing clear of the wheelhouse roof, so that the helmsman could have an unobstructed view. I wanted the cutter on the port tack. The wind was freshening all the time and backing north-west. I was afraid that the boat would be caught in irons with someone inexperienced like Jutta at the wheel but the sail took all my attention. Eventually, however, *Ichabo* came round slowly and clawed her away past the Broke and we moved out to sea by way of the narrow passage.

I took the wheel after that and we stood off the coast with the wind freshening still further and the squalls churning up the water in the rebound from the land, as Kaptein Denny said they would. Behind Elizabeth Point – the old ghost town site – the land was a dreary waste. *Ichabo* handled well: she came from the same yard as *Gaok* and probably had much the same underwater lines. But with that ugly menace of the storm on the southern horizon I could have wished for someone better than a girl for my crew. Still, I had gone into it with my eyes open, and by resorting to sail had made my commitment complete to the in-shore route. Yet, looking at the grim, deadly shore and the growing line of white breakers, I wondered with some trepidation what the next twenty-four hours would hold.

By afternoon it was blowing a fresh gale and the wind was steady in the south-south-west. Kaptein Denny's forecast might have been computerized for accuracy. *Ichabo* had begun to run towards the coast in the final leg of a somewhat S-shaped course to pick up the entrance to the inshore route, which lay well to the north of Elizabeth Point. The scud and overcast were down to mast-height. *Ichabo* was riding well: waves would come up astern and her bow would dip on the summit as if she were crouching for some stupendous leap, then she would career into the trough, bucking and shredding the seas. It was an exhilarating and frightening motion, all at once, to be caught in the gigantic crossflow of energy between wind and sea. It was an uncomplicated challenge of survival. It clarified my senses and I didn't feel tired any longer.

Alabama Cove was once the famous Confederate raider's funkhole. It is roughly a funnel-shaped affair with the broad end of the funnel in the north and the narrow end in the south. The coast forms one side of it and a discontinuous line of reefs and sandbars the other. There are gaps of deep water between these hazards. From end to end the place measures three or four miles. There is a safe channel up the middle. This can only be entered via the narrow section in the south. At the other extreme is Tuscaloosa Islet, a low-lying group of rocks which offers a safe anchorage in almost any weather. The islet is named after the *Alabama's* auxiliary and one-time prize, the *Tuscaloosa*. If you could put a trapdoor across the entrance, nothing could winkle out a ship inside. That half-mile-wide gap is a death-trap. You have to negotiate it – Kaptein Denny had briefed me in detail – by steering for a strange beacon made out of whale skeletons, set up at the foot of a solitary sandhill. It's called New Bedford Point. The bones were put there by American whalers that frequented the Sperrgebiet before the Declaration of Independence. The dry, salt-impregnated air has preserved the bones ever since.

I checked the briefing in my mind as I headed for the point. The suspicion also arose, when I saw the holocaust ahead, that it might be a death ride Kaptein Denny had organized to take care of me. But the time for choice was almost past: astern loomed a wild, bleak and rain-scourged sea; chunks of it kept slapping in our faces like wet clothes. There was a continual lash and splutter of spray past the wheelhouse and *Ichabo* writhed and twisted in the mounting seas. The sky was a solid wall of cloud.

'There!' I pointed, to show Jutta.

The landmark I was homing in on – a fan-shaped patch of white among some curious black hummocks behind the whale bones – came into sight. I felt easier. They were spot on where Kaptein Denny said they would be. Once again.

Jutta didn't share my relief. She hung on to the grab-handle in the wheelhouse, her oilskins streaming. I had the windows open because the wipers didn't work.

'In . . . *there*?'

I had to admit to myself it didn't look too good. To myself alone. Spray was exploding forty or fifty feet high on the outer chain of sand-spits and reefs. A clear line of white water demarcated it all the way down to that savage little blinder off the southernmost point. A patch of breakerless water near it was the entrance-way. *Ichabo* was like a wild animal being driven by beaters into the mouth of a *boma* thornbush trap. Violent gusts and squalls bouncing back from the land stirred up the channel like a gigantic swizzle stick.

'Kaptein Denny said it'd be okay.' I couldn't think of anything else to say.

'We'll never make that tiny gap.'

'We will and we must.'

Tuscaloosa Islet, where we intended to anchor, was low and close inshore and difficult to make out. That didn't help Jutta's fears or mine. First we had to reach the channel leading to it.

I spotted discoloured water right ahead of the bow. That meant twelve fathoms – so Kaptein Denny had said. Every warning of his was at a premium now.

'I'm going to snug her right down.'

I had to shout for Jutta to hear.

'Hang on to the wheel for a moment while I fix the sail. Just hold her steady. I won't take a minute.'

I was a fool, of course, to have entrusted the steering under such conditions to a novice, but it seemed simple enough and I didn't intend to be long. I felt the gale cool the sweat inside my oilskins when I got outside the wheelhouse. That should have been a red light, telling me how hard it had been to work the wheel.

But I went on to the sail.

At that moment *Ichabo* must have hopscotched over a shallower bit of bottom. From being merely storm-triggered rollers, the sea became a battering-ram. *Ichabo* caught it on the port quarter. She yawed wildly; the boom thwacked me in the rib-cage. I felt as though I'd been kicked by a mule.

I was hurled off the wheelhouse roof on to the foredeck. I caught a glimpse, plunging past the windows, of the wheel spinning out of control. Jutta's hands were in the air semaphoring her helplessness.

Where I finished up I was swamped and soused immediately by torrents of water. The cutter's head fell off. She started to swing beam-on to the sea – the most dangerous position for a boat under such circumstances. The peril made me try to rise but I fell back, helpless.

Then Jutta was there, holding me to her. Another ice-sharp, hissing deluge poured over the deck. *Ichabo* bucked like a demented rocking-horse.

'Get back! Get back to the wheel, for Chrissake! Leave me!'

But she wouldn't, and hugged me to her. I fought her and I fought for breath.

'Struan! Struan!'

Ichabo lay beam-on to the swell. I managed to get to my knees. I longed to take advantage of the full count to recover my wind but the awful motion of the boat made me throw aside all thought of it.

'Get me up! Get me on my feet! To the wheel!'

I hauled myself upright by throwing all my weight on to her shoulders. And I went on doing so unmercifully, using her as a kind of human crutch to jack me up the ladder to the helm. I battled to get air and give her orders at the same time but I only achieved a whisper because the salt water I'd swallowed had dehydrated my throat.

Finally we made it to the spinning wheel but because of my nausea I couldn't stand upright on the canting deckboards. So I got behind her and clamped my hands over hers on the spokes and tried to steady them. I stayed on my feet by hanging on to her like that and jamming my chest against her back. I whooped; the boom banged; the sail tried to blow itself away with reports like rifle-shots. Every time we fought a wave the pain ripped up my side. Every one of them seemed to pack maximum punch. But we won out. Finally the out-of-control twisting of the boat eased and the seas stopped scouring the decks.

We'd only bought a temporary reprieve, however. We'd lost our critical moment; there wasn't a hope now of hitting the mouth of the channel. The safe bearing on which Kaptein

Denny had red-lined the passage was past. We were careering straight towards the chain of hazards on the seaward side. It was impossible even to try and claw away from them. *Ichabo* was carrying far too much sail, anyway. She crashed through the troughs like a cart through potholes: she was being blown along like a paper boat on a pond.

'Dial a prayer, Jutta.'

'Is it so bad?'

'Odds are ninety to one against.'

Jutta had lost her sou'wester in our scramble for the bridge and her hair was tangling in my face. It smelt of sea, sand and ships. Then I became aware that she wasn't only using her body as a makeweight to steer: it was clinging to mine, saying its own message, in the few desperate moments we had left before *Ichabo* struck.

'Do we swim when she strikes, Struan?'

'Not a chance. It'll be over quickly.'

'Then don't let me go.'

'I won't . . . Jutta . . .'

'Struan?'

'Sorry I made you come.'

'I'm not. Only that I found out too late.'

'Me too.'

Ichabo bored in at the terrifying barrier of driving, rearing water which walled off Alabama Cove seawards. It was leaping so that great chunks of it were breaking off the crests and shooting into the air, like shapes.

'Birds!' I yelled. 'Birds! Millions of 'em! Back from the great migration!'

They were beating the sky apart with their wings. I saw an outside hope.

'Look, Jutta, they're at the fish!'

Maybe she thought I'd gone crazy because she just stood dazed. I threw my weight and hers on the wheel spokes, trying to bring *Ichabo* round a point or two. That would be enough, if I could get her among the birds.

'Help me! Everything you've got!'

She did so, and it helped.

'There's a shoal of fish going through a gap there between the sandbars! The birds are after it! If it's deep enough for them it's deep enough for us!'

Ichabo came round a trifle more, but the deck went clean

under beneath the press of sail.

Water, spume and spray exploded as the sand-spit took the sea's force, and we hurtled into the breakers. About a bucketful of fish was thrown bodily out of the sea on to the deck. There was a crash and a gannet the size of a turkey dive-bombed after them into the planks and broke its neck. Its mates pulled out of their dives in time and the boat was surrounded by white blobs until I couldn't distinguish which were birds and which were bits of spume.

That blind rush through the sandbars and reefs can't have lasted more than a couple of minutes, but it was the longest voyage I've ever made. I expected at any moment to hear the crash of her keel on to the iron-hard sand. A bird went slap through the sail. It rent it across but this had the good effect of making *Ichabo* ride easier.

Then we were through, safe; through the breakers and into the channel beyond. It didn't look safe, though. The shore-line was a wall of black rocks. The surf leaped spectacularly against them and threw spray high over the beachfront dunes. The rocks looked like teeth sticking out of frothy gums.

I got control of *Ichabo* with Jutta's assistance – my side hurt like hell – and we coasted up-channel under short sail towards the anchorage at Tuscaloosa. The birds were every-where, following the same up-channel course as ourselves to-wards the islet: they were there by the tens of thousands.

There was another tricky moment when finally we got into the lee of the islet and felt its blanketing effect on the wind. I couldn't do much because of my side, so decided to bring her up by the simple method of cutting sail and anchor loose at the same moment. Jutta took the sail and I the anchor cable.

The plan worked. The sail came down and the anchor roared out, simultaneously, as if they'd been linked to some synchronizing mechanism; *Ichabo* came to rest at a spot which I reckoned would have been a natural also for the *Alabama*.

Behind Tuscaloosa the wind's roar diminuendoed: the islet formed a splendlid natural bulwark against the gale, which was now nudging peak velocity.

The place appeared to have been thrown up by some mighty volcanic convulsion. It was simply a confusion of great loose blocks of stone, basalt and lava. It was so low on its exposed side that the rollers came smashing half-way over it. Nevertheless it was high enough to constitute a gale-break. *Ichabo* plucked and strained at her cables and a lot of loose gear sloshed about on deck. I made it fast in a hap-hazard sort of way because my side began to hurt as if one of Tuscaloosa's blocks of stone had fallen on it.

Jutta made me leave off before I was properly finished, so she could have a look at it. The day was gone and the storm made it too dark topside to do much good, anyway; so I went down with her to the shabby oil-lit cabin where she had coffee and food ready.

My suspicions towards Kaptein Denny had abated. He'd provided us with the perfect funk-hole. If he'd wanted to get rid of me he could simply have kept his mouth shut about Alabama Cove.

'Let's have a look at your side.'

I stripped off my oilskins and shirt.

'You were terrific, Struan.'

Her fingers, massaging and exploring the injury, continued the tell-tale messages of her body at the wheel.

'You weren't so bad yourself.'

'It's an awful bruise. I don't think the ribs themselves are damaged, though.'

'It feels as if a squadron of seals had made a racetrack of me.'

'It was my fault. I let you down.'

Her fingers were soothing – and charged. They were betray-ing something exciting going on inside her.

'No post-mortems. We're safe in one piece and that's what matters.'

She was very close to me, concentrating on the damage. Concentrating more than was really necessary. She'd got rid of her suède jacket. Her breasts swelled under her sweater, firm and tight.

'I'll rub you with some warm oil.'

'Aboard this outfit you'll find nothing better than engine oil.'

'I'll dig up something. There's a first-aid kit in the engine-room.'

I didn't want to spoil the relaxed moment. I'd never seen her like this, and I didn't want it changed. My rib-cage felt ringed with a steel band when I filled my lungs; but the injury didn't really merit the fuss she was making of it.

She returned with some smelly ointment.

'Horse-doctor!'

'Horse!'

We just couldn't help turning one another on. We grinned at each other.

But I overbid my hand by bringing up *Ichabo*'s narrow escape.

'Old Captain Semmes was a crafty one, to have holed up here in the Alabama. It would have been impossible to flush him out. I wonder how he discovered it? One thing's certain – he didn't get the help of any Yankee whalerman, being a Southerner himself.'

'Lost causes like his always bring out one's inventiveness.'

I should have stopped short and kept to the soft-core talk when I heard the note in her voice but I didn't expect a sudden deadfall after what her fingers had revealed.

'At least Semmes couldn't even have missed finding his way back here – he had seventy chronometers.'

She stopped massaging. 'Seventy? How'd you know that?'

'Prizes. He always took his victims' chronometers as personal loot. He gave my great-grandfather one for his services.'

She sank to a squatting position on the floor. I was on a locker. Her hair burned brighter than any light.

'How'd your great-grandfather come into it?'

'He was the *Alabama*'s Number One gunner. Ex-Royal Navy: he'd been a gun captain aboard HMS *Furious* a couple of years before the *Alabama* started raiding. Half Semmes's crew were British recruits. He was in *Furious* when she annexed Ichabo Island for Queen Victoria.'

'So the Weddell roots really go deep into the Sperrgebiet?'

'If you put it that way.'

That emotive little spot was back in the corner of her eye. 'I do put it that way! It burns me up! You've got this place in your blood – but you want to deny it to me! Why? You're throwing me out like an empty bottle!' She jumped to her feet and stood over me. 'Why'd you have to bring in your blasted *Alabama* gunner? Why couldn't you let us be . . . us?'

I also got up. I pulled on my shirt: that part of things was over.

'You make me sick!' she exploded. 'I wasn't trying to steal

your bloody wreck! Or anything else! I've got a claim, like you! I was only looking . . .!'

'Calm down. It's not my Sperrgebiet. If it was I'd let you stay.'

I was seeing her with clearer eyes than I had before. Her face was more fragile than it had appeared out there on Doodenstadt. Her teeth were very fine and regular and there were several tiny skin blotches on the line of her scalp and forehead. Her mouth looked the sort better suited to smiling than accusing. Up to now there hadn't been much of the first for me.

'You've bawled me out over every nit-picking point you could lay your mind to. Even having a bath.'

'I've got a job to do. You think I'm a bastard, don't you?'

It was the sort of point-scorer one throws around in a quarrel. Neither her fingers nor her body had said that.

'What's the use of going on? We're not getting anywhere.'

'It takes two to tango,' I said. 'I'll listen.'

She said carefully, 'I don't know what you want me to tell you.'

'I think you do.'

She sat down. Her eyes met mine briefly, slid away, and then came back. 'It'll sound like a confession. It's all about myself.'

'That makes me want to hear everything.'

She seemed surprised – and pleased.

'My life, really. I was beginning to find some pieces. I don't know where to begin.'

'When we met is good enough for me.'

'The tape? You do believe it, don't you?'

'Yes.'

'Here it is then, Struan. This isn't a tale I'm pitching you. Neither am I trying to bamboozle you into taking me back to the Bridge of Magpies.'

'I can't, anyway, in this gale. We're here for a couple of days at least.'

She took her time about beginning, her face wearing a withdrawn expression.

'You know about me and the *City of Baroda*. Maybe I sound slightly "schizo".'

'What's really at the back of all this, Jutta? Diamonds? Treasure? The old shakeroo of dead man's gold in a space-age wrapping? Captain Kidd was on Possession once. You're not chasing that sort of moonbeam, I hope?'

'No. The story's unfinished, perhaps unfinishable. Let's first get the record straight. It's taken me years of saving and scrimping to get together enough cash to reach South West Africa. I'm not trying to sound heroic, because you don't feel heroic bashing a typewriter all day and selling house-to-house at night and giving up your holidays in order to earn a few extra pounds. Six thousand miles is a long way to come. I *had* to see the Bridge of Magpies. Everything about me for the past few years has been geared to that one objective.'

'They must have missed you around parties, with your hair.'

'That's the nicest thing you've said to me.'

'You're giving me some unrelated facts plus a motivation which isn't really motivation at all.'

Her look met mine squarely. 'Back there at the wreck I told you about my mother in the single cabin. I never knew who my father was – is.'

'Good God, Jutta! You don't have to be hung up on a thing like that – not in these days!'

Her voice changed in pitch and register. 'You're rather sweet, you know. No, it isn't that aspect of things that worries me. You see, my mother was on her way to South Africa to marry him. They would have been married earlier, in England, but he was suddenly sent out to the naval base at Simonstown . . .'

'A naval officer?'

'It's one of the few things I know about him. I've been searching for clues about him very hard for a long time.'

'Your mother's parents . . .'

She smiled ruefully. 'They didn't know. About him . . . or about me, until it was too late.'

'He never showed up afterwards?'

'Never.'

'And I told you to run home to Daddy!'

'You didn't know then how it could hurt. I felt I might get some clue to his identity at the Bridge of Magpies. Those things of mine you confiscated are a file on my father. Rather, clues that might lead to his identity. It's been a long time. British Admiralty, German Admiralty, Japanese – for what it was worth. Nuremberg Trials photocopies, U-boat records. There are all the false leads I've chased; notes on all the scores of people I've interviewed and corresponded with . . . The more I gathered the more necessary it became to see the wreck and the Bridge of Magpies for myself. The whole thing snowballed once I became deeply involved. It's been the main purpose in my life for years now.'

She was easing up all the time, as if she'd had it all bottled up inside her and had been waiting for the right listener to come along: it gave me a strange, elated feeling to think I might be the one.

'Only a super-sleuth could have dug up that U-boat tape,' I said. 'I didn't know that anything like it existed.'

'It was luck. I've had it only a few days. Part of the luck I've had ever since I started out for the Bridge of Magpies.'

'Go on.'

'My own story is tied up with the way it came into my hands. You see, after my mother died nobody really knew what to do with the wartime waif. A woman called Emma Hasler in Luderitz became my foster mother. I lived with her until after the war, when my grandparents took me away to England. Things didn't really work out with them. They tried their best, I suppose, but my father's name was a dirty word to them. I had a pretty miserable childhood.'

'An odd womanhood, too.'

'You think I'm a bit of an oddball, don't you, Struan?'

'You said it, not I.'

Her eyes were full of broken lights, like a sea with the sun on it.

'My researches have brought me into contact with only one type of man. The old casting-couch principle: information in return for an easy lay.'

'The tape,' I reminded her gently.

She laughed, a little shakily I thought, at something she was remembering. I wanted to know what it was – and I didn't want to know.

'When I landed in Luderitz the other day I went straight to Frau Hasler. We'd kept in touch. She really loves me and it's a shame my grandparents ever took me away. Of course I told her why I'd come back, and that I intended getting to the *City of Baroda* somehow to look for possible clues about my father. At that she produced the tape. It had been left in her husband's care by the spy Swakop all those years ago.'

'Spy?'

'The man who made the recording itself: Swakop. His name's mentioned at the beginning, remember? He was a Nazi spy. He was sent in the U-boat to stir up trouble and lead a pro-Hitler movement among the German population of South West Africa.'

'That tape was dynamite if he'd been caught.'

'Also an insurance policy.'

'What d'ye mean?'

'If he'd been captured he could have used it as a bargaining counter with the authorities. With all its top-secret information it was worth more than solid gold in a currency crisis. I think that really must have been at the back of his mind because he kept the spool though he dumped the recorder after he left the Bridge of Magpies. He had a hazardous desert crossing before reaching Luderitz, Frau Hasler said.'

'I'd also have dumped a bulky war-time tape recorder – pre-transistor model.'

'Swakop was an opportunist. It was pure chance that the U-boat's ship-to-shore radio was left transmitting and he was able to record all that happened inside the U-boat herself during the final action.'

'It cost *U-160* her life.'

'That's part of my puzzle.'

'Why should a Nazi spy go and see Frau Hasler?'

'Her husband was the boss of the pro-Nazi underground movement. Emma Hasler wasn't one of them. Swakop holed up with the Haslers in Luderitz. She warned her husband he was playing with fire and backing the wrong horse. She was right: only a few days after they'd taken me in, someone stabbed Hasler to death.'

'Swakop?'

'No. He was in the clear. He vanished only later – Emma Hasler said he always had an eye to the main chance. She's never seen or heard of him since. Never knew his real name, even.'

'I begin to see why you felt you had to play it back where you did. What happened to the other guy, the Jap they came to pick up?'

'He is one of my file's blind alleys. Every lead on him

has run dead. But he must have been important. There's mention of him in German records – a conversation in the early summer of 1943, when Hitler offered his official condolences to the Japanese Ambassador, Oshima, on the death of Japan's great naval hero, Admiral Yamamoto.'

'Yamamoto! Your man must have been a big shot!'

'The lead runs dead there – again! The Japanese navy records are hopeless. Who or what Tsushima was I can't find out. The Japs didn't follow the Germans' practice of logging all details of U-boats and their movements. The best I can do is to say that *U-160* sailed from the Japanese base at Penang for the Bridge of Magpies on what was called "an exchange of technical information". Technical information! Here! in the desert!'

I felt as if I'd been coshed by the past.

'Why go into all this, Jutta? Surely the answer lies – or lay – with the naval officers stationed at the Cape?'

The enthusiasm she'd shown up to then ran flat and dry.

'There were 687 British officers who served at Simonstown from 1943 until the end of the war. Try asking 687 men, married and unmarried – years afterwards – whether they sired an unwanted brat who is now trying to find out who her father is! Take a look in my letter file if you want to see what the big brush-off really means!'

'Surely the naval records . . .'

'Of course I worked that angle too. But just you watch the Navy clam up when along comes a girl trying to pin parenthood on one of its boys!'

'Right,' I said. 'You've done all this sleuthing and delving and what have you got?'

'I don't know. You threw me out before I could find out.'

'Jutta . . .'

She hurried on. 'I'm just a woman who hasn't found herself. The search has turned into the main thing in my life: a way of existence programmed by a couple of torpedoes which lammed into a ship's side; a mother who died giving me birth; and a father who didn't show up. There've been men of course. Men – and men. I told you about one type, the *quid-pro-quo* lot. There've been a couple of the other sort: you don't get to my age without being turned on. Then, when I thought I'd found something that was going to stick, my heart fired blanks. I couldn't.'

'So you want to find your father, in the hope that it'll put your own pieces together again?'

'That sounds a bit crude for something as deep as what I feel. Maybe you're partly right. Maybe after I've found him I'll get direction and meaning. All I know is that the not knowing acts as a drag on me. Or perhaps I'm one of those people not lucky enough to know love. But I do know this, Struan: out there on Doodenstadt I was within reach of something . . .'

She made a V of her hands and thrust them hard into her groin, too carried away to guess at the extent of the sexual charge the gesture threw at me.

'And I got in your way.'

'You, or your job.'

'I wish you'd told me what you were after, there by the wreck and the grave.'

'To a stranger, a policeman?'

'What's different now?'

'Nothing, really. Everything maybe. I don't know.'

She'd begun to talk as though I were thinking of changing my mind about taking her on to Luderitz: I wasn't. But she'd said enough – and hinted enough – for me not to want to leave an image in her mind of an unfeeling bastard – not any more.

'I've been a drifter for years . . .' I told her about the Greek islands. 'My bivouac was a boat or a bar, whichever was handier. On the primrose path to the Alternative Society, I was pretty close to becoming a juiced-up drop-out. This job is a challenge.'

'So that's why you're acting tough.'

She was unresponsive, so I went on to the story of the *Walewska* oil-spill. I explained that it was the C-in-C's faith which had backed me for the Possession headman's job.

'Good old C-in-C! It takes courage, loyalty and devotion to duty to protect a lot of birds!'

I was losing her, fast. I had to choose quickly. So on impulse I broke the secret of the lost city and explained why Koch and I had banished her and Kaptein Denny. I swore her to secrecy but I wasn't fool enough not to realize that I'd given her a weapon to use against me if she chose.

Her eyes kept going over my face as I spoke. After I'd finished she came and put her hands on mine. I wanted the

100

gale to go on for ever, so that I need never take her to Luderitz.

'Thanks,' she said huskily. 'That makes everything different. You too, thank heavens.'

I was a little sandbagged by the way she'd come over to my side. But it wasn't the sort of takeover I particularly minded.

'Maybe you'll find out – for me. I'll wait at Emma Hasler's.'

I couldn't meet her eyes. I knew it would be a lie if I said yes.

'I wouldn't know where to begin.'

My reply made us both miserable and after that she closed up. There wasn't any more to say and we sat silent and uncomfortable for a long time, while the gale roared overhead and plucked and boomed over Tuscaloosa as if trying to ape the sound of guns. Later I lay broad awake for hours in my bunk listening to the tumult – so similar to the one going on inside me – and to the quarrelling and clucking of myriads of birds descending out of the night and making for their old nesting-grounds on the islet.

The gale lasted two days. You couldn't have called the *Ichabo* a lovers' hideaway during that time: Jutta and I were shut off from one another; so found small jobs for ourselves round the boat, discussing them in impersonal voices. The mast and boom were badly strained and kept me occupied fiddling them and fixing the rigging; and I think Jutta felt relieved when I asked her to stitch the torn sail. It was wet and unhandy, so we brought it below into the big cabin where she worked on it. I could have tinkered with the engine but didn't. It was an excuse (which I wouldn't have admitted to myself) for delaying as long as possible at Alabama Cove.

On the second morning Jutta had gone on deck while, down in the cabin, I put some final touches to the sail.

I heard her call above the wind. 'Struan! Struan! A boat!'

The white sail and the breakers combined to look like a split image, far away near the channel entrance, until one saw the flared bow and characteristic black strake of a Nieswandt cutter. The way she was being handled and the press of sail made me certain it was Kaptein Denny. Then she came a little closer, and I spotted *Gaok*'s unmistakable figurehead.

'That boat's in a hurry, Jutta.'

'He's alone. I don't see anyone else.'

Goak finally came almost alongside at the same cracking pace before Kaptein Denny spun her round and tossed me a securing line.

He jumped aboard. His eyes were strained and red and his mouth was bracketed with fatigue. Salt had made a white fuzz on his beard stubble and round the neck of his heavy turtleneck sweater; it emphasized the rough planes of his face. However, there was a jauntiness about his stocky figure which I put down to excitement at the storm and his triumph over the sea's challenge.

'Dr Koch sent me. Urgent. You're to come at once. There's a strange ship at the Bridge of Magpies. She's up to no good.'

CHAPTER EIGHT

'What sort of ship?'

'A deep-sea trawler, so she says.'

'Why, so she says?'

'I'm used to seeing all sorts on the fishing grounds. Not one like this, though.'

'What's different about her?'

'Big. Too big for a trawler. Perhaps a thousand tons. And too small for anything else.'

I could sense Jutta tensely wondering while I questioned Kaptein Denny, whether I would return to Possession. I intended to, but hadn't committed myself. The summons let Jutta off reprisal and me off the hook as far as she was concerned. It was my big face-saver. It solved one problem and created others. Yet I was uneasy that Koch felt he couldn't cope.

'What was she up to?'

'Nothing that I could see. She came in during the storm and anchored in the channel as far away out of sight of the huts as she could.'

'That's no reason for me to rush back.'

It was curious that Koch hadn't sent me a note giving the reasons for his anxiety. Disquieting, too, that he'd dispatched Kaptein Denny, post-haste and unrestricted, when he'd been so keen to keep him incommunicado on Possession.

'No, it's not. She's foreign built and decked-in for'rd with a kind of whaleback. You don't get that in a trawler. She's also carrying a lot of heavy gear on deck.'

'What sort of gear, man?'

'I didn't go aboard, Dr Koch did. With Breekbout.'

'And then?'

'He came back to Possession looking worried. All he said was, take your boat at once and go and find Captain Weddell. That ship stinks.'

'You asked no questions?'

'You don't, when the jail doors are suddenly thrown wide open.'

'Also you knew exactly where to find me?'

'You used sail from Possession. That left one answer in the storm: Alabama Cove.'

'My engine packed up.'

'I thought so. But that didn't stop you.'

Jutta said, 'We had a narrow escape getting here. Struan hurt his side.'

'Bad?'

'I can still handle a ship.'

'Good. Let's go then. I'll tow you out.'

'You'll – what?'

'Tow. The gale's dying. I know a way back close inshore all the way.'

'You're a devil for punishment.'

'It's safer, really. After a blow like we've had you have to keep a weather eye open for rogue rollers. They seem to come out of nowhere. If one caught us out to sea, towing, we'd be in big trouble.'

'By the same token, why wouldn't that happen inshore too?'

'The shoals and reefs would break up a wave before it could reach us there.'

There was a controlled zest about the man: he was itching to go. Either I was going to put my trust – possibly my life and Jutta's too – in his hands or I wasn't. He hadn't let me down over Alabama Cove.

'Coffee,' said Jutta. 'We can talk below.'

'No time.'

His hurry reawakened a tiny spark of suspicion in my mind. Why was he so anxious to move out? One would have thought a couple of hours' wait, until the wind finally dropped, wouldn't do any harm. I let it ride. Perhaps it had something to do with negotiating the coast?

'Right – shoot!' I said. 'Give me a hand with the anchors first.'

He came for'ard to help me. His eyes were everywhere – on the sea, on the land, on the sky.

I said, 'Towing will use up a lot of your fuel. We'd better transfer what's in *Ichabo*'s tanks before we start. Her old clanker's had it: it won't want fuel this trip.'

'No time.'

Again there didn't seem all that much need for his bustle. I must have shown something of what I was thinking because he added, with a grin which disarmed me, 'If I run out of gas I'll piss in the tanks.'

The down-channel tow wasn't a milk-run. It was a sweat, even in the relatively calm water of Tuscaloosa's lee, to fix the rope so as to avoid snarl-ups. But Kaptein Denny knew his business: he handled things surely and expertly. I sent Jutta aboard *Gaok*, to be safe in case we ran into trouble and had to cut *Ichabo* adrift. She wanted to stay, on the grounds that my injury needed further attention. It didn't, but it was nice to hear her.

Within half an hour of his arrival Kaptein Denny dragged *Ichabo* clear of her funkhole, at the end of a tough manila hawser. We left the miserable little island behind, with birds clustered over it like flies on a kill. Near New Bedford Point the sea showed signs that the gale was on its way out: the water glistened darkly instead of breaking white and there were patches of green amidst the universal, monotonous grey.

Kaptein Denny took the hazards of the whalebone point in his stride but the way he squeezed the two cutters through, until white water came churning over *Ichabo*'s side, almost turned my seasoned stomach! *Ichabo* cavorted at the end of the hawser like a yo-yo free-falling in space with only a string to bring it up short. He repeated the act a little farther down the coast at the cost of much adrenalin. I never guessed there were such routes. The wind decreased; our speed increased.

By afternoon the wind had fallen to a fresh breeze. Denny and I had agreed, on leaving Tuscaloosa, that when this happened (he had slated Seventy-four Rock, another half-submerged islet well down the coast as the place where it would happen and he was right) we would drop the tow and use sail, so as to make better time. But the wind was veering west, and with my injured side I couldn't manage the short, sharp tacks that were necessary. So *Gaok* took up the hawser again and strung *Ichabo* along that frightening shoreline, working up to a useful speed of six knots. Seals appeared as the water smoothed: one huge fellow, a sort of cheer-leader, led his pack round the cutters for nearly an hour, playing waterborne ring-o'-roses.

When night came I didn't want to blow our luck by carrying on, but Captain Denny wouldn't hear of anchoring. His knowledge of the way was uncanny. He rigged a light in *Gaok*'s stern and I held station on it – as tense and nerve-racking a business as flying a plane dual control when you can't hear the pilot and don't know what his next move will be.

About midnight – I hadn't an idea where we were – Kaptein Denny hailed me to say we were about to anchor. He cast off: *Ichabo* freewheeled on, and I felt utterly helpless. But I needn't have worried. Kaptein Denny ran the smartest shop, *Gaok*'s guide light did a quick flipper turn, disappeared, and then the boat was back alongside *Ichabo* again, made fast, and sheep-dogging my powerless craft to anchor.

We had a quick hard-tack supper aboard *Gaok* and turned in. The last sound I remember hearing before dropping off was the thunder of the surf close by.

We started off again in the morning before the sun broke up the fine spidery structure of the fog. There was no wind and an almost uncanny quiet. Jutta joined me in *Ichabo*. Kaptein Denny told us that the switchback part of the trip was over and that it wasn't far to Possession, but he made a minor mystery out of the ship's position. I thought it boosted his ego.

Jutta stood by me at the wheel, watching the silvery splash from the hawser as it dipped and tightened, dipped and tightened. In the confined space the sweet slept-in woman's clothing smell of her stirred my senses. The fact that my attention was on her made it all the more remarkable that my subconscious should have thrown up something about Kaptein Denny.

'Jutta! For crying out loud! He said, *U-160*!'

'Who?'

'Kaptein Denny, of course. He said, *U-160*!'

'Why shouldn't he?'

'There at the grave – *U-160*!'

'After all, he knew it.'

'But he didn't, Jutta! That's what I'm saying! He was aware that the *City of Baroda* had been sunk by a U-boat. A U-boat. He didn't know specifically *which* U-boat! Then, before he has heard your tape which identifies it, he comes up with *U-160*. Not any old U-boat, but a particular one. What a give-away!'

'I don't get you, Struan.'

'What I'm saying is that if Kaptein Denny knew the U-boat's number he wasn't at the Bridge of Magpies that wartime night, just fishing as he'd have us believe. He's playing a very deep game. He must have been part of that spy operation. Don't you see what I'm driving at?'

'Yes, I do now. That he came to the Bridge of Magpies knowing all about *U-160* and her rendezvous to pick up one spy and land another.'

'His function may have been to ferry the Jap Tsushima from Luderitz under cover of his fishing; then take back to port the man they landed – what was his name?'

'Swakop. It jells, Struan! Then everything came unstuck for him when *U-160* tangled with the liner and *Gousblom*. Maybe that's why Swakop had to make his way across the desert to Luderitz. Frau Hasler said he was nearly all in when he arrived.'

'Kaptein Denny's liner rescue act could have been a blind. He'd have been obliged to provide a very sound reason for being around that night. He'd also have had Tsushima on his hands after he'd missed the U-boat. That's why he remained so unbelievably modest about the whole business. It was a gigantic bluff!'

'He even dodged the warships.'

'With reason, if he had a Japanese spy aboard. But all that doesn't really concern us, Jutta. What does, is the fact that he's back here now – as he's been every winter for thirty years, on his own admission. What's the drawing-card? Loot from the lost city? Loot from *U-160*? Whatever it is can't be easy to get at, because he keeps coming back. And only at one season of the year, when conditions must be favourable for his operations.'

'I wasn't going to tell you, Struan, but he wouldn't charge for bringing me here.'

'Ah! How did he react when you first approached him about chartering his boat?'

'Surprised. Pleased.'

'He wasn't worried about operating in forbidden territory?'

'He laughed it off. I was touched by his willingness to help.'

'We're beginning to discover why.'

'He's kept his nose clean up to now. He didn't object when you ordered him off the shore.'

'With reservations. He still wasn't going to shift from his boat, remember.'

'It doesn't add up, Struan! If he wanted you out of the way, why has he made such an effort to bring you back again? Why risk his neck in the storm? It would have been an easy enough excuse to say he couldn't find us. Why be in such a hurry to get back to Possession?'

'Koch's no-good ship seems to have complicated the issue.'

'Look, there she is!'

We broke clear of the wisps of fog and I realized immediately where we were – off Elizabeth Point's ghost town. There were only about four miles of open water now between us and Possession. In the channel, somewhat to the south of the usual anchorage, as though avoiding the huts ashore, was the ship.

'Sure, that's no trawler.'

The vessel was too far away for me to make out her name but my glasses showed a low black hull with a whale-back fo'c'sle, a straight up-and-down outmoded cutwater, and a single, high, old-fashioned stack with a white band painted round it. Two very tall ventilators towered almost as high as the marking. She had a very square bridge and a box-like structure in the stern which on a warship would have been a radio or radar shack. But she wasn't a warship. Her masts were squat and sturdy, with heavy booms and derricks, their strength out of keeping to her size. No crew was visible.

'She looks . . . sort of sinister, Struan.'

'All black ships do. I'll find out soon enough. I'll go aboard once we've tied up.'

Possession advertised its presence in its usual nostril-assaulting manner. The two cutters plugged slowly across the sea to the anchorage. They were white with salt, as if they'd taken a pasting on the Iceland cod run. We remained visible for miles but there was no sign from the stranger that she'd sighted us. Her decks remained empty of men.

'Where the devil's Breekbout?' I asked irritably. 'He should be getting out the whaleboat to fetch us.'

Jutta took a look through the binoculars.

'Not a sign. Having breakfast in bed, perhaps, while the cat's away.'

I tried to relax.

'Baths are on the house today.'

She smiled back. 'Think of all that lovely drinking water

going down the drain.'

'You tempt me to rush in on you and switch off the tap.'

'Possession chivalry to ladies-in-the-nude.'

I wanted more of her in that mood. We'd taken up where we'd left off in Alabama Cove, but the business of making the two cutters fast cut across it, and Kaptein Denny had us rushing backwards and forwards in the process of manoeuvring up to the mooring buoys.

When it was done we went aboard *Gaok*.

'They haven't hung out the flags for our return, Kaptein Denny.'

'Breekbout I could understand: Dr Koch puzzles me.'

I'd come prepared to read anything into his words but they were neutral enough.

'I'd have expected him to be chewing his nails waiting for us to heave over the horizon, the way you spoke.'

'He was, when I set out.'

All the time his eyes were scanning the anchorage, the channel, the black ship, the shoreline and the island. There was no smoke from the bunkhouse chimney and a gobbledygook of bird noises floated across the water. The place had a never-never air, like a stage with props but no actors. They might all have been there for ever. The Sperrgebiet has that trick of making time scales wobble.

After ten minutes' waiting I'd had enough. The others were uneasy too.

'We'll use your dinghy,' I told Kaptein Denny.

Even the splash of oars sounded unnaturally loud as we rowed to the jetty. So did our footsteps on the concrete path leading to the bunkhouse door.

I threw it open.

'There's no one here. You two scout around. Koch may have left a note for me. I'll take a look-see at the cottage.'

The door was half-open and Breekbout was sitting at the radio transceiver. His eyes were half shut and his mouth had the beginnings of a silly grin, as if he'd shaken loose a laugh out of his own death.

His head was smashed open like a pomegranate.

The radio was also wrecked and bits of its innards lay around like Breekbout's brains.

I wanted to puke. But I had enough remaining sense not to leave before I'd taken a look at the remains of the radio.

The transceiver switch was on 'Send'. The dial pointer stood at the Silvermine frequency. No one on Possession besides myself knew that frequency. I crashed my rifle butt into the dial's face so as to make it unreadable.

I went back to the bunkhouse.

'. . . he had *three* ghost lights burning,' Kaptein Denny was telling Jutta when I entered.

'It didn't help him,' I said. 'Besides, ghosts don't bash in heads with sealing clubs.'

'Oh God!' she'd seen my face.

Then hot and cold sweat chased one another across my face and body and reaction shakes set in.

Jutta grabbed me by the sleeves of my jersey. 'What . . .!'

I passed my rifle to Kaptein Denny, whose face was a mask. 'You'd better take this for the moment. I couldn't manage to fire it even if someone was about to kill me too.'

'Struan! What happened!'

I tried to pull myself together and tell them but I made such a poor job of it that Jutta went for some brandy. She found the bottle but it was empty. Breekbout had seen to that.

'I could have grown to like that stupid sonofabitch.'

I managed to say it and it helped the mind-numbing shock of that hideous object at the radio, plus my wavelength discovery. Breekbout had been a clown pointing his laugh lines in the appealing idiom of the *gamat* and that seemed somehow to make his dreadful end the worse.

Kaptein Denny left Jutta to do the fussing over me. He took up guard just inside the door where he couldn't be seen, with my rifle in his hands and an ugly commando knife in his belt.

When I'd got my composure back I said to Jutta, 'Blow out those lights. They give me the creeps. They may have guided the killer.'

She did so. I turned to Kaptein Denny. 'He can't stay like that . . . a piece of sail or something to cover him.'

He handed me back the gun. 'There's no one around – absolutely nothing.'

I took over his observation post but it did seem rather ridiculous. There was no sign of anyone ashore and no activity aboard the black ship.

Kaptein Denny found a tarpaulin.

'We three stick close together from now on,' I said. 'You stay outside the cottage, Jutta, while we see to him, but close enough to yell if you spot anything. But anything.'

Kaptein Denny and I went inside and masked the bloody cameo. I watched him closely but he paid no special attention to the transceiver.

'Look at the bloodstains,' he pointed out. 'They're old and dried.'

'The birds have been at him too.'

'That means he's been dead a couple of days.'

'That makes it as soon as you left.'

'He was fine then. One loses track of time in a storm.'

What did he mean by that sidestep? I asked myself. Could he have killed his jailer and escaped . . . no, that line of argument broke down when you thought he'd come after me and brought me back. As a bluff, though? A cover?

'No one had anything to gain by killing this poor bastard,' I said.

'No?'

'Who, then?'

'He was the only one except yourself who could work the radio.' He gestured. 'Whoever it was made it clear that he didn't want you to communicate.'

'Bastard,' I said automatically. True, I'd myself taught Breekbout to transmit. But neither he – nor anyone else – knew about my hot line to the C-in-C.

'Where *is* Koch?'

'Most likely on his way to Luderitz to report this.'

'And very considerately sent the whaleboat back empty across the channel and let it tie itself up at the jetty.'

'Then possibly he's over at that ship.'

'We've been back for over an hour. The cutters were in sight long before that. Koch's had plenty of time to make his number if he's around.'

'Why shouldn't he be?'

'That ship. Not a man's visible. Either the crew's devoted to the 'tweendecks or they've been ordered to stay out of sight.'

'Why?'

'We'll soon find out. I'm going across to her – now.'

'Alone?'

'All three of us. As I said, we keep close. '

I checked that the rifle's magazine was full and worked a shell into the breech. I put the safety-catch on.

'Let's get cracking.'

We rejoined Jutta, who accepted my decision without comment. We used Kaptein Denny's dinghy instead of the heavier whaleboat, since he had to do the rowing because of my side. It was a long pull. Not much was said. All kinds of random explanations and accusations wheeled through my brain. Some of them were so way-out as to be pure nonsense. It was the carry-over of shock, of course. I was prepared to suspect Kaptein Denny's silence, even. Cut it out, I told myself, the man's simply saving his breath for rowing. By the time we were half-way across I'd got control of my thoughts and dumped my overheated fears overboard. My mind was empty and cool and ready for what I'd find aboard the ship.

'They're coming up on deck!' exclaimed Jutta.

If they'd been as shy as the ten virgins up to now, that's where the resemblance ended. They were as tough and motley a bunch as could be raised in any waterfront bordello. A man in a peaked cap – presumably the captain – joined the population of the hitherto empty decks. He took up station on a narrow cat-walk surrounding the bridge, and watched us approach.

Kaptein Denny read out the vessel's name: *Sang A.*

'Never heard it before. Where she from?'

'I can't make out – it's some sort of Eastern writing.'

'She could be, with those lines and a name like that.'

It wasn't her lines, though, which caught our interest when we came closer, but some big tarpaulins concealing unknown bulky objects abaft the bridge. There was another big, mysterious hidden hump near the foremast. An armoured rubber hose snaked across the whaleback from some machinery in the bows, and ended up looped in the forward rigging.

'Those men are Chinese,' said Jutta.

They certainly looked it, but more obvious than any national characteristic was the rough-tough unwelcoming look on their faces. They didn't offer to make us fast when we came alongside. However, it was not really necessary because about fifty feet of heavy chain cable hanging in scallops from the rail offered a natural securing point. More of the cable was lying on the deck. There was also a clutter of wire rope, cables and powerful block-and-tackle gear. If the ship had been bigger I'd have thought she was a cable-layer.

'Attention!'

The arrogance of the Teutonic form of address made me dislike the man on the catwalk before even I knew his name.

'You the captain?'

'*Ja*. Come here.'

We had to skirt round to reach the ladder leading to him. There was clutter everywhere and more tarpaulin-masked objects. The shack aft which had puzzled me from a distance intrigued me more from close to. It didn't appear to have a deck entrance and its portholes were so high you couldn't see in. However, it was inhabited: a face looked out from one of them as I mounted the ladder.

'Emmermann. *Sang A*.'

The captain was a chunk of a man in his middle fifties; as tall as my own six-foot one, with a craggy face, big nose and short iron-grey hair. His lips were indrawn and his very large eyes were trenched with crow's feet at the corners. A scar ran from the corner of his left eye to his ear. His manner was one of controlled hostility.

I introduced the three of us.

Since summoning us to the cat-walk he'd been joined from inside the bridge by another man, like the rest of the crew an Oriental.

'First Officer Kenryo.'

His introduction was as unwilling as the rest of our reception had been. If it had been on Kenryo's account, I could have understood it. He had a flat, golliwog face, with a smashed nose and the emptiest black eyes I'd ever seen. He was short and stocky and wore jeans and a greasy flannel tartan shirt. And I didn't care for the way he undressed Jutta with his eyes.

'Is it all right to speak English?'

'For us, but not for the crew.' There was a trace of American in Kenryo's accent.

'They're Chinese?'

'No,' replied Emmermann. 'Korean. *Sang A* means shark. Our home port's Pusan.'

'We're here with the Korean trawler fleet offshore,' added Kenryo.

A couple of the crew had gathered under the cat-walk, which

wasn't very high above their heads; and seemed to be idly listening, despite Kenryo's statement that they should not understand our conversation. He leant over the rail and said something to them. A flash passed through Kaptein Denny's eyes but it was gone again as quickly as it had come. One of the crew came back with a repartee and they all sniggered. I guessed it had something to do with Jutta.

'No fishing is permitted here. There's a strict twelve-mile offshore limit.'

Maybe I pulled my authority too hard, out of reaction over the crack about Jutta.

'So?'

'That's the law.'

'So? And you carry out the law?'

'If necessary. I'm the island headman. These waters fall under my authority.'

'You come aboard my ship with a gun and threaten me, eh?'

'I'm not threatening: just getting the record straight. There's no problem, provided you don't fish.'

'The record is straight then. Good morning!'

'If you don't know the law, you should.'

'Now I know it.'

'Good. Another thing. There's been a death on the island. One of my men . . .'

I left out the details and purposely made Breekbout's end sound more like an accident. I wanted to hear what they had to say before I started talking about murder.

Kenryo cut me short. 'None of our men has been ashore. *Sang A* isn't in a hot seat.'

'I didn't say you were. I'm investigating. I was away when it happened. It could be something more than an accident.'

Their faces remained blank.

'I'm also looking for a colleague of mine who seems to have disappeared: Dr Koch.'

'Never heard of him. We saw no one.' Kenryo's eyes were black and beady.

'Didn't you see the whaleboat being ferried around?'

'There was the storm. You couldn't see much. If he used the boat in the gale maybe he drowned.'

'The boat's safe at the island.'

'Then he didn't drown.'

This sort of thing was getting me nowhere. The ball was back in my court – if I'd ever managed to get it into theirs.

'Fair enough. This becomes a police matter, of course.'

They shrugged as if they realized, as I did, just how much that meant on the Sperrgebiet! There was nothing else to do but leave. We headed back to our boat. The group of plug-uglies, who had been standing chinning between themselves, fell silent; I'd get no more change out of their sullen faces than I had out of the officers.

We pushed off. I took the oars because I wanted to test my side. It was one of Possession's rare beautiful days: birds trailed over the anchorage like a king-sized paper-chase, fishtailing down after the shoals in the water. I hadn't much inclination to admire: I was smarting inwardly at the way my show of authority had fallen flat on its face on *Sang A*'s deck.

'Captain Weddell!' Kaptein Denny was straining and peering at the land. 'It's the Land-Rover!'

Before I could turn to look, Jutta exclaimed. 'There's been a fire.'

I looked. 'Not a fire. A conflagration.'

The blackened skeleton of the vehicle stood out clearly against the champagne-coloured sand.

'No sign of Dr Koch,' Kaptein Denny observed.

'We'll soon check. Help me with the oars. We'll take the boat in.'

'It would be a mistake.'

'Mistake! Koch could be lying there . . .'

'Keep your voice down! They'll hear you aboard *Sang A*.'

'Well, say it, for pity's sake!'

'If *Sang A* wanted to fix us by taking a crack at our cutters while we're ashore, we'd be playing right into their hands by going there now.'

I eyed him with a new respect. The more so when I noted that *Sang A*'s hoodlums were still lining the rails, watching us. 'What do you suggest?'

'We'll go ashore all right but we'll use both cutters for the trip.'

'It'll look pretty silly towing each other across such a small stretch of water.'

'It'll be sillier still if we should lose them. Without boats we'd be hamstrung.'

'Right.'

'It will also be a subtle demonstration of no confidence in our new neighbours.'

Jutta never stopped looking at the burnt-out vehicle. She was very withdrawn.

When we reached the cutters, Kaptein Denny took *Ichabo* in tow and made as wide a detour of *Sang A* as possible. The water was deep off the landing beach and we anchored close in. From our position a sandhill barred further view of the Land-Rover.

I took the rifle and made as much show of it as I could, for the benefit of *Sang A*. I was sure every move of ours was being watched through binoculars.

We landed. When we obtained our first clear sight of the vehicle I ordered Jutta to stay right where she was.

It looked like a charred tree-trunk behind the wheel.

It was Koch.

I didn't feel the same revulsion for his remains as I had done for Breekbout's. Maybe the earlier shock had conditioned or numbed my reactions. It was only a faceless, blackened outline, really. We'd also come half-prepared for tragedy.

Kaptein Denny and I fanned out to approach the Land-Rover from both sides, I with the rifle cocked. As I walked cautiously through the sand I had a curious impression – one of those ready-made pictures the mind throws up in times of stress – that I'd seen it all before. It was coupled with the foreboding of a pattern of future tragedy, into which these two deaths were inexorably grooved.

I reached the driver's side of the Land-Rover at the same moment as Kaptein Denny got to the other.

'All clear!'

He straightened from the half-crouch he'd gone into when he'd circled round, and put away his knife.

'Look at this!'

The steel fascia was blackened and buckled. The bonnet was also starred with glass fragments from the windscreen.

'An explosion did this,' he said.

I tried not to give way to my doubts and suspicions before testing all the every-day possibilities.

'Of course it did. The tank went up. It's right behind the driver's seat.'

'If it had, the force of it would have thrown him forward and out.'

'Some sort of freak accident.'

'It wasn't an accident. Come over to my side and see. His left leg's gone.'

I went round and joined him.

'Someone sneaked up alongside and threw something next to him on the floor.'

'Something?'

'Grenade. That would account for all the buckling and glass out front.'

'Bastards . . .!' I began and then took hold of myself: cursing wasn't going to help. 'This was done days ago.'

'*Seker* – for sure. The gale swept away the footprints. You couldn't prove anything against anyone now.'

'Except the grenade.'

'The trail's already cold. By the time the experts sort that one out it'll be in deep freeze. And *Sang A* will be over the horizon.'

'She's not bloody well going over any horizon! I'm going right back on board!'

'A lot of men have died in unexplained ways on the Sperrgebiet, Captain Weddell. You don't want to be among them.'

Our eyes locked. I felt instinctively he'd not had anything to do with the killings.

'Thanks,' I said. 'I needed that reminder. Now let's do something about Koch.'

'I've got some spare canvas aboard *Gaok*.'

We went to Jutta, who had been waiting behind the sand-hill, and told her what had happened.

'Why?' she burst out. 'Why kill him? Why kill Breekbout? They didn't have any secrets worth murdering them for . . .' She caught my warning glance and remembered the lost city and that Kaptein Denny didn't know about it. What *did* he know, though? He'd now moved right out of my area of suspicion and was firmly aligned with us against *Sang A*. That was merely the end of the negative aspect, however: he'd done nothing positive yet to win my confidence. And he often indulged in a mannerism which, from my point of view, wasn't at all positive; a trick of quartering the anchorage as if he expected to see something there. His quick survey always began down by the Bridge of Magpies and worked its way up-channel. His eyesight was so phenomenal that I was sure he'd spot anything long before Jutta or I.

'I'll fetch that canvas.'

Kaptein Denny went off in the dinghy, leaving Jutta and me.

'Keep out of sight of *Sang A*,' I warned.

'The fact that they're a lot of weirdies doesn't turn them into murderers, Struan.'

'Who else could it be?'

'Who knows?'

A very uneasy present had blown up in my face and swamped a very puzzling past. Until I'd been confronted by the two murders and the mysterious *Sang A* I'd felt mentally like a castaway wandering on the dim shores of that past – Jutta's past, Kaptein Denny's past, Doodenstadt's past. Now, however, I'd snapped clean into the present. In doing so a new suspicion the size of Possession Island hit me: was the C-in-C's mission itself not a blind? Maybe it was a front for something much more sinister and deep-rooted that he couldn't – or wouldn't – reveal at our interview. That would make sense of the underhand way he'd brought me from Santorin and his insistence on secret, single-handed investigation on my part. All this carried the implication that Koch was part of his conspiracy. Then he would have been the one who had attempted to get off that emergency radio signal to the C-in-C, via Breekbout. Why not send it himself, though? It was confusing, but possible; and what the time sequence of events was in regard to the two killings I'd never know. I wondered if the little admiral was gambling on the expectation that I would see the lost city mission for the blind it really was, and get his real message when things started to hot up? They had now.

Jutta and I stood around without saying much more until Kaptein Denny returned. He and I shrouded Koch in the canvas and left the body in the Land-Rover. It was so charred that we reckoned the jackals wouldn't scent it.

Then we rowed out to *Gaok*.

I sought a topic to defuse the underlying tension.

'Why'd you call her *Gaok*, Kaptein Denny?'

'It's short for *Gaokhaosib* – Hottentot for the Bridge of Magpies.'

Everything always seemed to come back to the Bridge of Magpies! That past again!

We went on in silence, each wrapped in his own thoughts.

Finally when we three were seated in *Gaok's* cabin drinking coffee, I said, 'Priority number one is for me to go aboard *Sang A* again.'

'What purpose will it serve, Struan?' asked Jutta. 'They will deny any knowledge of Koch – they have already done so – just as they did in the case of Breekbout. It's a foregone conclusion.'

'It would look odder if I didn't inform them there'd been another murder. It mightn't sound too good in court one day.'

'They know already. It's a long way from here to court.'

'What if they did kill them both? What do you intend to do about it?' asked Kaptein Denny. He'd been very reserved up to now. 'You haven't even a radio link, now, with the outside world.

'You'll scare them off if you go at it like a bull at a gate,' said Jutta. 'They'll up-anchor and vanish. That won't do anyone any good.'

'They won't.'

There was something about Denny's flat assertion that made the small bell of mistrust tinkle again at the back of my brain.

'What makes you so sure?'

I had a feeling he'd overplayed his hand and he knew it. He back-pedalled on the answer and merely said, 'It's a move which could backfire disastrously on us.'

'How?'

'Look what happened to Breekbout and Koch!'

'They wouldn't dare . . .'

Jutta interrupted me excitedly, 'Look! Look! *Sang A* is getting up steam!'

We rushed to the nearest porthole. There was a thin wisp coming from the tall funnel, and a bow winch was taking in the slack of the anchor cable.

'That does it!' I rapped out. 'Move! She mustn't get away!'

CHAPTER NINE

I slipped *Gaok*'s cable and Kaptein Denny had the diesel roaring in under a minute. We got under way and tore off in the direction of *Sang A*.

Jutta joined me on the bridge. I took a long look at the black ship.

'We're in danger of making fools of ourselves. That ship's not up-anchoring at all.'

'What's all the activity about then?'

I shouted to Kaptein Denny to cut our speed and join us. *Sang A* wasn't more than a mile and a half away now.

'They're trimming her head,' I pointed out. 'Look, it's beginning to point towards Doodenstadt.'

'There's another mooring buoy astern.' Denny could make it out but I couldn't. 'There's a cable out to it and they're winching her stern round.'

'What the hell are they up to?'

'There are a couple of boats, too,' added Jutta.

They were light launches and they were putting off from *Sang A*'s side, trailing something between them. I saw what it was as Denny spoke.

'A hawser. They're dragging for something.'

'We don't want to break up this interesting little party,' I said. 'We'll just stooge around with the engine off.'

While Kaptein Denny attended to the motor Jutta and I kept watch on the launches. They worked their way slowly and deliberately between *Sang A* and a point on Possession, holding so straight a course that it was clear they were steering on a fixed bearing. *Gaok* lost way and lay rising and falling in the easy swell.

'Looks as if they're dragging for something on the sea bed,' I said.

'Perhaps they lost an anchor in the storm,' suggested Jutta.

Denny paused before replying, until the launches had made more progress towards the island.

'No. They're much too close inshore. Any skipper who

anchored there would need his head read.'

'Maybe he does anyway,' I retorted. 'See what they're doing with the ship itself.'

Sang A's head was pointing all wrong, to lie meeting the upchannel current but it was clear that was the way it was intended because they'd now secured her stern to the buoy and I could make out the tight thread of cable out of the water between the two.

'Take us close now,' I told Kaptein Denny. 'The top of *Gaok*'s crow's nest is about level with the portholes in that odd shack of *Sang A*'s. I mean to find out what's inside.'

'A sneak look seems the only way to do it, judging from their previous reception,' said Jutta.

Kaptein Denny grinned. Whatever *Sang A* was up to seemed to have put him in a relaxed mood.

'There's nothing to prevent us sailing round and round *Sang A*. You could always be looking after the interests of your darling birds.'

The way he put it could have implied anything or nothing. Anything being that he guessed I was no more a headman than I was a gannet.

'Let's go.'

Our run-in was from astern of *Sang A*. I'd circled over towards Possession to get into position, and Kaptein Denny was to take the wheel while I made my eye-in-the-sky inspection.

We were chugging along at about four knots.

'Steady!'

I glanced up to take my line.

'I'll be damned! Look at that!'

Sang A's masts and the stumps of the *City of Baroda*'s were in a line.

'They've deliberately trimmed *Sang A* on the liner's old course!'

Jutta was afire, now that the liner had come into it.

Denny said, 'We too are on that course – exactly.'

'The liner had already been hit by the time she reached the position where we are now. She was heading for the rocks to beach herself.'

Jutta gripped me tightly by the arm. She was looking everywhere as though she hadn't already memorized every detail of the anchorage!

'What's the sense of it? Struan . . .? Kaptein Denny . . .?'
Neither of us replied, because there wasn't a reply.

'What's the point in mocking up an old course? It doesn't help . . . I don't see . . .'

'I do see something, Jutta: that there's more to *Sang A* than meets the eye.'

'You're going to cut that stern buoy mighty fine, Captain Weddell.'

'Shave it to a whisker, if you like. I want the best view.'

'It's like treading in old footprints made by someone you knew!' exclaimed Jutta.

'Take it easy,' I said, hearing the excited pitch of her voice. 'There are no footprints in the sea. You've crossed and re-crossed the line's course a dozen times already and it's meant nothing. Don't start imagining things.'

She replied with a gesture: you didn't need a pelorus to see how the six masts of the three ships stood in a neat line.

'Take her in now,' I told Kaptein Denny. 'I'm going up aloft.'

Sang A's crew came running when they saw us boring straight down on their stern. They did more than run when we seemed likely to ram. They yelled and waved us off and shouted obscenities. Kenryo was among them.

I ignored them and concentrated on the shack.

The racket brought one man inside to a porthole. He'd forgotten to remove the headphones hanging loose round his neck. The giveaway was complete when Kaptein Denny skimmed *Sang A*'s quarter so close that I could almost have reached out and touched two other head-phoned operators seated at big consoles.

The shack was jammed with electronic equipment.

I left the crow's nest and descended to the wheel-house.

'Give her the gun and pull well clear,' I told Denny. 'The place is stuffed with electric gear. *Sang A* is no more a trawler than I am Captain Kidd.'

'Then what's she up to, Struan?' asked Jutta.

'I'll reserve judgement until I know what is under those tar-paulins.'

'Then you'll have to go aboard her again, Captain Weddell.'

'Not today. Let 'em cool off. Tomorrow. We've got two bodies to bury now.'

The burials went wrong right from the start. I would have

122

preferred to have buried them at sea but there would have had to be post-mortems when the law came into it; so that meant land burials. Possession was out, for the simple reason that there is no soil over the island rock in which to dig a grave. So we decided on the mainland, alongside the charred Land-Rover. Kaptein Denny and I couldn't manage to dig the graves more than a couple of feet deep because the sand kept pouring back. There wasn't a Bible or a prayer-book and I could only remember stray holy-sounding phrases like, dust to dust, and in the midst of life we are in death. So after a couple of false starts I said the Lord's Prayer while Jutta wept and kept looking back towards her mother's grave, away in the old cemetery. The only other sounds were the soft chording of the breeze and the faraway clatter of *Sang A*'s winches and the chug of her launches. They were watching us, of course.

I expected Kaptein Denny to do better in his own religion for Breekbout, but his contribution consisted of some rice balls and bright sticky sweets. It was probably reaction, but I wanted to laugh when a group of beetles emerged from the sand and started rolling away the rice balls and became entangled in the sticky sweets while Denny intoned in a language I didn't understand. I thought of the belly-laugh it would have given Koch. Then the whole thing backfired on me and all I wanted was to get my hands on the swine who had done it to him.

There was no decisive finale, and Denny stood around looking awkward when he'd stopped his half-chant. We just grabbed the spades and shovelled the sand over the two canvas bundles and then I remembered, 'I am the resurrection and the life,' and something about the sea giving up its dead, so I said aloud the parts I could recall, and slurred the rest. Then Kaptein Denny and I wired two boards, with their names and the date, on to the wrecked vehicle.

When we'd finished, Jutta asked me to take her over to the official little graveyard. Kaptein Denny retreated – he sensed that Jutta wanted to be alone with me – but asked for the rifle and some spare shells, and went and stood guard by the shoulder of the big sandhill from which we'd first spotted him at the graveyard. The precaution seemed strange in that emptiness – until one thought of Koch.

Jutta had brought some smooth white stones from Possession in her handbag, and she laid them out on the mound in the form of a cross. She asked me to say some of the words I had said for Breekbout and Koch, but I tailed off because, being so disconnected, they sounded ridiculous. Suddenly Jutta came close and clung tightly to me, then turned and walked fast and straight, back across the sand to where Kaptein Denny stood guard.

I didn't follow immediately. I stood and stared after her – she'd changed for the ceremony, before we came ashore, into a pale green slack suit, which was her only decent outfit, and which offset her hair. I felt a sudden tide of emotion, as criss-cross as any on the Sperrgebiet's coastline. One thing I was sure of – Jutta wasn't just a sudden infatuation on my part. What I wasn't so sure of was Kaptein Denny. What I was least sure about was *Sang A*. Already my one-man assignment had ballooned into squad size: a murder squad. Nor had I even got to grips with whatever lay behind the thing whose deadly sharp edges had revealed themselves in the two killings. Should I leave things to simmer until someone put a foot wrong and enabled me to play the right card? Or act decisively on the plan which was starting to take shape in my mind?

I walked back to Jutta and Kaptein Denny.

'I intend presenting Emmermann and Kenryo with an ultimatum tomorrow,' I told them. 'I'm going to ask them to signal the fisheries frigate and report Koch and Breekbout's deaths, and at the same time request clearance for *Sang A* to be at Possession.'

'That isn't an ultimatum,' answered Jutta. 'It's simply an admission that you're without a radio and therefore cut off from outside help.'

Denny too was sceptical. 'Where will it get you?'

'If they refuse, which is likely, we needn't look any further for the murderers.'

'Of course they did it,' Jutta was emphatic.

'Furthermore, a refusal would prove that they haven't any right to be doing whatever they're doing at this moment.'

'And then?'

The rest of the plan was mine, and they were involved: it wouldn't do to reveal it yet. 'We'll play it by ear. I may get some clue tomorrow as to what all their hidden gear is for.'

But in that I was mistaken, because early next day, when Kaptein Denny took *Gaok* through the thick fog to where *Sang A* had anchored, she had disappeared. It was the right spot, too, because her stern mooring buoy was still there.

Kaptein Denny cut *Gaok*'s engine. The only sound, magnified by the fog, was the slap of waves against Possession's cliffs, and some other unidentifiable noises from the channel. None of us had slept well and Jutta's eyes were tired. She was wearing her favourite suède jacket and her shoulders and beret were beaded with moisture.

'Blast!' I exclaimed. 'But I'll bet *Sang A* hasn't thrown in the towel and pushed off altogether.'

'No,' Denny replied, 'she hasn't.' He stood listening a moment and then went to the bridge door. 'I don't see her. But I smell her. There!' He jerked his head in one direction but it didn't mean much to me: I'd lost all sense of direction in the fog.

'Go after her, Captain Weddell?'

'Naturally.'

'Wait!' Jutta came to me. 'Isn't there some other way . . .?' She indicated the loaded rifle which stood near the wheel.

'Sooner or later there's got to be a confrontation between us. Better sooner, Jutta. You're not involved, so don't worry.'

'Not involved! And if they clout you over the head with a sealing club you think I won't get hurt?'

I turned away from her eyes. I was on an emotional seesaw and my end was high in the air.

'Think you'll locate her?' I was unjustifiably abrupt with Kaptein Denny.

'Yes. We'll stalk her. We use sail: good, silent sail.'

That killed the moment with Jutta, of course. She went and stood by herself, looking out.

We made sail and slipped slowly and silently down-channel. Denny was everywhere: a sea-challenge always stirred him up. He knew his way, too, and gave us – me, rather, because Jutta held herself apart – a running commentary on the wrecks we were passing by, or over. There was the *Nautilus,* a World War I coaster stuffed full of treasure-recovery gear; a sailer named the *Maridahl* which couldn't beat a Possession gale when she tried to claw her way out; close by her the *Lovely Amanda,* a Yankee whaler; and finally the *Black Prince,* a 1915 mercy ship from Luderitz which had finished up on the island's southern tip and had given her name to Black Prince Cove.

Some of the holiday air went out of Kaptein Denny when we left the island astern without sighting *Sang A*. He went to the side and took a sip of seawater and announced that we were over the spot where Bol Islet – once positioned on Admiralty charts – had suddenly vanished.

He made several fiddling alterations of course which kept *Gaok* in the fog curtain. He seemed to be getting uptight about something.

'*Sang A* is around,' he said. 'I smell her still. But I reckon she's over towards the mainland.'

'It makes no odds. Go after her.'

'There's a dangerous *skietrots* there . . .'

'*Skietrots* – what sort of *gamat* word is that?'

'Shooting rock: it's untranslatable really. It's a rock on which the seas break and shoot high. It's called *Pikkewyn se Draai* – Penguins Turning.'

'I hope *Sang A* is turning too by now.'

'Ready then, Captain Weddell?'

'Any time.'

Something was eating him, though, and he still hesitated to break clear of the fog. Instead, he hung around on the wispy fringe of the bank for some time. Then he seemed to make up his mind and everything grew light all at once, and we were blinking in broad sunlight, with a long view of the Sperrgebiet's desolation ahead.

Sang A was there all right.

She was moving southwards parallel to the coast, close in-shore. Her passage ahead was blocked by an irregular chain of islets. Two stood out at a glance from the rest. One of them was shaped like an outsize conical highway post and the sea clawed and foamed against it and gave it the name *skietrots*; the second, bigger, was almost a third of a mile long and half a mile offshore.

Kaptein Denny indicated the latter. 'Albatross Rock.'

Jutta broke her silence. '*Sang A* isn't worried at seeing us.'

'Not yet.' I swung my glasses through a wide arc. There was something very determined about the way she was plugging along on a dead straight course. She might have been on rails, rather than negotiating as bad a patch of foul ground as I'd seen on the Sperrgebiet. She was changing course now, coming about a little short of the dangerous fang.

'Engine,' I requested Kaptein Denny. 'We'll go alongside now.'

'Is she aware of us at all, Struan? Look at the way she's behaving.' That was clear, even to Jutta's unnautical eyes.

Instead of sheering clear of the rocks and reefs, as any normal vessel would have done, *Sang A* completed an inward U-turn which would bring her still closer inshore, and among them. She then steadied on a new course, still parallel to the coast but this time heading back towards the Bridge of Magpies and Possession.

On rails, I thought, on bloody rails!

Kaptein Denny's eyes were slits. 'She's following a plot.'

It was clear that her new reverse up-coast course overlapped slightly on her previous down-coast one.

'And I'm going to find out what it is. That engine, please!'

He went to see to it.

'The lost city, Struan – is that what she's after?'

'On this pitch? . . . It's miles away.'

'Kaptein Denny's not happy either.'

'Why isn't he, do you think, Jutta – why? What gives?'

She clenched one of the bridge window catches until her knuckles showed white.

'I'm scared, Struan.'

'Of what?'

'I don't know! I don't know! Scared about your going aboard that ship. Scared about my staying. I want to run away, but I want, more, to stay.'

I took her by the shoulders and pressed my thumbs into them.

'I'll sort it out. For us. That's a promise.'

'Promises are easy. This isn't.'

There was no time to say any more because just then Denny returned from the engine-room. The distance between the two vessels began to narrow.

'This isn't going to be easy. *Sang A* won't stop.'

Denny spoke almost mechanically. Ever since sighting *Sang A* he seemed to have fallen into a mood of deep preoccupation. His earlier enthusiasm for the chase had evaporated.

'I'll jump when we come alongside. You hold station until I'm ready to return. What I have to say won't take long.'

Gaok bored in on an interception course; *Sang A* held hers, ruler-straight. She was doing about eight knots and could easily have got away from *Gaok* if she'd wanted to. But not if she was doing what I thought she was doing.

Emmermann and Kenryo rushed out on to *Sang A*'s cat-walk when we drew level, and the crew began giving their vocabularies a work-out.

'What d'ye think you're playing at?' roared Emmermann. 'Keep clear! Keep clear!'

Gaok was thrashing along right alongside *Sang A* and both vessels were bucking in one another's wash. Only a couple of feet separated them. I picked a gap between the threatening crewmen, and jumped.

Two toughies made at me. The nearer aimed a roundhouse swing at my head. I dodged and made a staggering lunge across the bucking deck, missed my footing, and fell on my knees. My man came on. I was a millisecond ahead of him; grabbed his foot and rode the kick aimed at my neck. Nevertheless, it caught me under the right armpit with the force of a car's bumper. I was tossed backwards and half under one of the tarpaulined objects. Only my peripheral vision registered what it was because my main attention was focused on the two men rushing at me, the first one having disengaged his foot. It wasn't a winch or a bollard I saw, or any of the other things you'd expect to find on the deck of a ship going about her lawful occasions. It was a twin-mount machine-gun.

I'd slipped into a crouch to meet the attack when the men stopped like dogs called to heel. Angry dogs, snarling dogs. Only then did I hear Kenryo shouting at them.

I got up, brushed past them, and started to walk towards Emmermann and Kenryo on the cat-walk. That walk could have been in millimetres, not feet: it seemed to last for ever. Not because of the menacing crew but because of my racing thoughts. That machine-gun put the clincher on what I suspected about *Sang A*. It certainly didn't fit in with Emmermann's story about trawling. It also wrote the C-in-C's brief to me in much broader and more dangerous terms. Ships don't go around with high-powered electronics gear and mounted guns, searching for lost cities. *If* there was a lost city at all. I wondered whether there'd ever been one, in point of fact, and what really lay behind my assignment. Whatever it was it began to look rough. I decided to tackle Emmermann and Kenryo first about the electronic gear, and hold back about the gun. I'd never get off *Sang A* alive if I mentioned it. They weren't to know I'd glimpsed it: the tarpaulin cover was still in place. Their answer to any request for use of their radio was both a back number and a foregone conclusion now, but I intended to go ahead because it provided my excuse for boarding *Sang A*.

I finally reached Emmermann and Kenryo. Emmermann's face was livid; the cords in his neck stood out and there were little nicks from a bad shave.

'Order that ship of yours to sheer off or I'll ram her,' he rasped.

'Get off or I'll throw you off!' added Kenryo.

I gave his stocky figure a quick once-over. His threat wasn't an idle one. And I'm a big man. You murderous sod, I thought, it was you who killed Breekbout and Koch. He looked as if he'd come at me any moment.

'See here,' I said. 'There's been another death. I want you to signal the fisheries frigate.'

'Who the hell do you think you're ordering about!' Kenryo started towards me but Emmermann stopped him.

'It's no business of ours, whoever it is,' he said.

'It was Dr Koch. I'm making it your business.'

'Why don't you use your own radio?' Kenryo's eyes were hot and sly.

'It's out of order,' I admitted. 'Well, yes or no?'

'No,' replied Emmermann.

'Fair enough.'

They both seemed surprised at my ready and unquestioning acceptance of their refusal. But there wasn't any point in pressing the demand, plus another for *Sang A* to request clearance to operate in non-fishing waters. The answer to that one lay back on deck, hidden under a tarpaulin. Also, I wanted to keep communications open between myself and *Sang A*, so that I could still come aboard under some pretext or other. The whole situation had changed radically since I'd spotted that machine-gun: I'd have to handle things very carefully indeed.

I was wondering how to play my next card about the electronics business when a man walked on to the cat-walk carrying an echo-sounder, or sonar record – the sort of cardboard cylinder device that revolves on a drum while a pen traces graphs on it. It also proved my point why *Sang A* couldn't speed up to escape *Gaok*; because above twelve knots the noise of a ship's engines confuses the sensitive instruments.

I said, keeping my voice as level as I could, 'You're not a trawler!'

Kenryo's eyes were dirty with anger but the cool way he played the situation showed me what I was up against. He took the cylinder from the newcomer, held it out briefly to me, and then thrust it out of sight into his pocket. But I'd seen enough. It was different from and more sophisticated than the ordinary type of echo-sounder record I'd known in the Navy.

'Who said *Sang A* was a trawler? Not us. You came aboard blowing your top about fishing inside the limits, when we're not fishing at all. *Sang A*'s job is to spot shoals for the fishing fleet. You've probably seen this sort of record. Echo-sounder.'

'Your fancy equipment is a waste of time where you are now,' I retorted. And pointing seawards I indicated a patch of water over which the birds had gathered hunting for fish. 'A little local knowledge would be much more profitable.'

'We prefer technology.'

My attempt to lower the temperature seemed to be paying off because Emmermann said, less aggressively.

'You fouled up our run by barging alongside. Sonar cannot . . .'

'I know. Above twelve knots you can't get a decent reading.'

'You're very well informed for a simple island headman.'

(Steady, I reminded myself, steady. Not so simple, as you will discover.)

'These waters are full of ships fitted with special gear.'

The man who had brought out the echo-sounder cylinder came to my rescue by asking Kenryo a question. Now that the heat was off I wanted to get back to *Gaok* and think — hard. I'd found out what I'd come aboard for. Plus. The man was a Korean like the rest of them but with the air of authority which never brushes off a naval officer. His question was clearly about me; his presence as a neutral bystander helped also to defuse the explosive potential of the situation.

Kenryo hesitated a second, then said with a feeble attempt

at sociability, 'Captain Miki, our liaison officer. He asks to be introduced.'

Miki held out his hand with a puppet-like action as if he'd been trained to it and to the words he now shot out. 'Glad to know you, sir.' Like Kenryo, he had a slight American accent.

I shook hands perfunctorily. I couldn't work up much enthusiasm for being buddies with anyone aboard *Sang A*. All I wanted now was to be gone. But Captain Miki just stood there in front of me – I guessed he'd run out of further English – with an odd dazed expression in his eyes as though he were trapped in a mental cage. Either he'd been kicked around a lot or else a 16-inch gun had gone off next to him and he'd never got over the shock.

'Lend me a megaphone,' I asked Emmermann. 'I'll call up my boat to come alongside.'

'Good. Your birds and seals will be starting to miss you.'

'No one can accuse us of disturbing them,' added Kenryo with a sneer.

Except when that machine-gun of *Sang A*'s opens up, I told myself. Except when all this mysterious gear hidden from sight goes into action. Except . . .

With a derisive half-smile, Kenryo handed me the loud-hailer. 'Satisfied?'

His remark made me surer than ever that he was unaware I'd spotted the machine-gun. I wouldn't be leaving *Sang A* if he'd known. I didn't want to spoil things at the last moment, so I didn't answer; merely took the megaphone and busied myself calling up Kaptein Denny. While I did so I was noting the deck lay-out and the various entrances and exits.

Gaok drew alongside.

'So long.' Captain Miki found two more English words. He seemed to know what they meant, too.

'*Totsiens*' – which means no more than *au revoir*; I meant to be back.

I reboarded *Gaok* and we headed for Possession.

I told Jutta and Kaptein Denny about the machine-gun and echo-sounder. In my own mind I'd resolved to take a closer look at *Sang A*'s other concealed deck gear but didn't mention that. It could wait. I had other things laid on for them.

Kaptein Denny's reaction to my news was to become completely silent.

But Jutta asked, 'What can they be after on the ocean floor, Struan?'

'Not a clue. But if it's fish it's illegal and if it's treasure or diamonds it's doubly illegal.'

She was still on the lost city tack; she wasn't to know that I now discounted it. 'What's left – where they are now?'

'I don't know,' I replied. 'But the whole thing has got out of hand. Kaptein Denny, I would like you to take a message from me to the police and port captain at Luderitz. You can make tracks at once. I'll write it down so there won't be any mistake.'

He didn't answer.

Jutta's eyes were all over my face. 'And me?'

'I'd like you to go along too.'

Her eyes called me traitor.

'Not again. I went once.'

Kaptein Denny had given the channel one of his long quartering surveys. Then he said, 'I'll let you know my decision in an hour when I've had time to study the weather.'

'Hell's teeth!' I burst out. 'Weather! Temperament! Mood maintenance! Both of you! You'd think we were a crowd of kids playing cops and robbers and deciding who's going to be next to hide! This is murder! Two men are dead!'

'There may be a third, Struan, if we leave you alone. No dice!'

The emotional seesaw I'd ridden previously now came up and smacked me hard under the chin. The first part of my plan had worked but the second was in danger of being sabotaged by my own side.

I thought I'd give them a cooling-off period so I switched to a neutral topic – so I thought.

'One of their own people gave away the echo-sounder,' I told them. 'An odd-looking guy came on to the bridge carrying the cylinder. I'd have thought he was an ex-navy type. Kenryo introduced him as Captain Miki.'

'Who did you say?'

I almost felt Denny's shock-wave strike me.

'Captain Miki.'

He'd half-turned from the wheel and now he put in a terrific effort to pretend he was concentrating on *Gaok*'s course. It meant I couldn't see what was going on in his face. But his hands on the wheel gave him away. The knuckles were white and the fingers tight clenched.

'Mean anything?'

'Nothing.'

But it did. It changed his mood from preoccupation to reserved consternation. He didn't speak again all the way back to the island and when we landed, went off by himself. It gave me the opportunity to speak alone to Jutta. We went and sat on some rocks by the bunkhouse.

'I'm not side-lining you, Jutta, I'm front-lining you by asking you to go to Luderitz.'

'Don't twist my arm, Struan. It isn't that way.'

'Why I want you to go is that you must get on the blower direct to the C-in-C. I'll give you the Silvermine code number. Tell him what's happened. Say *Sang A* is fitted with a sophisticated echo-sounder and is searching the sea-bed for something with it.'

'You don't need me to do the legwork. Denny can do that just as well. Have him tell the police what he knows. They can pass it on to the C-in-C. He'll then make his own deductions about the echo-sounding gear.'

'No. I want you to describe to the C-in-C Denny's reactions all along the line. Especially after I returned from *Sang A*.'

'He seems burned up about Captain Miki.'

'I mean to find out about that too. He's playing a lone hand, Jutta. I can't get on to his wavelength. Sometimes I think that weather line of his is a bluff: at other times I fall for it. I just don't know the key to the man.'

Jutta said nothing, but wouldn't meet my look.

'Ask the admiral, too, whether he saw Kaptein Denny's boat the day after he rescued your mother.'

'What did you say?'

'He was in the corvette *Vygie* off Possession . . .' I explained briefly his war-time association with Convoy WV.5BX. She was all ears.

I added, 'By speaking direct to him you can give your search for your father's identity a big boost. If anyone is in a position to help you it could be the C-in-C. By doing this for me you have a unique opportunity of getting his ear.'

That ended her objections; and her eyes were very bright, as if the sun's reflection off the sea were being mirrored in them. Then she knelt down impulsively and found one of the smooth, white, marble-sized pebbles penguins roll to each other when courting. She squeezed it into my palm and touched my knuckles with her lips.

'I'm a stupid clot . . . I'll go . . . I won't mistrust you again.'

But she did.

She and Denny sailed a couple of hours later, after he had come to me and announced, to my surprise, that the weather signs were right. He was as reserved as before. I didn't know whether to believe him or not; nevertheless I gave him a written message for the authorities in Luderitz.

After *Gaok* had sailed I began to feel Possession's special quality of loneliness. Not even *Sang A* was in sight. The island seemed as ancient and companionable as a sabre-toothed tiger. I hung around while it was light and at sunset *Sang A* returned. She kept well away from the lost city area and made straight for her mooring.

When darkness came I lit Breekbout's ghost lights. I rationalized my action as being a kind of tribute to the dead.

The fog came, the wind ceased, the sea boomed.

Every time condensation splashed off the roof I thought it was a footfall. I loaded the rifle after I'd heard the noise half-a-dozen times. Listen, I told myself, you'd better get a grip on yourself or you'll be heading the same crazy way as Van Rensburg. It didn't help my hyper-acute state of alertness, though, and I went to bed with the gun by my hand. I slept dressed, on a hair trigger.

It was a real footfall outside the bunkhouse which woke me around midnight.

I groped for the gun, set my finger to the trigger, and went in a low crouch to the door. I eased it open and edged out.

The ghost lights were a yellow reflected patch against the fog. There was also a blurred human outline.

My bare feet made no sound. I went closer. The figure started to move away, back to me. My pulse rate doubled. It was a woman. Automatically I looked for the ghost hounds.

She didn't hear me before I was right up to her and threw my arm in a stranglehold round her throat.

I dragged her into the light.

It was Jutta.

CHAPTER TEN

I didn't know whether to hug her or hit her.

Since in fact I'd already half-scared her to death, I supported her indoors.

She slumped on to a stool and rubbed her throat. 'I pity the real ghost.'

Seeing her nearly on the point of passing out did something to my heart, and I found my hands were shaking.

'Lucky I didn't take a knife to you.'

'Thanks for the lights, Struan. I was lost in the fog.'

My anger thinned. 'You little idiot! You could have fallen over a cliff, broken a leg – anything. Been savaged by a bull seal, even.'

She tried to smile. 'My throat feels just like that.'

'Where'd you come from?'

'Auckland Cove.'

'Has *Gaok* run ashore? What's happened? Where's Kaptein Denny? Is he safe?'

'He's okay. He's on his way.'

'*On his way?*'

'I talked him into putting me ashore. We waited till dark. He dropped me off on the other side of the island. I walked. Then I spotted the ghost light.'

She'd started, with reaction, to shake like a wet dog.

'You're cold.'

'Scared too.'

'I'll fix some coffee.'

'Struan . . .'

'It can keep.'

I blew up the embers and we sat on stools in front of the fire.

'You must have done a lot of talking. Kaptein Denny's not an easy subject to persuade. And what about the chance you've thrown overboard: the chance to learn about your father?'

She spoke into the coffee mug she'd cupped between her hands. 'Can't you see why I came back?'

'The whole point of sending you to Luderitz was for you to explain the situation personally to the admiral. Your short-circuit blows the fuses on my plan.'

She went on as if she hadn't heard me, 'It probably sounds wet. You.'

We didn't look at each other for individual reactions: we simply sat and stared into the fire for a long time.

Finally, I said, 'If it's going to be a rough party with *Sang A* I'd rather not have a woman around.'

She got up and stood behind me. She pressed against me so that I could feel her breasts and belly against my back. She rested her throat on my head so that when she spoke softly, as if to herself, I still got the words because it had the effect of a throat microphone. It was as intimate, too. She locked a wrist round my neck, a sort of caressing affectionate imitation of my stranglehold on her earlier.

'If you'd broken my neck out there I'd have died happy, thinking you'd be glad I'd come.'

'I'm glad but I'm mad.'

'All glad is what I want.'

I pulled her round to kiss her but she fought me off.

'Heart firing blanks again, Jutta?'

She slipped out of my grasp and went round behind me again. This time she ran her fingers over my lips and nose and eyes.

'I'm not at the firing stage, Struan. I'm loading up. I don't know with what. Shot or blanks. Could be either.'

'But you came back.'

'I came back.'

'If you don't know, who does?'

'Ask the Bridge of Magpies.'

That was the answer, of course.

She stroked my head, and I could feel her breasts against my back. I wanted to lose myself for ever in the valley between them – down, down, down.

After that, there wasn't much more to say. But there was a lot to think. I lay awake through the small hours, wondering whether I wasn't the biggest sucker ever: sleeping almost next to a woman I was more than half in love with, and doing absolutely nothing about it. Mystics, they say, keep virgins in their beds. I'm low on mysticism, myself. I wished I could hear her breathing but I couldn't because of the grumbles of the gannets and penguins close to the bunkhouse. The ghost lights still burned because Jutta thought them beautiful. I tried to sort out my feelings towards her and also to unravel the Kaptein Denny-*Sang A-U-160* tangle, as well as that of the sound of guns we'd heard that other night, but I got nowhere.

In the end I gave it up and fell asleep.

The next day was a Saturday. Because the pressure was off – it would be at least twenty-four hours before the frigate arrived, provided Kaptein Denny made average time – there was a purposeless air about the day. It was warm, windless, with a few cats-paws on the surface of the channel. Nothing could be seen of *Sang A* before mid-morning, because of early fog. We rose late and I fixed the trouble with *Ichabo*'s engine – a faulty injector.

Then we went down to the landing and rubbernecked at the birds and at a group of cute seal pups that came sporting round the jetty. Neither of us knew how to handle our situation of emotional hiccoughs. Jutta was very serious and sweet to begin with and then gay and sweet when the seal pups cavorted about. We idled, but it wasn't the same as during the storm in Alabama Cove, when we had tried to sink ourselves in chores about the cutter. We were on the way to being in love – and we both knew it.

There was nothing idle or purposeless about *Sang A* when the fog lifted. Three or four boats were darting in and out from her side like jackals snooping at a kill. There was also a lot of activity on deck. Through my binoculars I could make out the crew working winches and arranging heavy chains and cables. Those tarpaulins were still firmly in place, however.

'Maybe they've discovered an outcrop of the lost city, Struan.'

I strung along with her. 'They're a long way from Doodenstadt. But it's shallow where *Sang A* is – not more than fifty feet.'

'Perhaps the lost city was overwhelmed and submerged at some time in the past, and most of it is now beneath the channel.'

'Could be. Koch's cave was supposed to be half-in and half-out of the sea.'

'They must be pretty sure about it, to have come here with all that expensive and elaborate equipment.'

Too elaborate and too expensive altogether, I reminded myself. But I couldn't tell her that.

'Relic-robbers are professionals these days, make no mistake,' I replied as convincingly as I could. 'I've seen them at work in the Aegean. I once got caught up in a shooting off the Turkish coast where they'd looted an underwater town. Maybe the same thing's going on here.'

'And you're all that stands between them and whatever they're after.'

'I mean to find out what that is – today.'

'Struan – don't stick your neck out! Please!'

'I was sent here to do a job. I shall go on doing it until the frigate takes over. If, meanwhile, I can find proof about *Sang A*, so much the better.'

'For my sake!'

'I'm going to throw a firecracker right into that black elephant's trunk. I'm boarding her tonight. Secret recce. Objectives: one, equipment under tarpaulins; two, electronics shack.'

'They'll kill you if they catch you.'

'I'll see that they don't.'

'I'm coming too.'

'Not on your life!'

'I came back – to be with you. Isn't that enough?'

It wasn't . . . after the night before! I told her, however, that she could be of very real help in ferrying me to within boarding distance of *Sang A*. 'I'll swim the last bit,' I added. 'You can pick me up on the way back. I could lose my way in the fog otherwise. We'll fix a pick-up signal. Right?'

That pleased her, and the day didn't seem too long, as we sat on the rocks and watched *Sang A*'s activities. The launches darted about purposefully at first, and we could almost sense the crew's expectancy, but after a time interest appeared to flag. Finally the launches gave up and the ship itself came into the picture. She up-anchored and made several runs in different directions in the vicinity of the area in which the boats had been working. It became clear to me that she wasn't using the type of echo-sounder I'd been accustomed to; because each time she all but reached the spot indicated by the launches, she would sheer off to one side. This manoeuvre was repeated several times, and totally mystified me. The picture, as I saw it, was that the launches' sweep had snagged on a promising ocean-bed object and *Sang A*'s passes were intended to plot it. Why, then, veer away just when it was reached? Perhaps the electronics shack would provide the answer.

Sang A's crew knew we were watching them. Canvas dodgers were rigged on light stanchions on her rails, further to mask the tarpaulined objects. Several times I caught Kenryo and Emmermann studying us through binoculars.

Sang A kept it up all day. The weather was glorious, and I was content just to sit there with Jutta.

By the late afternoon the fog bank had started rolling in from the sea: *Sang A* used her radar to continue with her plotting runs.

I got up and stretched. 'That's it! I'll have the wraps off her after dark – both literally and figuratively, I hope.'

'What do you hope to find, Struan?'

'Catch-as-catch-can. It's a toss-up whether I go for the shack or the tarpaulins first. Depends.'

'You were going to teach me to row with muffled oars.'

I checked the channel. 'Fine. *Sang A* can't see what we're doing any more. Come down to the jetty.'

When it came to the point, the drill wasn't necessary. Either *Sang A* regarded Saturday night as party night or else they had some other reason to celebrate, because shortly after dark boozy sounds started to float across the water; pin-pointing her position was thus no problem. I made do with black shorts and jersey, though I would have preferred a rubber suit. I made sure I had a knife for the tarpaulin lashings; the rifle I would leave behind in the dinghy with Jutta.

Jutta became more and more edgy as the deadline approached. When finally we were at the jetty and almost ready to board the dinghy she exclaimed, 'You'll need a torch. I'll get one.'

She doubled off into the fog before I had time to protest that a torch was the last thing I'd require. My arms were full and I offloaded my things into the boat. By that time Jutta was overdue – it was only a short distance to the bunkhouse. Irritated at the delay, I climbed up the iron ladder to the top of the jetty. She wasn't around. I went to the bunkhouse. It was empty. I started back towards the cottage with a feeling of uneasiness. I'd almost reached it when there was a chatter from the birds and Jutta came hurrying down the path, torch in hand.

'Struan?'

She was breathing heavily as if she'd been running.

'Where the devil have you been?'

'I lost myself in the fog . . . I went the wrong way . . .'

'Uphill? With the bunkhouse lights to guide you?'

'I couldn't see . . . I'm sorry . . . I heard you coming . . .'

It was an unconvincing performance and killed the fun approach to the *Sang A* escapade we'd had all day.

'Let's go,' I snapped. 'We've wasted enough time as it is.'

We made our way in silence to the jetty and shoved off, still without speaking. We could safely have whispered but I chose not to. Whispers are for someone very close, and she was very far away from me that night: just an outline crouched in the boat's stern.

We'd only gone a little way when I thought I heard the sound of a distant engine. I couldn't be sure: fog plays all kinds of tricks. I shipped the oars. We waited. A long time. Nothing came. We went on.

Then there was another long wait when a sound like the wash of a bow-wave – possibly oars – came through the darkness. The night seemed full of presences. Again it proved to be nothing tangible.

Soon we were close enough to make out the loom of *Sang A*'s portholes – a series of bright circles in the murk – though her decks were in darkness.

I shipped the oars, checked my knife and got ready to go.

Jutta sat silent, an amorphous silhouette, not a woman. It was better that way.

But I couldn't just slip over the side without a word; I whispered, 'Fire when you see the whites of their eyes. Make sure they're not mine.' That was mean; I meant it to be.

I went over the side – the water wasn't as cold as I'd expected. I hung on to the side for a second, my face level with the gunnel.

She crouched down to me. 'Take care of yourself, darling.'

I'd already let go and had given myself a push to get clear of the boat: Jutta had become a dim ghost before I'd taken in what she'd said.

All the way out I'd been spoiling for an encounter with

one, or more, of *Sang A*'s toughies to work off the roil inside me; now I had to stop myself from going soft. I deliberately shut out Jutta, and concentrated on the job ahead.

The *Sang A* crowd were certainly beating it up. There were whoops and shouts and laughter, and the occasional thump. Several launches and dinghies were tied up alongside her and it was as easy as going up stairs to find my way to the deck. I couldn't see overmuch because the decks were so dim, so I used one of the big chains as a guide, following it until I came to the big seven-ton anchor shackled to its end.

I decided to investigate the electronics shack first because it was less exposed than the deck, and the racket below provided me with my maximum opportunity for indoor reconnaissance.

I headed at low crouch for the shack, my bare feet silent on the planks. The shack hadn't a deck door and its portholes were blacked out. There was, however, a gleam of light through a roof skylight. I shinned up the stern mast ratlines – they were only a few feet away from the shack – and dropped down cat-like on the roof. It took only a moment to force the skylight with my knife, and slip in. The light wasn't coming from the shack itself but from a door a little ajar which led to the 'tween-decks below.

I hung by my hands from the sill and the soles of my feet touched one of the big electronics consoles. I detected lettering. I dropped down and read, 'Transit sonar – Kelvin Hughes.' Now a transit sonar is a sophisticated instrument – big brother to the echo-sounder – which has nothing to do with fish but is employed almost exclusively for salvage work; and Kelvin Hughes is a well-known manufacturer. Pieces of the jigsaw fell rapidly into place. *Sang A* had made those odd directional approaches to the launch area because a transit sonar doesn't throw a straight up-and-down pulsed echo wave like an echo-sounder but, instead, an inverted V-shaped beam, offset to one side of the ship. So *Sang A* had to make her runs to one side to obtain a trace of whatever she was after. The size, depth and position of an underwater object is plotted automatically on graph paper – as on the cylinder Captain Miki had handed Kenryo.

The other instruments were: conventional Asdic echo-sounder, radar, and electronic navigational gear.

My discovery of the transit sonar also blew the secret of that heavy gear on deck: the powerful derricks and three-sheaved tackles. They were for salvage – peaceful salvage, though that didn't explain the mounted machine-gun. The armoured hose was an 'air-lift' used for clearing mud round a wreck on the sea-bed.

There was so much racket coming from beyond the door that I didn't have to move about too cautiously; I decided also to have a look-see at the party.

The door led to an exceptionally long cabin, stretching the entire width of the ship, which appeared to be used as a general messroom. Tables and chairs were stacked against the walls and there was a thick carpet on the deck.

The air was rancid with the sweat-smell of active men.

The whole crew – about twenty – seemed as high as a moon probe. It must have taken some exotic Eastern drug to have sent them on a trip like that – an Einstein, the hippies call it: way out and beyond the farthest stars.

They were all wearing loose things like karate gowns and were lamming into one another with long wooden staves and yelling bloody murder as they did so. Some leapt high into the air like dervishes. Then, at a whistle signal, the mêlée sorted itself into groups, like a possessed ballet chorus: first of six men, then four, and finally two, all shouting and bashing. Eventually all but one pair fell back against the walls, sweating and stamping.

Kenryo was one of the two remaining in the ring. He and the other Korean circled one another like wrestlers looking for an opening. Kenryo's opponent lashed out suddenly at his legs, but Kenryo side-stepped the blow with a vertical take-off and from shoulder height hit the other man a vicious crack across the forehead. Kenryo's man wasn't out, but he was as near to it as anyone could be after a haymaker like that. He stood dazed and swaying. Unfortunately for him the Queensberry rules weren't in operation and he couldn't make for a neutral corner. The mob shouted like madmen; Kenryo swung his stave with both hands into the other's left side, near the heart. That finished him. He started to sag and Kenryo went up and kicked him in the testicles. He went down, screaming with pain. Kenryo kicked him again. Then the spectators were all over both men and chaired off Kenryo, shoulder-high. The only two who didn't seem to be having fun were Emmermann and Captain Miki, who stood together on the sidelines. Miki's remote air was apparent to me even at that distance.

I took a firm grip of my knife and got out.

I shot through the skylight, down the ratlines and on to the deck. There was some faint illumination by virtue of the portholes' reflection off the fog curtain. I started to head towards the bow of the ship where the machine-gun was. But where I stood, still aft, was an intriguing bulky object, concealed under a large tarpaulin. Another weapon? I cut loose the lashings: underneath was a long cylindrical metal object, about eight feet long and three in diameter, with a large yellow '4' painted on its conical top. It was a salvage mooring buoy. They are generally numbered in sixes according to the type of mooring to be laid down.

Then I went for a bundle wrapped in black plastic, next to the buoy, and ripped it open. It contained a stack of four-inch metal tubes of varying length – some over a dozen feet and some as little as three. I started to explore by touch, and my fingers came upon a gnarled surface at the end of one of the tubes. I froze. I knew what I'd struck: special underwater explosive charges, designed to blow open wrecks. I'd seen Navy specialists using them. What I was fingering was an adjustable, sensitive membrane which explodes the device by water pressure. There was enough high explosive in the stack to blow *Sang A* on to the top of the Bridge of Magpies.

I decided to go for the gun for'ard. Before leaving I selected the smallest tube I could find. Souvenirs have their uses.

The tiny burn on the nape of my neck felt like a hypodermic needle. At the same instant a cold circle of steel pressed under my left ear. Pistol muzzles have their own special sort of caress you don't forget in a hurry.

The man – probably the anchor-watch – was standing over me with a long-razor-sharp knife that had nicked me like a cat's claw ripping a captive mouse for fun. I kept so still that I didn't even unclasp my hands from the bomb. But my upward view took in, in succession, the guard's bare feet, dark baggy pants, heavy, short-armed body, black leather jacket and balaclava-encased head.

He brought his knife against my other ear so that the two

weapons made a pincer on either side of my head. Any movement of mine would have telegraphed itself immediately to him. He was a professional and as wary as a panther. He stood far back enough to prevent my sideswiping his legs, but close enough to retain full command over me.

He made a gesture with the pistol which I misinterpreted until he reinforced it with the knife. I thought he wanted me up, back to him. I reckoned he was mad to let me hang on to the bomb.

Then he gestured again. He was showing me over the side!

I couldn't believe it. But I had no intention of inviting knife-thrust or bullet. So I mimed my query. He gestured back impatiently: I was to go.

Not crediting my luck, I clambered on to the rail and paused. He was standing there, a dim, grim, masked figure with a weapon in each hand. I lowered myself overboard.

I swam clear of *Sang A* and orientated myself on the dinghy.

In reaction to the last few minutes' events, I found myself treading water, trying to get control of my arms and legs and at the same time keep hold of that bomb, with its pressure-sensitive mechanism. If it sank it would explode right under me.

According to my water-proof watch, I was early for our rendezvous, so after I'd recovered I swam slowly. The pick-up signal was the low-pitched sound obtained by blowing in an empty cartridge case. We'd decided it wouldn't carry far and was sufficiently like the prevalent bird-noises to escape attention.

All at once the underside of the fog curtain took on a strange silver-blue colour. The sea around me became as silver as a young salmon. I raised an arm: it dripped luminosity.

My fish-eye view of the channel was necessarily limited, but I guessed that the whole of its surface was being lighted up by a multitude of minute fire-bearing creatures that were being swept in by the current from the south. The fog made a low-ceilinged black dome above the sea's silver shield.

It was pleasant to admire but no good for escape.

I struck out strongly and swiftly. Then I heard Jutta's signal, ahead and to one side. I gave a cautious whistle back and then spotted a beautiful, luminous arc of watery fire spilling from an oar as Jutta began to row.

In a moment I was alongside. Jutta's face didn't look lovely in the weird light but dead and colourless like a materialized spirit at a séance. Maybe I appeared lovely coming over the side trailing phosphorescence but I was too anxious to get away to care about the personal beauty stakes. I pitched the bomb in the bottom of the boat without explanation or greeting, grabbed the oars and begun to scull.

We hadn't gone far when the world went black. The silver magic vanished. At any other time I might have regretted it. I guessed we had broken out of the light-giving mainstream coming up-channel and must, accordingly, be quite close to Possession's cliffs.

We were. It wasn't long before we heard the wash of breakers. We were well to the south of the jetty, of course, so I followed the coastline by the sound of the breakers to port, and after what seemed an endless row came at last to the landing-place.

Jutta and I hadn't exchanged one word, all the time. I still couldn't be close to her with that torch business eating me – in spite of her parting words. The torch itself lay next to the bomb, on the bottom-boards; we both shunned it as though it were a black mamba.

I led the way to the bunkhouse and, after I'd changed, joined her at the fire for food and coffee.

She started the ball rolling. In a neutral voice, she said, 'I've never seen anything so lovely as that sea, Struan.'

'I expected, any moment, to be shot at.'

Her eyes seemed to find lots of places to look at in the fire. They never met mine.

I said, 'I had a bummer of a trip . . .' I described what I had found in the shack; on the deck; the sadistic scene in the mess; my incredible let-off. 'Search me why he didn't make a killing. I'd written myself off as a goner.'

'What did he say?' Her voice was strained and apprehensive.

'Nothing. I saw nothing either. He had the cap pulled right down over his face.'

'Thank God for him!'

Her relief still didn't bridge the gap between us.

'Why that gun-toting bruiser didn't turn me in I'll never know.'

'I sat waiting in the fog for a hundred years.'

She was giving me all the openings but I couldn't take them.

'Don't start throwing your hat in the air yet,' I replied brusquely. 'I can't imagine he'll go on keeping his mouth shut about me.'

'He may have to, to save his own skin.'

We might have been light years away, judging by the lack of warmth between us.

'Anyway, I'm going to beat him to the chequered flag tomorrow,' I said. 'I think I know now what *Sang A* is up to.'

CHAPTER ELEVEN

What we saw spread out round *Sang A* next day underscored my discoveries of the previous night. The salvage part, at least.

It was a six-pointed pattern of cables and chains stretching out about half a mile to the main points of the compass with the black ship in the centre. It resembled a gigantic spoked wheel on the sea's surface, with *Sang A* as its hub. Half-a-dozen moorings had been made ready, and numbered buoys were in position – a typical preliminary salvage lay-out. It had all been done some time before the fog lifted. The *Sang A* crowd had certainly sweated out their hangovers.

Echoes of the previous night hung a little drearily on the morning air between Jutta and me. I'd tried to fling away the thought of her possible duplicity, but the nagging suspicion of the torch affair still stuck.

She stared at *Sang A*, and across the channel to where the *City of Baroda* lay. I couldn't fathom the expression in her eyes.

She said, 'My search is snowballing into something far beyond what it originally was. I'm scared for the future.'

I replied – to reassure her – not to convince myself, 'There are too many ghosts around. Those salvage preparations are a complete give-away. The frigate will be along any time now and that will be that.'

She didn't answer. The sunlit anchorage seemed so peaceful; even the day was unnatural in its continued calm. It was hard to credit the other side of the *Sang A* coin.

'Why go then? Why not wait?'

I might have found a reply of sorts, before last night. Now I shrugged.

'I'm going aboard *Sang A*. Stay if you wish.'

'Never.'

We left it at that.

I rowed us out in the dinghy to *Sang A*. Her boats were fussing about. Some of the crew stood at the rails watching us approach, their dull, sullen faces so similar that I couldn't pick out individuals. If I hadn't seen them going to town the night before I couldn't have credited what a bunch of rowdies they could be.

We made fast. Emmermann and Kenryo were on the cat-walk awaiting us. Even less than before did I like the look of *Sang A*'s number one hatchet man. The whites of his eyes weren't white, but murky yellow.

'I've been expecting you all morning, Captain Weddell.' Emmermann smiled sarcastically. 'It would be unlike a go-getting headman to stand aside from this.' He indicated the preparations.

'That's what I've come about.'

'Salvage is no doubt within the province of island head-men also?'

'Don't beat about the bush, Emmermann. You know damn well you can't undertake salvage operations here.'

'So . . . now?'

Kenryo regarded me with his glum face and dirty eyes. I wanted to give a medal to the guy who'd smashed his nose. Now that I was near him I smelt the acrid odour of stale sweat and burned-out drugs. I wondered how good he'd be for a fight, without a drag.

But Emmermann wasn't out for trouble.

'Please to come to the chart-room. I would like you to examine our legal papers.'

'They don't need vetting,' rasped Kenryo.

Emmermann almost apologized for him. 'Our information was that we would find a more . . . ah, accommodating headman on Possession.'

I directed my reply to Kenryo. 'There was. He's gone. He granduated to mainlining. They usually start soft.'

Kenryo's yellow skin had a sort of dull, oily gloss on it – and he didn't have jaundice. He spat over the side.

'So . . .?' persisted Emmermann.

'Dope, booze – that's Possession.'

He smiled indulgently at Jutta. 'I have some of the latter inside. We will use it for less serious purposes than the in-cumbents of Possession.'

In the chart-room he produced a bottle of *schnapps* and three glasses. Kenryo wasn't included. Maybe he didn't want to overburden himself with vices.

148

'*Gesundheit!*'

I raised my glass to Emmermann, wondering where all this spurious bonhomie was leading to.

Emmermann kept it up. 'Documents! You shall see. We have plenty.'

'Be specific,' I replied. 'Tell me what you're after. I know most of the wrecks around here – *Maridahl, Nautilus, Lovely Amanda, Black Prince* – and *Auckland* on the other side. None of them's worth a packet of matches.'

'All oldies, as the jargon has it.' But Emmermann's next words snapped Jutta out of her aloof and detached mood. 'No, Captain Weddell, we're searching for a submarine that was lost here during the war. The U-160.'

Emmermann missed her reaction because he'd risen to open a wall safe. But Kenryo didn't. His eyes narrowed as hers came alight and bright colour rushed into her cheeks. He must have used a good brand of dope, to be so alert the 'morning after'!

Emmermann thumped down a wad of documents in front of me. If they were calculated to impress, they did. Parchment: stamped, watermarked, letterheaded, scripted, with red seals and ribbon. A couple of the documents were in Oriental writing which I imagined to be Korean. It looked good and convincing . . . I couldn't read a word.

'Right,' I said. 'You've done your homework. But as far as I'm concerned this is so much bumff. These are Sperrgebiet territorial waters. You can't operate here without authority. I can't find that authority among these – '. I indicated the pile of documents.

He pointed to a particularly impressive-looking one which sported a coat-of-arms and drop-lettered Gothic capitals. 'I am authorized by the German Ministry of Marine to salvage any metals, machinery, fitments and tools from *U-160* in consideration of the sum . . .'

'Fine, fine,' I broke in. 'I'm not a maritime court. I have no discretion. You can argue with the fisheries frigate. She'll be here at any moment.'

'How d'ye know, if your radio's out of operation?' demanded Kenryo.

Emmermann's temper showed through his smooth social façade, enabling me to side-step Kenryo's punch question.

'It may interest you to know that at dawn today the frigate was two hundred miles away. At the northern end of her patrol beat.'

That knocked me. It meant Denny hadn't sent my signal. Or, if he had, the warship couldn't possibly be at Possession by that day. It also revealed something equally disquieting – *Sang A* was monitoring the frigate's movements.

Emmerman realized that at the drop of a hat Kenryo and I would be at each other's throats. He said in a conciliatory way, 'That's as may be. The important matter is that *U-160* was sunk in the Possession channel during the war . . .'

'She wasn't sunk.' Jutta's reserved mood had now completely dissipated, like the fog. She was alert and animated. Up to then neither Emmermann nor Kenryo had regarded her as being in their league. They probably thought she provided me with Possession's only distraction.

Her words poured out. '*U-160* first sank the *City of Baroda*. She then sank the frigate which pursued her. The last that was heard from her was that she was making for the open sea. She was badly damaged and losing oil. But she was afloat.'

There was something – more imagined than real perhaps – behind Kenryo's eyes I didn't care for. He spoke rapidly to Emmermann . . . all their attention switched away from me . . . I wanted to yell at Jutta to stop.

Emmermann's restraint was obvious. 'You are informed about *U-160*? How strange for a woman!'

'I . . . no, that part of it doesn't matter. I know however that Captain Schlebusch fired a spread of four torpedoes at the City of Baroda and then used the U-boat's two stern tubes against the warship. He got her too.'

Kenryo's voice had a dull, flat note, like a counterfeit coin's dud ring.

'*U-160* sank. She is –' he thumped a heel on the floorboards – 'right under us at this moment. We have located her.'

'That's what the buoys are for,' added Emmermann.

'No!' exclaimed Jutta. 'No! You're wrong! She got away. She . . .'

'Yes?'

She had the sense, at least, not to reply to that bit of Emmermann's prodding. I tried again to signal her to play it cool but she was being driven along by some inner compulsion.

When she hesitated Emmermann repeated, 'She is here. Right under *Sang A.*'

'Transit sonar,' I jibed.

He looked startled but let it pass. He was far too interested in Jutta. He found a lead weight in the safe and brought it for her to inspect.

'Sounding lead,' he explained. 'Look! Look at what came up from the wreck below.'

Mixed in with the typical sand and shell of the channel floor were some red and grey flakes.

'Paint. Red lead underneath, with grey above it. U-boat grey.'

'No,' I said. 'British naval grey. *Gousblom.*'

Emmermann and Kenryo's attention switched back to Jutta when she added, 'Her magazine blew up. It's she you've located, not *U-160.*'

'So now! So now!' They were only four short words from Emmermann but they said everything.

Kenryo addressed Jutta with the controlled menace of a panther stalking. 'You are extremely knowledgeable about naval matters.'

Emmermann helped himself to some more schnapps. 'Would you know what *U-160* was carrying?'

'A couple of prototype torpedoes. Samples of new explosives. The latest counter-measures to Allied submarine devices. A Nazi agent.'

She had them riveted. If she went on they'd never let us off the ship. So I brushed aside the rest of what she had to say. 'Technically, all of it was old hat within a year. Nothing that's worth salvaging in this day and age.'

'Her phosphor-bronze torpedo tubes are worth £100 apiece at today's prices,' replied Emmermann.

'She had six. Six hundred quid. That wouldn't even pay your way for a couple of days. It's also peanuts compared with your outlay.'

Emmermann looked across at Kenryo for the go-ahead: he got it.

'Captain Weddell. We are men of the world. If I told you that *U-160* was carrying something which – if you choose to co-operate – could help you to be comfortable for the rest of your life, would you believe me?'

'If you're going to say she had aboard Captain's Kidd's

treasure or the *Alabama*'s gold or a trunk-load of diamonds, you can keep it. It's just another Sperrgebiet yarn when the lights are low and the brandy goes round.'

'You are sensible not to be gullible. No. *U-160* was carrying two hundred tons of liquid mercury, as ballast. In canisters. Attached to her keel.'

'So what?'

'In the early days of the war mercury was dirt cheap. Cheap enough to be ideal ballast. Germany bought a lot from Mexico at bargain basement prices. Today . . .'

He let the rest of the sentence hang.

Kenryo completed it. 'At today's prices two hundred tons of mercury is worth over a million dollars. Tax-free.' He gave a tight-lipped grin. 'With your co-operation.'

'See here, Captain Weddell,' Emmermann punched home the offer. 'We're not asking you to do anything. Anything, you understand? All you have to do is to sit and watch us from Possession – if you want to watch. If you agree in principle, we can discuss terms. We will be generous, I assure you.' He turned to Jutta. 'You have information about *U-160*. Information is also a saleable commodity. For example, if we knew more details of the action in the channel we could plot *U-160*'s firing angles. We could obtain transits. That in itself, by narrowing down possible areas, would be worth thousands of dollars of search time.'

Something had come over Jutta since they'd started their talk about buying us. She'd been all fired up at the start – unstoppable almost – now she'd gone cold.

'I . . . I . . . need time to think.'

Kenryo spotted the change in her, too. All I wanted was to get away. I rose to my feet. 'We'll talk it over . . .'

I was nearly thrown to the floor. *Sang A* shimmied under a hammer-blow concussion from outside. I felt as if someone had tapped me on the head with a rubber truncheon and at the same time thumped me in the diaphragm. There was a white photo-flash of light across the cabin. My ears reeled.

We threw ourselves at the portholes.

A few hundred yards away a geyser-spout of water – it had a dirty, curly black top like a giant ostrich feather – stood up higher than *Sang A*'s stack. One of the boats that had been fussing about was tumbling sideways out of the mess, men and timber falling in all directions.

'Christ!' I exclaimed. 'They've tripped one of *U-160*'s old mines!'

They had indeed, with that wire sweep of theirs.

We rushed on deck; Emmermann and Kenryo shouting orders. They'd forgotten us amid the general uproar.

'Beat it!' I said to Jutta. 'Now's our chance!'

We slipped over the side and sneaked away in the dinghy towards Possession.

We'd gone nearly half-way when Jutta suddenly exclaimed, 'Struan! *U-160* didn't have mercury ballast: she was built too late. She was a Class IXC boat. Mercury ballast was confined to earlier types.'

CHAPTER TWELVE

I rested on my oars. 'It's the chopper, Jutta.'

'I don't understand.'

'You've put a short fuse under us. Any moment the powder keg will explode. We couldn't be more vulnerable.'

'What I said back there?'

'What you said. You went up like that old mine yourself.'

'I couldn't stop myself: everything came bursting out when they brought up the subject of *U-160*.'

'You're the best strike they've made since they hit the Bridge of Magpies. Don't imagine they won't be following it up.'

'I only said . . .'

'You showed you were loaded with enough information to make a salvage man's tongue hang out. You didn't only hint – you positively shouted it – that there was a packet more where it came from.

'I can't see how a harmless tape recording . . .'

'Harmless! Listen! Sound travels at five thousand feet a second in sea-water. All you have to do is put a stop-watch on that tape and it's a piece of cake to plot exactly where, within a given radius, *U-160* fired from. Then there's a U-boat coxswain's firing countdown – perfect check! Datum point. Listen to Captain Schlebusch's orders: course, speed, changes, the lot. Plot 'em. Allow for his D/A during the attacks – that's a firing angle lay-off – and mark it down. Our stop-watch man now has a chart full of points and intersecting lines – transits. Join 'em up and, voilà, there you'll find *U-160*. Need I say more?'

'*U-160* got away.' Her voice was small but emphatic.

'Maybe. Maybe not.'

It flashed through my mind, even as I said it, that, had she escaped, the C-in-C wouldn't have sent me to investigate; because the U-boat seemed to be the kingpin of the whole business.

'Our immediate problem – it's almost superfluous to say so – is that Emmermann and Kenryo will come after us.'

'For what?'

'You. They don't know about the tape and I don't intend that they shall.'

'We could drive a bargain with the tape . . .'

'Be your age, Jutta. There's not only harassment in the *Sang A* pipeline. What they can't buy they'll beat out of you. That tape could sign your, our, death warrants if they got wind of it.'

'I still think . . .'

'You want to get your perspectives clear. Once they have it we become expendable; of no more use to them. They'll have got all the information they need. Emmermann and Kenryo are after something big. It's not a million in mercury – we have your assurance for that. And a million's big. They know *U-160* wasn't carrying mercury. You don't launch a salvage project of *Sang A*'s magnitude without first checking your target. There's nothing secret any longer about Class IXC U-boat plans. What they're after is big enough for two men to have been killed already. Another couple – you and I – wouldn't make any difference.'

And mounted machine-guns are capable of killing plenty more, I reminded myself.

'You've let Kaptein Denny off the hook, I see.'

'No. My guess is that he's on to *U-160,* from a different angle. Somehow the winter weather governs his operations. If he's come fishing here for thirty years I'd say he's been busy netting enough lolly every time to sit for the rest of the year with his bum in butter. He *knows,* Jutta!'

'There wasn't anything aboard *U-160,* Struan – nothing! I've checked and checked! Nothing at all!'

'It's too late now to bring that up with Emmermann and Kenryo. The longer you say that the longer they'll try to wring out of you what you didn't really know in the first place. And, judging from what I've seen of their party manners, it won't be a pretty operation. Where's the tape?'

'Aboard *Ichabo.*'

'Then we're going aboard to get rid of it – now. The cutter will be a natural for them to search.'

'You can't dump it overboard, Struan!'

'I agree: it's too valuable. We'll stash it away. The best hiding-place is always under the light. Of course they'll search the huts once we're gone . . .'

'Gone?'

'Once we've shed that tape we're high-tailing it out of here in *Ichabo*. Provided they don't get here first. We'll make a break for the inshore shoals beyond Elizabeth Point where we can still be within striking range, and can spot the frigate when she arrives. They can't pursue us there in a big vessel like *Sang A*, and their launches haven't the range.'

'But the tape, Struan?'

'Into a penguin rookery. Safe as the Bank of England. They'll never think to look there.'

I took the oars and we streaked for *Ichabo*. It took Jutta only a moment to bring the tape from the cabin once I'd got alongside. Then I pulled for the island jetty. I made good time because of the calm sea. That sea worried me. Possession weather should be sour, not sweet: something was brewing. There was a sultriness about that rasped the temper. The waves slopped like bath water against the piers of the jetty. Activity round *Sang A* was dying down. That in itself spurred me on.

We sprinted up the concrete path past the bunkhouse to the high ground near the cottage. Over the skyline we were out of *Sang A*'s range of vision. When we veered off the path into the breeding-flats every bird and penguin seemed to join in resisting our invasion of their territory. I secreted the tape away under a big rock, while Jutta, using the rifle barrel, fended off the attackers when they tried to slash at our ankles. Their protests were deafening!

That was the reason for our not hearing *Sang A*'s launches. We spotted them, though, the moment we crossed the rim-rock of the skyline.

I pulled Jutta down beside me on the path. 'Look!'

One launch was almost up to *Ichabo*; the other was already alongside the jetty. Coming along it at the double, fanned out in attack order, were half-a-dozen of *Sang A*'s crew, led by Kenryo. Some had sub-machine-guns slung at the hip; others, automatic rifles. One way and another, *Sang A* certainly packed a lot of fire-power.

I loosened the safety catch of the rifle with my thumb, and signalled Jutta to crawl towards the cottage for cover.

I wasn't quick enough. Someone gave a shout: I caught a glimpse of fire-flashes lancing from muzzles and sunlight glancing off a cascade of spent brass hulls; and heard the characteristic spat-spat of automatic fire. At the same time the birds' uproar doubled as bursts tore into them.

I rolled sideways to join Jutta. 'Keep your head down! Roll! Behind the cottage!'

I loosed off a shot at random as I dived away. There wasn't time to aim but I heard a ricochet and a yell of pain from one of Kenryo's men.

Then we were behind the cover of a stone wall encircling the cottage. I heard orders shouted, probably by Kenryo; and a concentrated burst of fire spattered and chipped the cottage's stone chimney.

I put my arm round Jutta's shoulders. 'They're not trying. Look where they're firing – high and wide.'

'They want us – alive?' Jutta's voice was choky.

'Damn sure. We're no use to them dead.'

More bullets clattered and whined off the chimney and walls but I noticed they left the windows alone. Maybe they thought we were inside.

I eased myself into a better position to see what was going on. Jutta's fingers clamped on my arm. She gave a soft gurgle and the edges of her lips twitched. For a moment I thought she'd been hit until I followed her terror-stricken eyes to the rocky high-point we'd crossed.

Kenryo was standing there, holding on us one of those deadly snap-collapse weapons which street snipers love. It was a stubby-barrelled thing that could be stripped down to pocket-sized parts and reassembled in seconds. A thug's weapon for a thug. It wasn't the only thought of mine to beat the speed of light. I tossed my rifle from me. That weapon of Kenryo's could cut a man in half before he got to opening the breech for his second shot.

'Up!'

We got up. Kenryo shouted and we heard heavy feet thudding up the path. In a moment we were surrounded by men pointing either sub-machine-guns or automatic rifles at us. They were a mixture of PPSHs and AK-47s – all Russian.

I tried making my tone incredulous and outraged.

'What the hell are you playing at?'

'Leave it alone!' Kenryo snapped. 'We want you. We've got you. Rather . . .' he leered at Jutta. 'You.'

Jutta imitated my line. 'You might have killed us!'

'Not a chance. We know what we're doing. Forget it. What concerns you more is the future. The more you have to tell us the less you'll get hurt.'

'A million in mercury!' I scoffed. 'How to win friends and influence people.'

'Shut up! You'll both tell everything before I've finished with you.'

I found my breath coming quickly and jerkily, and felt a bead of sweat run all the length of my spine from neck to coccyx. I was afraid for Jutta. Nervous compulsion made me speak.

'We've nothing to hide. I'll see you answer for this when the frigate arrives.'

He banged me lightly on the chest with the barrel of his nasty little automatic.

'That frigate is as far away as she ever was. Now – where's your kit?'

'In the bunkhouse mainly. Some in the cottage.'

He gave an order and a couple of men left the group and went off to search. I guessed *Ichabo* was being ransacked too.

'Get moving!'

We had no choice: we walked down to the jetty, Kenryo and the others covering us. He motioned us into the launch. I was glad to see Jutta looking more angry than scared.

When we came close to *Sang A*, Kenryo slowed the launch, then stopped altogether. A diver was being lowered over the side. He stood for a moment, in his heavy helmet and space-man-like suit, before giving the thumb's-up signal and disappearing into the water in a stream of air bubbles.

Kenryo indicated the air lifeline. 'Compressed air.'

I eyed him speculatively. Kenryo wasn't the type to dwell on modern marine marvels.

'I know.'

'That's for him. There may be some for you.'

'What d'ye mean?'

He answered as conversationally as his rather stilted way of talking permitted: he gave the impression of transmitting mentally before committing himself to English. He might have been describing a diving technicality.

'He's going down about fifty feet. That means the water pressure on him will be about forty pounds to the square inch. Of course, the compressor is designed to cope with that.'

'So what?'

'I imagine the same thing inside a man.'

'I can't.'

'You'd be surprised to see how a little compression up the rectum will make a man talk.'

I'd been right about him that first time: a sod, a murderous sod.

'Women talk sooner – they've got more inlet valves.'

He relished Jutta's silent shock reaction. I sized him up: he'd take some beating, I reckoned. He was stripped down to a towelling T-shirt because of the warmth, and his chest and arm muscles bulged. I knew what he was capable of in action.

When a derrick swung out one of the tube-like explosive charges and started to lower it into the water, Kenryo went on.

'There goes your luck. Soon we will blow off a piece of plating from the wreck, for identification. If it's the U-boat, you're in the clear. If not . . .' he shrugged.

The launch negotiated the complex of mooring cables and made fast. There was no sign of Emmermann. We were escorted below through the long mess-room, and past the sonar shack door, to two cells over the screws which faced each other across a narrow passageway.

Kenryo locked the grilled doors and left an armed guard behind. It wouldn't have been too bad except for the stifling heat. Perhaps this was the unusual weather which was part of Kaptein Denny's plan of operations. I'd written him off as a two-timer who'd run away to save his own skin and had no intention of getting my signal away.

We'd been brought aboard *Sang A* about mid-day and all afternoon the 'tween-decks grew more suffocating. They'd also screwed the portholes closed. We could see out, of course. We weren't sure whether the guard understood English, so we stuck to commonplaces.

We'd been in the cells about an hour when there was a sharp crack as if the hull had been tapped with an outsize hammer.

'Underwater bomb,' I reassured Jutta. 'They're working on the wreck.'

Then it struck me – what had happened to the small one I'd filched from the pile on deck? I'd left it lying in our dinghy under one of the thwarts. Had the very obviousness of its position caused it to be overlooked? Kenryo had not mentioned it.

'There's nothing to see, Struan.'

Jutta, from her porthole, could watch what was going on, but I couldn't because I faced the mainland. After that the never-ending afternoon was punctuated by sharp cracks and long silences, as fresh charges were lowered and manoeuvred into position, then detonated.

'Best weather in the world for salvage,' I said to Jutta. It didn't make any difference whether the sentry understood or not.

'How long will it go on, Struan?'

'Not long. There's an upwell cell starting to build up . . .' I explained the phenomenon to her. 'It always begins with this type of impossible hot weather: it brings the east wind off the desert. I've known it on occasion be a hundred degrees ten miles out to sea.'

'This place is a sweat box already.'

'It'll become worse. The fog gets thicker, too. Warm air on icy water. Tomorrow will be a humdinger.'

'It all sounds very complex.'

'Not really. There's the build-up, then the actual process of the upwell cell lasts a few days. Once the desert wind gets going, however, everything seems to take wing – sand, sea, the lot.'

'Struan!'

'What is it?'

'They're bringing something up out of the sea!'

I craned to try and see through her porthole but couldn't. The guard eyed me sourly.

'What, Jutta, what?'

'It's a chunk of metal . . . ragged . . . covered in seaweed and stuff . . .'

'Colour?'

'Black. Rusty.' She was very excited. 'Now it's gone. They've lifted it aboard.'

We both knew how much depended on that undistinguished piece of decaying metal. The thought killed my weather chat. There were no more underwater explosions. The afternoon dragged on. The cells became hotter. Towards sunset little puffs of wind started nibbling at the crests of the dunes. An east wind. A desert wind.

It also became darker earlier than usual, because the fog was thicker. The guard switched on a naked light in the corridor. The glass of my porthole was opaque with heavy condensation. The ship began to tug a little at her moorings. Upwell cell symptoms were beginning to show.

It became still hotter. I stripped off my shirt and shoes; the guard's face glistened with sweat – the place was like a sauna bath. Food was brought in, but we felt too hot to eat it. The best part of the meal was some iced, slightly scented tea.

Then Kenryo appeared with two more guards, and they took Jutta away. All their armament seemed absurd for one strained, wan girl.

I tried to help her morale before she left. I said to Kenryo. 'You'll know what a cell's like in this heat tomorrow – a warship's cell.'

'Save your breath,' he retorted in his unpleasant voice. 'No warship is coming to rescue you.'

I was afraid he was right. He wouldn't have been so cocksure if they hadn't been keeping tabs on her movements.

Jutta was away for over an hour. I forced myself to lie on my bunk. I don't know if my nightmare of what I imagined they were doing to her would have been less if I'd chosen any other way to wait. I couldn't stop the pictures of the torture-cell – the same sort of shadeless bulb blazing in Jutta's eyes as hung above me; her sitting there naked at a table with her arms clamped and two copper claws fixed to each nipple and the electric current shooting her mouth gaping wide and screaming every time they fired the switch. And Kenryo was there and the compressor tube was between her legs probing like an obscene penis . . .

I was at the bars then, yelling obscenities and every foulness I knew at the guard and clawing at the steel. He crashed the stock of his gun over and over against my fingers to make me let go, but it wasn't until he worked the lock of his automatic into a firing position that I sobered up enough to stop it.

Then it was all over because she was at the end of the passageway between Kenryo and the guards, coming back to her cell and smiling a little uncertainly at me; but still there

—alive and herself; not a naked torso taped with electrodes.

Kenryo locked her in; and the guard told him about me. He said nothing, only scowled at me. It was a good thing the man hadn't understood what I'd called him. Then all of them went, leaving a new sentry.

Jutta said, 'You look as if you'd just seen Dracula.'

'A roomful of them.'

'Poor love.' That made it right. All right. All the gnawing doubts over the torch business, too. The light was too harsh for me to read the messages in her eyes.

'Thank God!'

'Poor love.'

I got a grip on myself.

'Was it bad?'

'Not really. They called it an interview. In the chart-room. The same routine as before. Drinks. The iron fist in the velvet glove. More iron this time.'

All my muscles felt as though they'd been stretched and let go and were trying to find their way back to normal. I sat down. Jutta glanced inquiringly at the guard.

'His pal didn't react to my fo'c'sle language. I'll try some on him and see if he understands.'

I gave him a volley – brief because of Jutta – but he simply stared owlishly at me.

'Fine. Now tell me what happened.'

'First, of course, they pressed me about how I came to know so much about *U-160*. I said I'd been researching on behalf of a writer who was doing a book on U-boats which had disappeared without trace during the war.'

'Did they fall for that?'

'To begin with. Emmermann was persuaded when I came up with the answer to a question of his regarding the difference between German and British operating methods: a U-boat captain never stood at the periscope like his British counterpart but sat on a kind of saddle affair. I lost ground, though, when they demanded to know what I was doing alone in a place like Possession. How'd I got here? Where was my author? I said he'd been delayed through illness in Britain but would be along shortly. I made up a name and address. They were even more insistent about you.'

'Not the headman type?'

'Too right. I said you were an alcoholic who'd been kicked out of the Navy and were in the process of rehabilitating yourself.'

'It could have been true once.'

'That got by – just.'

'Not a hint about the tape?'

'No. They found nothing to implicate us, either at the bunkhouse or on board *Ichabo*.'

'Good. Our prospects grow brighter every minute.'

'Make no mistake, Struan, Emmermann is extremely clued up. He fumbles on the details of *U-160*'s action but he has the general outline spot-on.'

'What about that section of plating they recovered?'

'*Gousblom*'s. Hence the interview. They're pulling out from this area tomorrow and starting a fresh search in the channel.'

'Emmermann's sold on the channel?' I asked.

'Absolutely.'

'But you're not.'

'No, Struan, never have been. I can't back up my hunch: I'm just not.'

'The tape would be worth its weight in gold to them.'

'Every question seemed like a trap. It was nerve racking. But I'll keep stringing them along.'

Next morning, however, when Kenryo appeared, grim-faced, at the cell doors I thought she'd fallen into their trap. Until he explained.

'These cells are bugged, of course. We recorded your confidential chat last night. We deliberately put a man on guard who didn't understand English in the hope that you'd be lulled into feeling safe and open up. You did.'

He didn't wait for us to try and talk our way out of it.

'The tape – where is it?'

Neither of us replied. Then he tossed through the bars of my cell a garment he'd been carrying. It was made of leather like a pair of Tyrolean pants with braces.

'Put that on. Over your trousers. Take off your shirt.'

That was no hardship because it was warm already. All night the searing wind off the land had grown progressively stronger.

I was mystified and didn't carry out Kenryo's order.

He barked at one of his plug-uglies and snapped at me, 'Put

'em on or he'll do it for you. Take your choice.'

I felt ridiculous standing there in the peasant pants when I'd done.

He said, 'You'll do. The crew will love this.'

He addressed Jutta. 'The men need entertainment once in a while. They get bored with shipboard life. You'll be made to watch. You can stop the proceedings any time by telling us where you've hidden the tape and everything you know about the U-160.'

I gave her a reassuring glance because I thought I was being forced into one of their staves matches. I rather hoped so. I wanted to have Kenryo on the receiving end. But the purpose of the fancy pants was lost on me.

I found out soon enough, however, when we were marched out on deck. It was murky with fog and desert grit. The crew were gathered round the foremast. They'd lowered its heavy wooden boom parallel to the deck and a couple of feet above it. Three of them grabbed me at a word from Kenryo and frog-marched me to the spar. They compelled me to sit astride it and lashed my ankles underneath with rope. Then they fixed the legs of my pants to the boom with big flat-headed nails. My arms and hands were left free but I was immobilized from the waist downwards.

Kenryo supervised. Jutta was far back under guard and in the dimness I couldn't make out her face clearly. Emmermann stood beneath the bridge overhang with Captain Miki. Miki had a pistol on his belt. His immobility was so marked that it made him stand out amongst the comings and goings on the deck. While I was being nailed down the crew made a ring, chattering and laughing.

When they'd finished the three who'd been doing the job broke away suddenly as if they were afraid I'd take a swipe at them.

Then there was a burst of cheering from the crew. A tough emerged on deck and started walking towards me. He was clad only in the same Tyrolean pants as myself and stripped to the waist. The only difference between us was that he carried a ten-inch knife.

He sat himself down on the spar facing me. His eyes were dark and beady and his stare as impersonal as an abattoir hand's at an ox. He had a bruise on his forehead – Kenryo's staves opponent.

He put his knees to touch mine and they nailed down his pants.

'If you know how to fight with a knife it'll provide better sport,' said Kenryo. 'Otherwise you'll get carved up. The girl can save you, remember.'

I then saw that the crew were laying bets – on me. If there'd been a bookie he'd have rated me as the rankest outsider that ever ran in the *Sang A* stakes.

'You bastard!' I said to Kenryo. 'Do you expect me to fight with my bare hands?'

He signalled a crewman who came up with what appeared to be two long fish gutting knives.

'Take your choice. The moment you do, the game's on.'

The purpose of the pants was clear. Winner or loser, you *had* to fight!

I flicked a glance at my opponent before I took a weapon, trying to sum him up. It's difficult to trigger hate in a minute or two for someone you've never seen before. But his knees were touching mine; he was ready to kill me. Make it a grudge fight, I told myself; that's Kenryo sitting there, not a nameless thug. Go for Kenryo and that will be it. Right for me, right for Jutta. He did in point of fact resemble Kenryo – the same tough-as-teak, hairless, barrel chest and gorilla arms. His chest was dark with sweat and the brassy, dead-fag smell of his breath was in my face.

I reached out for a knife.

He switched his knife from his left hand to his right.

There was dead silence.

I'd never fought with a knife. My one experience was once seeing two drunken *gamats* tear into one another in a street brawl. If I was to achieve anything it would have to be by surprise tactics.

I snatched the knife and lunged at his stomach.

My wrist felt as if I'd bashed a stone wall.

My knife was held fast by its pommel in an iron grip. It's tip was an inch or two from the man's navel.

The crowd roared.

He shoved my arm clear by brute force, deftly flicked his weapon clear and jabbed me in the shoulder above the heart.

It didn't hurt much but it brought a gush of blood.

In reply I side-swiped wildly at him; he blocked me without trouble. The crowd catcalled and booed me. Above their noise I heard an order from Kenryo.

My man acknowledged it with a slight nod and the next thing I had a gash the full width of my chest. He was simply playing with me, chopping me up expertly.

The crowd yelled at me to go for him. I started a thrust with my right hand and then switched the weapon to my left in mid-stroke. He hadn't expected that. It was meant for his throat and I nearly made it. There was so much impetus behind the blow that I jack-knifed forward and our jaws cracked together. He held off my knife-hand with his elbow crooked at shoulder level. I hadn't the strength to ram home the tip and we hung together with our muscles cracking while the crew screamed and stamped.

He pushed me clear and we were back to square one, panting in each other's face and pouring sweat.

Perhaps his narrow escape or my crack on his jaw roughed up his temper; whatever it was, he'd give up playing now. The crowd sensed it. I thought I heard Jutta's voice in the background but I couldn't be sure.

He took the initiative for the next move, but was fool enough to telegraph it by a downward glance at his knife, which then thrust like lightning at my heart. Even a duffer like me could see it coming. I countered by striking hard against the back of his blade.

My knife stuck there.

Then he grinned.

He'd bluffed me with his stroke into doing just what I had done because the back of his knife was overlaid with a soft bronze ridge and my weapon was snagged fast in it. I was wide open to the *coup de grâce*.

All at once his face went slack and he gave a soft little noise like a burp and his head fell forward against my chest.

A knife stuck out up to its hilt between his shoulder-blades.

Kaptein Denny stood on *Sang A*'s rail. He had a pistol in his hand.

'Watch out!' I yelled. 'There by Jutta!'

But he'd already spotted the guards and their automatics and he'd fired before my words reached him. One of them fell dead and the other dropped his gun. Its clatter in the frozen silence was as loud as a grenade burst.

Kaptein Denny shouted something at the mob in a language

166

I didn't understand. They froze – with surprise, and fear too, judging by their faces.

'Miss Jutta! Here! Quick!'

She went to him and when she was close enough to be safe under his pistol he jumped off the rail and made for me. His movements had the same sort of deadly grace as I imagine a leopard has, going in for a kill. He used the body of my opponent for cover, keeping the pistol on the crew, and jerked him off me with a swift pull at his hair. He kneed the knife free out of his back and slashed my pants loose. My ankles were still hobbled, though.

'Use your knife – get free!'

I went for the rope.

Kaptein Denny went forward a couple of paces and faced Captain Miki. He placed his feet wide and deliberately on the planking as if he feared he would slip. His gun came up in a slow stilted motion to full stretch – a curious chest-high way of aiming – until it pointed at Miki's head. In his other hand was his knife, all bloody. If Miki had gone for the pistol in his belt he would have been a dead man.

From that moment there was no one else on deck that mattered but those two. An invisible beam might have been stabbing between them, holding them locked together. Miki's earlier immobility was there still, accentuated by the mortal danger he was in; it reached right up into the inert face and sinister hooded eyes. They were fixed on Kaptein Denny, held in the trance of some association which lay between them. Kaptein Denny was almost as still as he, poised in that deadly trigger-man stance. Kenryo was to one side but Kaptein Denny didn't seem to be worrying about him.

I was. I slashed myself free. No one paid any attention; all of them were transfixed at the silent exchange going on between Kaptein Denny and Miki. Any moment they'd all wake up and overwhelm us by sheer weight of numbers and fire-power. It couldn't last.

It didn't.

I moved, Kenryo moved, Jutta moved.

I to grab the dead guard's sub-machine-gun. Jutta to me. Kenryo at Denny.

Denny's concentration on Miki hadn't blunted a sixth sense of awareness of peril. Kenryo caught him only half off guard. But the shock attack knocked his pistol spinning. I

167

went after it. Kaptein Denny was off balance so he didn't get in his knife thrust at Kenryo. But although the blade missed, the hilt of the weapon crashed him against Kenryo's jaw and he cartwheeled over and, still carried forward by his rush, crashed to the planks.

'*Todome!*' yelled Kaptein Denny. '*Todome!*'

You didn't have to guess that the words meant the big chop, from the pole-axed figure jerking on the deck.

'Struan!' screamed Jutta. 'By the ladder!'

One of her guards – the man who had escaped unscathed – had retrieved his automatic. I had the pistol now.

Kaptein Denny shouted, 'Watch the pull!'

I might have missed my man crouched in the fog if he hadn't warned me, because I'd loosed off three shots before I'd aimed properly, due to the unusual long sweet pull of the trigger which was unlike the customary on-off kick. The first did miss; the second screamed off the flashguard of the PPSH; and the third ripped into his chest.

There was still Miki and his gun.

I raced to the guard, snatched up the sub-machine-gun and trained it from the hip round the deck, moving at the same time towards Miki.

'No one moves!'

I tossed the pistol to Kaptein Denny and got alongside Miki. Emmermann had moved away.

Miki's eyes were a couple of almond-shaped blurs in the fog. He'd already got his hand on the butt of his pistol when I jammed the stubby barrel of the PPSH into his ribs.

'Lay off! Don't move! I'll cut you in half with this if you do!'

His understanding of English improved remarkably under the gun's tuition. He let his hand fall away. It was like an animated puppet's movement, however; not a muscle in the rest of his body seemed to take part in the action. Nor did his head. I might not have been there at all with a magazine full of instant death. His marionette-like stare remained on Kaptein Denny. All he did was to make a curious sucking noise, a short intake of breath. A strange reverse hiss, full of sinister menace.

'Tell 'em – quick – any games from anyone and you're a dead man.'

He didn't pass on my message because Kaptein Denny did

so. The men were all round us, crouched in the fog. I was alert for the slightest sound or movement. Jutta and Kaptein Denny were with me now.

'Over the side!'

I threw an arm round Miki's throat and half-backed, half-dragged him to the rail, helped him along with the barrel of the automatic too.

We made the rail.

'Into the dinghy! See to him, Kaptein Denny. I'll hold 'em off.'

Denny took over and I mounted the rail, swinging the submachine-gun in a slow arc from side to side.

'Struan!' called Jutta from the boat. Her voice was hoarse and unnatural-sounding.

I paused a moment to see if the crew would attempt a last-minute rush. They didn't. I dropped over the rail and into the dinghy. Kaptein Denny already had the oars. Balanced over them he held his gun on Miki; and Jutta was making her shaky and largely ineffective contribution with Miki's own pistol.

'Beat it!'

At my words Denny gave a powerful tug at the oars and stroked clear. There was a shot from *Sang A*. I cradled the sub-machine-gun in my hands and knelt in the stern; and 'walked' my fire up *Sang A*'s side and along her rail and upperworks, grimacing as the recoil tore at my slashed chest. There were yells, oaths, screams and a couple more isolated shots.

We vanished into the murk.

CHAPTER THIRTEEN

Four's a crowd in a small boat, and so is an armament of two pistols, a knife and a sub-machine-gun, all trained on one man in the stern. Captain Miki sat there to one side, where I'd pushed him while I cased *Sang A* with my fire. There was about him still that frightening immobility which he'd displayed on *Sang A*'s deck. He reminded me of a puff-adder which had been trodden on. It rears up and then remains deadly still; when it strikes it is like lightning and at short range. It first hisses like a deflating tyre. Miki had already hissed.

We had to get clear of *Sang A* – quick.

I moved to help Kaptein Denny with the rowing.

'No,' he said. 'Watch him.'

So I stood behind him at the oars, bracing myself by splaying my feet on either side of the bottom-boards. I held the sub-machine-gun on Miki. Jutta was in the bow behind me.

We'd only gone a little farther when she gave a low cry.

'Struan! You're dripping blood!'

I was. It was coming from the gash in my chest. I'd not noticed.

In a moment she was alongside me, steadying herself on my arm and dabbing at the wound with a handkerchief.

'Oh God! Struan, Struan!'

'It's not much.'

'Bandages! We must have some bandages for it!'

Kaptein Denny rested on the oars.

'Here!'

He leant forward as he sat, took Miki's shirt by the collar and ripped it bodily down the front. He might have been tearing it off a statue – except for the shock-wave of hate which his action sparked.

Denny passed the torn material over his shoulder to Jutta, who started work on me.

'Keep moving!' I told Denny.

'We're far enough, for the moment,' he replied. 'We've got

some things to sort out first.'

'I'll say!'

We couldn't make out *Sang A* any longer, and the sounds coming from her were muted.

Kaptein Denny snapped a few words at Miki, who still didn't move. He raised his pistol.

'No!' cried Jutta. 'No!'

'I should: it's what he deserves. Instead he can take his chance, and swim.'

Kaptein Denny gestured again. Miki remained where he was.

Then he uttered the only thing he'd said all along. It was a harsh, venomous little explosion of sound.

'*Tenchu!*'

'Punishment of the gods!' echoed Kaptein Denny. 'Here it is – *tenchu!*'

He struck Miki in the face with his fist. Miki topped over backwards into the water. When he came up, I didn't know whether to be glad or sorry he was still alive.

'Struan! Here! Pull!' Kaptein Denny was back at the oars. I took station alongside him. My last sight of Miki in the fog was of two malicious eyes burning just above water level, like the illustrations you see of vanished prehistoric monsters' heads swimming in search of prey.

The dinghy sped through the water. The slop of sea in the bottom of the boat made the hot barrel of the sub-machine-gun I'd discarded sizzle. It threw off a kind of pinky foam, steaming off the blood on Kaptein Denny's knife. My blood wasn't contributing, now that Jutta had bandaged the wound.

The navigation was a bitch. If I'd been alone I'd have fouled the spider's-web of cables and chains which enveloped *Sang A*. But Kaptein Denny seemed to know at every stage what he was doing. He made his changes of course by pulling less or more strongly on his oar, like a rider guiding his horse by his knees. The cables and smaller marker buoys were virtually undetectable until the boat was upon them: we evaded them all, however, and eventually broke clear of the network when one of the big buoys with its yellow number hove up on the port hand. At this point Denny made a radical alteration of course: I knew it was to the north-west because up to them I'd been facing the east wind squarely and now it was to one side.

The heat lay on the water like a fever and our eyes were full of driving, blowing sand; rowing was as cooling as doing press-ups in a sauna. It was a good thing, though, because it flushed out of our pores the throat-tightening fear-stench of men who have been in the presence of death.

What it didn't flush out, however, were a thousand questions I had for Kaptein Denny. And a thousand suspicions which were mutiplying as fast as one-cell cultures in a test-tube.

'*Tenchu*.' Jutta uttered the word mechanically, like someone who, on waking, recalls a puzzling fragment of a bad dream.

Kaptein Denny anticipated the questions which I was intending to throw at him any moment. It didn't escape me that during our rowing he'd hooked the sub-machine-gun towards himself with a toe, so that it now lay within easy reach under his thwart. His pistol was in his belt, too – a Taisho, Japanese Imperial Navy model.

He said, 'Punishment of the gods. I was the instrument.'

'Instrument!' Jutta leaned forward so that her face was close to our oars. 'Now I've heard everything! You loved that fight back there! Oh, it was pleasant – as a meat tenderizing demonstration!'

'You've got a lot to account for,' I added.

He replied, not at all breathlessly, because he was breathing easily and economically as he rowed.

'You listen to me, both of you. The *Sang A* crowd aren't paper tigers. They're a *kamikaze* suicide squad attached to the United Red Army – the *Rengo Sekigun*. Hijacking and terrorism. The same bunch who were responsible for the Lod airport massacre and a dozen other atrocities – remember?'

'There's nothing to terrorize at Possession . . .' I began, but he cut me short.

'There is. There was. Let's begin with what was. Emmermann is in fact Swakop, the Nazi spy who was landed from *U-160*, then disappeared. I heard nothing about him and thought he must have died – or gone back to Germany after the war.'

'Tsushima the spy!' exclaimed Jutta incredulously. 'A Japanese!'

'Fortunately for me the Oriental and Malay faces are very similar: I've pretended to be a *gamat* all these years.

Kenryo and the others are not Koreans. They're Japanese, like me. So are the others in *Sang A*. They didn't know I understood them that first day we went aboard.'

'A brace of ageing spies, you and Emmermann alias Swakop!' went on Jutta. 'I don't know where Miki fits in but I'd guess he is part of the same set-up. Revenge for some dead-and-gone hatreds which you've kept festering all these years since the war – thirty years! And you try to pass it off as punishment of the gods . . .'

'This isn't an affair of the past but of the present . . .' he began. I knew that must be so since the C-in-C had got wind of it.

'You've turned the whole situation arse over tip,' I interrupted. 'Start at the beginning, for Pete's sake!'

'I repeat: I am Japanese, the man who got left behind on the mainland by *U-160*. Tsushima was only a code-name, like Swakop. My real name's Denzo. It's close enough to resemble Denny – the *gamat* who never was. Nor was I a spy. I'll come to that part of it in a moment. Let's stick to *U-160*. After she'd attacked the liner and been herself attacked by *Gousblom*, my cover was in serious danger of being blown. So I acted the part of the fisherman hero and rescued the liner's passengers. In the resulting confusion and admiration no one questioned my *bona fides*. But I had to silence the one man who knew who I really was. He was the head of the pro-Nazi cell in South West Africa. I returned to Luderitz and did so.'

Jutta said in a whisper, 'Hasler. The husband of the woman who adopted me.'

'I cut his throat.'

'Oh, God!'

'I had to.'

'Had to! Vengeance of the gods again, I suppose! How many others have you killed?' she asked.

I had to risk his closing up completely when I fired my question: 'For what? *Why?*'

He replied deliberately, weighing his words. 'Because *U-160* carried something more valuable than any treasure. It's what the *kamikazes* are after, of course.'

'I thought, almost from that first day we met, that there was more to you than fishing,' I accused.

'You nearly caught me out at Jutta's mother's grave. Those

173

were Japanese Shinto rites for the departed.'

'*What did* U-160 *carry?*' My voice was harsh with tension.

He gulped a great breath of the sandy wind as if he were trying to free a vice round his chest. His steady measured rowing said it wasn't for his muscles.

'I'll tell you. I'll have to explain it. Japan established herself as one of the great naval powers of the 20th century by annihilating the Russian fleet at the Battle of Tsushima in 1905. You could call Tsushima Japan's Trafalgar. We also have our Nelson – Admiral Togo. My code name was associated with the victory: *Tsushima*.'

'I thought Admiral Yamamoto was your naval hero.'

'Yes. Admiral Yamomoto. Japan's sea darling will always be Yamamoto although the glory rests with Togo. In its way Yamamoto's contribution during the Second World War was no less than Togo's nearly forty years earlier. He masterminded our other great naval victory of the century, Pearl Harbour.'

There was no sound but the baying of the wind.

'Tsushima and Pearl Harbour; Togo and Yamamoto. Yet what if I were to tell you that those victories were not theirs but the brain-child of someone else?'

The way he spoke made me wonder whether we had to do with a homicidal maniac. His talk about glory would fit into the pattern of megalomania, of illusions of grandeur. I calculated how far it was to the sub-machine-gun. It would be an even-steven bet who'd reach it first if a shoot-out blew up.

He went on, 'The basic winning strategy at Pearl Harbour and Tsushima didn't originate with either of the two victors, although of course they were responsible for carrying out the detail. No. It originated in a secret Japanese book of naval strategy – not a super-manual, as you'd be inclined to think, of battle moves and countermoves; but a kind of semi-mystical collection of symbols. An oracle, if you like to call it that. This book has been consulted and acted upon by all our great naval heroes for centuries . . .'

Now I knew he was crazy. 'Come off it!' I interrupted. 'Who won the bloody Pacific war anyway? Where was your mystic book after the Yanks thrashed Yamamoto at Midway? Where? . . .'

'In the Possession channel, in *U-160*.'

That put the skids under me. Jutta's face went all tight, like an instant face-lift. As expressionless, too.

'We lost because we lost the Book of Tsu. That's what it's called – the name's a shortened form of Tsushima. *U-160* has it aboard.'

I missed the significance of his use of the present tense because suddenly I felt cold all through. I wasn't dealing with a madman – something else. Worse, if he wasn't on your side.

He went on. 'Miki is trying to sell the sea-heart of Japan to a shower of thugs.'

'You're talking as if we knew who Miki was!' I exclaimed.

'Captain Miki was Admiral Yamamoto's personal staff officer and confidante. He probably knew our great admiral – and his secrets – better than anyone living. He was also one of a small group of Imperial Navy officers who were sworn to secrecy by the Emperor himself and ordered to arrange for *U-160* to collect the Book of Tsu at the Bridge of Magpies.'

'Collect?' I echoed. 'Then she wasn't carrying it when she sailed for the Cape?'

'Collect,' he repeated. 'From me. Ashore. I had it. The Book of Tsu was in my safekeeping. Then *U-160* went off without me, as you know from the tape-recording, taking with her the officer who'd come in her to escort me home. A few minutes before, I'd handed over the Book of Tsu to him and he had waded out to the U-boat's dinghy with it. Then the *City of Baroda* burst in on the scene and in the panic I was left behind. Left!' His voice was edged with bitterness. 'The whole plan wrecked! Miki, as I said, was one of the planning team and afterwards he went back into the front line as the Americans drove closer and closer to Japan. He went on fighting, even after the surrender. He was one of those war-time hold-outs who show up from time to time on remote Pacific islands. In his case it was Lubang in the Philippines. He was eventually flushed out of the jungle a couple of years back, after nearly thirty years of no-surrender. He was something of a hero when he returned to Japan. But he found it wasn't the place he'd fought for. In his disenchanted state he was easy meat for the *kamikaze* movement. So he teamed up with them.

I said, '*Kamikazes* are suicide killers, avengers, nothing to do with naval officers or naval strategy.'

'You're right. Revenge. Russian revenge for their navy's humiliation at Tsushima. The Reds have long memories. It's eaten into them for nearly three-quarters of a century. It runs through all Soviet naval thinking in Far Eastern waters – ships, bases, tactics, dispositions. Russia didn't have the opportunity to take her revenge against Japan in World War II, because she came in right at the end when the Americans had done the job. She still longs to take a crack at us. What better target could a *kamikaze* squad set for itself than to lay its hands on the almost sacred weapon which broke their fleet once, and use it against Japan herself when the chance offered? Miki gave them their opportunity and Soviet money paid for all that expensive salvage gear of *Sang A*'s.'

'And their hardware,' I said, indicating the sub-machine-gun. 'There's a lot more of these around on *Sang A*. Plus other, heavier metal. But how do you know all this background?'

'I was given a lead by something I overheard that first day we went aboard her – they weren't to know I understood Japanese, of course. My suspicions were confirmed when I searched her. We had the pleasure of meeting that night of the party, you and I, Captain Weddell.'

'The guard in the mask!'

'Aye. Miss Jutta knew I was around.'

'You signalled him with the torch.' It was a rhetorical accusation.

Jutta had sat aside while I'd cross-questioned Denny. I considered that the whole thing had become too big for her. Now her voice was remote and slightly mistrustful.

'Yes, I did. I was afraid for you, being alone. We'd made a plan beforehand. Kaptein Denny never left the vicinity of Possession.'

'That puts paid to expecting help from the frigate, then.'

'It's better this way,' said Kaptein Denny.

I went on rowing mechanically, just as a concussed Rugby player goes on playing, my mind in a daze. Then I jerked into the present again. From downwind came the sound of a boat's engine starting up. If half of what Kaptein Denny said was correct, the sooner we made tracks for the high seas the better. 'Where's *Gaok*?'

'We're almost there now: only a couple of cables' lengths to go, to starboard . . . easy as she goes.'

We pulled alongside the cutter and streamed the dinghy astern at the end of a painter.

'They're practically breathing up our exhaust pipe,' I said. 'Start the diesel. Perhaps they won't hear it, the way the wind's blowing. Find your way out to sea?'

'I'll start the diesel all right but I mean them to hear it. I want them to think we're heading seawards.'

'*Think?*'

'We're on our way inshore. Bridge of Magpies. After that, Albatross Rock.'

'Do you want to hand them *Gaok* – and us – on a plate?'

'Listen to me. We start the engine, rev it up and hope the sound does reach them. Then we cut it. We sail. After we've picked up *Ichabo*.'

'Sail! Two boats! You're out of your mind!'

'I say two boats. And we sail.'

That settled it. As far as another reef-grazing ride was concerned, I didn't need faith to trust him after our break-out from Alabama Cove.

His next words, though, drove my patience to the limit.

'We'll tow *Ichabo*.'

'God's truth! What next! Tow! Halve our chances! Halve our speed! Halve our manoeuvrability!'

'We tow.'

The only bright spot was that he appeared to have more to lose than we did. We had only our lives. What the rest of his stake was I intended to find out.

'Okay,' I capitulated.

At that he became more relaxed and easy again. 'Let's go, then.'

We gunned *Gaok*'s engine as hard as we dared and then set off under a scrap of sail towards a spot where, Denny maintained, *Ichabo* was at anchor. Except for the direction of the wind, I had completely lost my bearings. Most of the fog had gone now but the dust made a more tangible darkness which hid the sun and filled our eyes and noses and crunched between our teeth.

We located *Ichabo*, lashed her helm, and made *Gaok*'s towing cable secure. Then we set off, in a series of tight tacks, into the teeth of the wind and across the channel towards the mainland. The air was very hot, and dust blew like a rasp. Desert debris was everywhere. The wind was nudging gale force and had a dry rolling rattle to it – like shaking a giant version of one of the Sperrgebiet's own rattle bushes which clatter like castanets.

There was a steely precision about the way Kaptein Denny tacked and tacked again. He himself had the wheel and I tended the sail. But my mind was only half on the tricky operation: at every turn I expected to run into a *Sang A* search party. Jutta, too, was on constant watch from the bridge.

There was no time to think about the fantastic story Denny had told us. I was continually on the move because at every change of course *Ichabo* would stream away lumpishly down-wind and drag round *Gaok*'s stern. As an example of giving your enemy every chance to cut off your retreat Denny's strategy seemed hard to beat.

But we went on undetected and finally made a ninety degree turn, so close to Doodenstadt's rocks that spray from the breakers was added to the little which cascaded on to the deck. Now *Gaok* pointed southwards, hugging the shore, with *Ichabo* cavorting out to lee at the end of her cable.

A thought struck me and I made for the bridge. 'Radar! *Sang A* has radar! She'll pick us up for sure!'

'In these conditions? Never!' Denny replied. 'Her radar screen will look like a bead curtain across a bar, with all this stuff flying around. There are enough mica particles in it to make radar about as effective as a cross-eyed drunk.'

We drove south.

It wasn't more than ten miles to Albatross Rock, but a couple of crabs under sail would have followed a straighter course than *Gaok* and *Ichabo*. The Bridge of Magpies showed up. Visibility was so low that its legs appeared to have been amputated. When it disappeared astern I gave up trying to calculate where we were, from the amount of forward move-ment, sideways drift and wind thrust.

It is impossible for me to say, therefore, at what point off the fractured, fissured coast I saw, dead ahead on the sea's surface, the grey thing with rounded sides which looked like an igloo tent, or a hangar – one of those plastic struc-tures which are inflated to give them shape. Only this one was dirty and shiny and wet and there were lighter patches here and there on its bulging sides.

Gaok couldn't miss it the way she was heading.

What in hell was Kaptein Denny doing?

I threw myself off the bridge and roof where I'd been attending the sail and into the wheelhouse below. Jutta was there, staring transfixed at the object in our track.

'Put your helm down!' I yelled. 'Down!'

Denny didn't seem to hear and went on gazing forward without turning his head.

I snatched at the wheel – and I looked into the blue barrel of the Taisho.

'Back! Keep away!'

'The rock, man – you'll sink us!'

'Leave it to me . . . it isn't a rock . . .'

He never got any further because at that moment *Gaok*'s bowsprit pierced the grey bulk. The result was like putting your head inside Big Ben's biggest bell when the hour strikes. The boom stunned the ears and kicked the diaphragm. My resulting nausea wasn't only sound induced. The plastic-looking bubble threw off a flatus which was as sickening as it was unique.

The stench-patch *Gaok* had to cross wasn't bigger than a cricket field, and it couldn't have taken more than a couple of minutes but it seemed like hours. I was shouting things which I couldn't hear because my eardrums were paralysed, and I was holding Jutta, gagging and retching against me.

I lip-read the explanation of the thing, on Kaptein Denny's mouth – 'The sound of guns!'

The sea round about was thick enough to have matched *Walewska*'s oil spill, but once we had lurched clear of the patch and gone far enough to give our ears time to recover, Denny told us what the 'sound of guns' really was. He'd heard it a score of times before, of course, but to us it made *Gousblom*'s end sound more poignant.

'It wasn't guns *Gousblom* heard but the explosion of gas pockets which are caused by the upwell cell building up. What you saw back there was a small section of the mud floor of the channel which the gas lifts bodily to the surface. Gas is quickly generated by the action of the upwell cell's warm water on billions of minute, decomposing sea creatures on the ocean bed. Pockets form and push the mud upwards into giant balloons. When they reach the surface, where the pressure of the air is less, they explode.'

'If there'd been no "sound of guns" there'd have been no *U-160* action,' observed Jutta thoughtfully.

'True. It was luck, fate, call it what you like. It doesn't last for long, Miss Jutta. *Gousblom* was unlucky enough to be around at the wrong moment. Once cold water starts flowing it kills the process.'

'No lost Book of Tsu. No Kaptein Denny,' she added.

'Sometimes even I think of myself as a *gamat* fisherman. Denny-Denzo.' That triggered off something inside him and he spoke and steered and never looked anywhere but ahead while *Gaok* spooked her way through the sandstorm towards Albatross Rock.

'The first Admiral Denzo lived about 800 years ago,' Denny began. 'He fought for a Japanese emperor named Minamoto. Denzo won a great sea battle against the Taira clan and his victory gave Minamoto control over the whole of Japan. It is the first occasion on which there is a record of the Book of Tsu. Denzo is known to have based his successful strategy on its precepts. In recognition of his victory Minamoto appointed Denzo to be Keeper of the Book of Tsu. He also conferred a hereditary title on him. It's been in our family ever since.'

Then he said quietly, and not at all theatrically, and with no pose, 'Master of the Equinoxes, Lord of the Solstice.'

He raised the gun-hand which had gone out at such high stretch at Miki. 'I am the Master. I have my duty. The Book of Tsu must never fall into the hands of Emmermann and Kenryo and Miki.'

'Pearl Harbour – Tsushima. The story's full of gaps.' The hoarseness in my own voice surprised me.

'Yes, it is. I'm not telling you that the Book of Tsu which won Denzo his victory was the same as the one used at Pearl Harbour and Tsushima. It wasn't. Over the centuries after Minamoto the Book of Tsu became debased until it was regarded as a lot of mumbo-jumbo, simply a collection of incomprehensible medieval magic spells. An elaborate ritual – over which the Master presided – was built up and it became more important than the Book itself. Its meaning was almost totally obscured by the beginning of the twentieth century.

'Then my grandfather, who lived at the time of the Meiji

Revolution which made Japan into a modern state, revised and rewrote the Book of Tsu in terms of modern naval concepts. That was about twenty years before the Battle of Tsushima. Admiral Togo based his victorious strategy on this revamped, dynamic version of the Book of Tsu. So did Yamamoto at Pearl Harbour. He and the Japanese Naval Staff were already planning and playing war games five years before the Pacific War broke out. Yamamoto himself tasted victory at Tsushima. He was there; he lost a couple of fingers from a shellburst.'

'I feel like a spacecraft starting to come back to the everyday things on earth,' I said.

'I haven't got past the shock of re-entry yet.' Jutta looked it, too.

Kaptein Denny went on: 'It's probably easier for the Oriental than the Western mind to accept that one can receive valid guidance from extra-sensory forces. Maybe it's something to do with the ritual or the symbols of the Book of Tsu, which arouse and project the unconscious. Who knows? It might prove a rewarding modern study in ESP. All I can say is that it worked for Togo and Yamamoto.'

'The more you tell us the more unlikely it seems that the Master of the Equinoxes should find himself as far away from his hereditary shrines and what-have-you as the Sperrgebiet,' I said.

'Not when you realize that Luderitz has a direct association with the Battle of Tsushima. It was at Luderitz that Admiral Rozhdesvensky coaled the Russian fleet for the last time before it sailed to destruction by Togo's guns at Tsushima. You'll find his signature in an old visitors' book at the port.'

'Nothing of this makes it any clearer why you were at the Bridge of Magpies with the Book of Tsu, that night, waiting for *U-160* to pick you up. And it wasn't even a Japanese sub, as you'd expect, but a German one.'

'In 1936 there was an army *coup* in Japan – a palace revolution. Young Turks grabbed the government. They set about eradicating all the traditional things – except the Emperor, of course. He's sacred. The rest went into the fire. That included the hereditary office-bearers. The Master, my father, was a front ranker for liquidation.

'We lived a little way out of Tokyo at the shrine where

the Book of Tsu was kept. I was an ensign serving in the Navy. My father was tipped off by phone that a killer squad was on its way to eliminate him. He vowed they'd never lay hands on the Book of Tsu. So he swore me in as the new Master, after arranging with friends to smuggle me – and it – out of Japan. He also fixed with someone at the Imperial Palace for me to see the Emperor in order to ratify the title. He shot me off with the Book of Tsu, and calmly awaited his executioners.

'I remember that day like yesterday – the Imperial Palace in the snow, the patrols, the shooting, the street barricades. They let me pass because I was in full-dress uniform, and the Navy was supposed to be sympathetic to the revolutionaries. I was young and terrified during the audience with the Emperor, who made me promise that whenever he sent for me I would return to Japan with the Book of Tsu. Then I went back through the patrols with the Book wrapped in a brown paper parcel under my arm and friends smuggled me aboard a ship leaving for Cape Town. My ultimate destination was Luderitz, which my father had designated.'

'A Jap in pre-war Cape Town! You must have stood out like a sore thumb!'

'That's what I thought. Language was no problem – I'd learned English, French and German at the famous Nakano School for Spies. It was my face. But I saw my break when we actually reached the Cape. Malays are Orientals and there are thousands of them there. I'd easily pass as one. So I jumped ship and went to ground in Cape Town's *gamat* Casbah among the cut-throats. I had plenty of money and in those days, there, you could buy a man's soul for a dollar. A year later I emerged – a fully-fledged *gamat* myself, complete with patois. After that it was simple to ship to the guano islands. After a season among the zombies I bought a boat and started fishing out of Luderitz. My cover was complete.'

'The Master, the Book of Tsu, and no employment for them,' I said.

'It looked like that, after Pearl Harbour and the fantastic run of Japanese victories which followed. They were Yamamoto's, of course. Do you know we conquered the whole of South East Asia, from the Philippines to Singapore, from Burma to the outskirts of Australia, for the loss of one destroyer? The new admirals and captains believed it was due to their own fighting skill – who among them had ever heard, or cared, about the Book of Tsu?'

'Except Yamamoto,' said Jutta.

'Even the great Yamamoto overreached himself. He hadn't the Book of Tsu to rely on any more. The Battle of Midway finished him – and the Japanese Navy. Then Yamamoto was shot down and killed in a plane by the Americans in the Solomons. The writing was on the wall for Japan. Traditionally the Navy – the hard inner core of top brass – turned to consult the Book of Tsu. It wasn't there; it was with me at Luderitz. The Emperor knew; so in greatest secrecy the pickup was arranged.'

'But why a German U-boat?' Jutta demanded.

'Swakop – the man who was to raise a pro-Nazi rebellion in South West Africa – was in Japan. *U-160* was refitting at the Japanese naval base at Penang: we let the U-boats use our East Indies bases after they'd been driven out of the Atlantic and Indian Oceans. And *U-160*'s skipper was an ace who knew the Cape well. He'd served in two wolf-packs, *Seehund* and *Eisbar,* in these waters. The whole set-up provided perfect cover for *U-160*'s real mission.'

'No wonder my researches ran dead!' exclaimed Jutta.

'You know the rest,' added Kaptein Denny.

'Except why you were left behind.'

'The Japanese officer in *U-160* who was to be my aide was a stickler for rank and protocol, and the Master was more than someone. He was set on doing me all the honours; he wasn't even going to allow me to wet my feet. He'd first taken the Book of Tsu out to the U-boat's dinghy, intending to come back and piggy-back me out. Then the liner alarm went and the dinghy raced away back to the *U-160*. I was left standing on the beach.'

'That's that, then.' Jutta's voice was flat and empty.

I added, 'I appreciate now why you don't want *Sang A* to know where *U-160* sank.'

'She didn't sink,' said Kaptein Denny. 'She's due any time now at Albatross Rock.'

CHAPTER FOURTEEN

It felt as if there'd been some delayed blow-back into my brain from my paralysed hearing earlier. It simply wouldn't function to accept what Kaptein Denny said. The paralysis seemed to have spread to my vocal chords too.

Jutta's incredulity took the common form of demanding a repeat of a statement that you'd heard perfectly well in the first place, anyway.

'*What did you say?*'

Then her voice wobbled and went temporarily lame.

Denny said, '*U-160* didn't sink. But she didn't remain afloat either.'

'For Chrissake,' I interjected, 'you can't have it both ways!'

'You can – and the U-boat did.'

'I need a shot of *dop-en-dum* – without the *dum*.'

'*Gousblom*'s attack put *U-160*'s ballast pumps out of action and wrecked all her valves. It's there on the tape. I came to the same conclusion when I saw her first.'

'Saw? First?'

I felt a tide of excitement rising inside me. If I could get my hands on the Book of Tsu, the C-in-C would get more than he'd bargained for.

'I've watched her surface every winter for close on thirty years.'

'That accounts for the X-ray-eye weather watch.'

'Aye.'

'It's the upwell cell, of course?'

'Yes and no, but mainly yes.'

'You must have seen the spot where she went down, and marked it; and now with the upsurge of water . . .'

'That isn't the way it works. I myself didn't witness what happened to *U-160*. All I know is that there was a long oil patch next morning, after the action round Broke Rock, and a couple of mines floating about. Everyone said they'd got *U-160*. There was no reason to doubt it.'

'Until?'

'Until after the war and I was on my way home – sick

and disillusioned and feeling not a little guilty about the whole tragedy of losing the Book of Tsu. In fact, at one stage I seriously contemplated committing *hara-kiri*. I was taking myself to Cape Town in *Gaok*, preliminary to shipping to Japan. It was winter, as now, and the weather was the same. I didn't know about the upwell cell in those days; off Albatross Rock I sighted what I thought was a whale on the surface. When I got closer I saw it wasn't. It was a waterlogged submarine. And when I got closer still I made out her recognition number – *U-160*. I thought I had gone out of my mind. I nearly did, when I went aboard. The conning tower and its escape hatch were smashed fast. Inside that floating steel coffin was a whole crew – and the Book of Tsu. There was nothing I could do to get at it. The last straw came a couple of hours later when the U-boat started to go down under my feet and I had to abandon her. That was near the Bridge of Magpies, where the current had carried her. I followed the sinking hulk up the channel and to the open sea, when it vanished altogether. I think I was a little insane that night.'

'It's not possible – that she should go and come back?'

'That's what I thought. For the second time I'd lost everything that was most precious to me.'

'She'd got caught in a dense salinity layer and that brought her to the surface?' I asked.

'Yes, that's it. I didn't rationalize it like that at the time, though. You don't, when a ghost shows up and you live with it for a few hours and then it slips back again into its grave. *U-160* was damaged at the critical moment when they were flooding her tanks to dive. Because of that, she couldn't blow them and she couldn't fill them. She had to go on, half-submerged. The crew was trapped. It must have been an awful death. Escape was so near and yet so far.'

'That is why she never signalled U-boat headquarters as she promised,' interjected Jutta. There was a lurking dismay behind her eyes, as if she feared she had no option now but to live out whatever trouble was in store for us. I think she also secretly mistrusted Kaptein Denny.

'If she went down at the northern entrance to the channel, what are we doing here in the south?' I demanded. 'Perhaps *Sang A*'s location wasn't so far out after all.'

'They're wrong.' His eyes looked as old and tired as if he'd been watching over the Book of Tsu all its eight hundred years. 'I found it all out the hard way. I became possessed with Possession. I lived, sailed, sounded, searched: everything I knew; everything I remembered about the hulk's course; and about tides, winds and currents to try to find her again. Nothing. Salvage can be frustrating enough when you have modern gear; imagine what I felt like using primitive means like sounding leads and fishing trawls and nets, trying into the bargain, to bluff everyone that I was a simple fisherman!'

'But you knew where she went down!'

'So I thought, so I thought. It was only a year later that I discovered that *U-160* didn't go down, but away.'

'What are you saying?'

'The waterlogged U-boat was carried away from the coast by the current. The farther she went the less the density of the sea became, and the deeper under the surface she went. God alone knows where in the South Atlantic she drifts, underwater, all year – Brazil? Antarctica? The Falklands? The West Wind Drift? I've given up trying to work it out. All I know is that it's a regular cycle, because she comes back and surfaces each year when the Bridge of Magpies wind blows.'

'It's blowing now.' There was a curious tightening in my throat.

'And she's coming. She always does. Her landfall's always the same – Albatross Rock. Captain Schlebusch himself couldn't do better. Then she works her way up-channel, on the surface.'

Jutta said, in a carefully controlled voice. 'You need have no fear that you haven't kept faith with your office. Keeper. Watcher. Isn't it enough? Thirty years – it's a whole life.'

He said, more gently than I'd ever heard him speak, 'Keeper. Watcher. True. But it's *not* enough, Miss Jutta. I wonder if you or anyone else could know how it feels to have an inch of rusty steel plating of a dead U-boat's hull stand between you and everything that matters in your world – and your country's?'

The wraps were off him now.

Snap out of it, I told myself, don't buy this Eastern line of a magic staff in one hand and a gun in the other. He's had nearly thirty opportunities, on his own admission, to take

186

a crack at opening up *U-160* – alone, or with the help of others.

I couldn't keep the scepticism out of my voice. 'From what you say *U-160* should have been a piece of cake as far as salvage goes. A tug or a ship to assist and the Book of Tsu would have been in the bag.'

He gestured at the coffee-and-cream whitecaps streaming in from the south; and the desert gale overhead sandblasting their crests to dirty foam.

'Take a look at the risk element. As an ordinary salvage proposition a U-boat is worth peanuts. You've said so yourself. Just after the war you couldn't have sold one for a thousand pounds, even to a film company. With the exception of the Book of Tsu, *U-160* carried nothing of value. Add to that the fact that you can only attempt anything with *U-160* just at a time when all the risks are at their maximum. The skipper of a Japanese trawler I prevailed upon to try it nearly lost his ship on Penguin's Turning. He was an ex-Navy man himself, and I sold him a yarn about *U-160* carrying important naval documents. I think he's cursing me still.'

'You're not the only one in all this time who must have seen *U-160* surface,' I said.

'No? Think! It's never for more than a few hours that she shows up. A necessary accompaniment is a sandstorm. There's fog. By the nature of things, she submerges shortly after the Bridge of Magpies wind drops. *A few hours.* Zero visibility. The most dangerous shore probably in the world.'

'The guano workers . . .'

'Forget it. It's the birds' breeding season. Possession's deserted. I don't have to tell you that. The mainland's Sperrgebiet, *verboten*. There's not a soul about.'

'Except *Sang A.*'

'You're wrong. Except us. We're going in to take the Book of Tsu out of *U-160* when she shows up.'

I, too, had to get in there with him. Intelligence-wise, the Book of Tsu could be the biggest bonanza since American Combat Intelligence broke the Jap code before Midway, and had the fleet's plan of attack handed to them on a plate. *If* it was all Kaptein Denny claimed, it was bigger than even the C-in-C himself could imagine. The odds against two men and a girl pulling it off were astronomical. Three's a crowd, ten's a team. And you'd need a damn fine team of ten experts, backed by a shipload of equipment, to swing the *U-160* odds in our favour.

When I stood turning all this over in my mind and did not reply immediately, the pupils of Kaptein Denny's eyes contracted like a cat's out hunting when confronted by a sudden light. As sinister, too.

Jutta noticed it and said quickly, 'Come down to the cabin a moment, Struan. I've something to say to you – alone.'

The light in the cabin was dim because of the sand cloud, and the dark mahogany panelling didn't help what little sunlight penetrated it.

Jutta stopped, turned, and faced me, looking as if there were something very complicated in her mind which had to be brought out into the light of day. She had about her a remoteness which made her seem vulnerable – and dear. I looked in the deep green of her eyes but found no answer.

She made a little gesture which was half-deprecation, half-something I couldn't define.

'My search for a father has turned into something else. It's still open-ended and likely to remain so.'

'*U-160* . . .'

'I wasn't meaning *U-160*. Me. I tried to tell you before I was a woman who hadn't found herself.'

'Was?'

Her tone was quite different from that night we'd been alone in the bunkhouse.

'I came to Possession looking for one thing. I found another . . . bigger . . . no, biggest.'

'Go on.'

'I'm someone who grew up by fits and starts, painfully. I've waited a long time to establish where I stand in the world.'

'Where is that?'

She came close to me and touched my lips with hers. She could control that, but not the tremors that rippled all down the length of her neck and breasts and thighs when I held her tight.

'Here.'

'Darling, darling.'

'I'm not firing blanks this time, my love.'

We couldn't hear the swishing of the gale past the port-

188

holes for the sound of our hearts beating, together.

She said, 'All these years I've felt I've been playing a part; not being an insider to myself because of it. Now you've come along and transplanted a heart into me and everything is bright and fresh and new. I'm scared of losing it through Kaptein Denny and *U-160*. Scared for you too, my darling.'

She held me fiercely with her hips and thighs. If all this was a revelation of the sort of woman she really was, she was my woman.

'I'll make it work – for you.'

'Maybe I love you too much or not enough yet. I can't go along with this crazy *U-160* business. I can't be sure in my own mind about Kaptein Denny.'

'It's too late to go back on it now.'

'That's what I'm afraid of. We're being squeezed between Kaptein Denny and *Sang A*.'

'Not if we get the Book of Tsu.'

'What if you do? Kaptein Denny won't let you keep it, you can be certain. Did you see his eyes just now?'

I had. Once we'd salvaged *U-160*, the chase might only be starting. I hadn't planned that far.

I said, 'I have you. That makes all the difference now.'

'I want it to, my very dear love. Just look after what's most precious to me, will you?'

We held one another so long that I was worried Kaptein Denny would come looking for us. So we went back to the bridge.

'What's the drill for *U-160*?' I asked him.

The contraction started to go from his pupils when he heard my acceptance. He kept his voice on a neutral level for the reply. The effort it took showed how keyed-up he'd been.

'We can't be sure when she'll show up. She may be coming our way at this very moment.'

There's no such thing as zero visibility but the Bridge of Magpies gale was doing its best to create it. The sand being carried along doubled the normal effect on the sea's surface, of a gale tearing in one direction while a current drove against it from the opposite quarter. It was milky-coffee, churned-up, short and steep; and the sand had a stinging, maddening quality like wind-fired birdshot. You couldn't get away from it, even inside the cutter.

Ichabo was corkscrewing at the end of the tow, and every time it went slack and took up again she jerked and lurched violently. In spite of the fact we were so close, we couldn't make out the scimitar-like curve of the coast, as there was only a frail wash of light from the sun. Waves of a hundred centuries had fragmented the rock of the coastline into a loose series of offshore reefs, stacks, pinnacles and blinders. The biggest of them is Albatross Rock and the worst, Penguins Turning. They form a half-circle of about three-quarters of a mile from land, extended in a south-westerly direction only, like a comet's tail. Between them – apparently known to Kaptein Denny – ran a deep-water channel, scoured, since the Sperrgebiet was young, by the action of the incoming stream of the upwell cell. Even the *Africa Pilot,* whose language is usually as unemotional as a judge's verdict, becomes charged when describing the dangers of the patch we were heading into.

'We go in the moment we sight her,' Denny said. 'You'll take *Ichabo*. I'll have *Gaok*. We make the cutters fast, one on either side of the U-boat. We rig a couple of cables under her keep and secure them to the boats. They'll act as pontoons. They, plus the lifting effect of the upwell cell, will combine to keep her above water while we cut open the hatch.'

'With what?'

'I've brought along an oxy-acetylene cutting torch, with special long leads to the gas cylinders. That means we won't have to carry them around.'

'A lot depends on the state of the metal.'

'Her hull's in fine nick still.'

'All the worse for us.'

'No. All the better. Otherwise it might collapse underwater – anywhere, any time.'

'Will two cutters be enough for a U-boat's deadweight tonnage of – how much?'

'Eleven hundred and twenty on the surface, twelve thirty submerged.'

'Trust Jutta to know,' Kaptein Denny permitted himself a smile.

I persisted. 'You're well heeled. You could have got the services of all the *gamat* fishermen and their cutters from Luderitz on the basis of winner-take-all from the hulk . . .'

'Listen –' I'd been misled by that passing smile – 'Listen very carefully to me! The Book of Tsu is a secret – *one of the world's great secrets*. My country's secret. It's not for spreading around a bunch of blab-mouthed wreckers! Or among prying officials who'd follow them once the story of a floating sub spread from the pubs. Only five people in the world, besides myself know about it: you two, Kenryo, Miki and Emmermann.'

We drove on, the silence in the wheelhouse thick and heavy. Later, the tension eased a bit when we had to exchange technicalities about the final run-in to Albatross Rock. At Penguins Turning we swung starboard on to a south-westerly heading. The fang looked like its name, a penguin who had turned its back to the land all black and shining and its chest to the sea, all white with the smash of the upwell cell.

The manoeuvre – a keel-shaking jolt which had the two boats weaving like drunks while they shaved past the outliers of Penguins Turning – brought the wind fine on the port quarter. It also put us heading dead-on into the current. This race created a whirlpool in the lee (or landward side) of Penguins Turning that didn't help our sea-keeping problems.

We inched onwards, a dreary yard-by-yard slog.

Visibility was no more than a couple of hundred yards. But that was good for morale, because though we could hear, we couldn't see the crash of the seas on every hand.

Albatross Rock finally heaved in sight.

I said, 'I understand now what the pig-boat saying means – "by guess and by God".'

'*U-160* can only come this way.' Kaptein Denny was very tense.

'So can *Sang A*.' Jutta voiced the doubt which had been nagging at the back of my mind all the time.

'Leave it alone!' snapped Denny. 'Leave it alone, Miss Jutta, I say!'

I speculated what his reaction would be if I asked what he intended to do if *Sang A* surprised us working on *U-160*, with both cutters immobilized. I only hoped Emmermann was an ardent reader of the *Africa Pilot*. At best Kaptein Denny couldn't count on more than a few hours in which to slice open a hull specially toughened to withstand four hundred feet of water pressure and the explosion of enough amatol in depth charges to blow the bottom out of the attacker's own hull if you didn't get clear quick enough after dropping them. How deep the U-boat would lie depended on the density of the water in the upwell cell. Only the tip of the conning-tower might emerge if its density was weak. That, only God and *U-160* knew. Also, once the radar-blinding screen of sand fell – as if must do with the decline of the gale – we'd be a sitting duck for *Sang A*'s search scanner.

Silence fell again.

We cased the ocean for *U-160*.

Finally Kaptein Denny brought both cutters to anchor. It was a back-breaking, muscle-fagging business and the spot he chose could have been anywhere except that there was a triangular blur to seaward which he said was Albatross Rock. His hard-line approach was an effective question-stopper.

All that lead-footed afternoon the gale roared over us like a dirty snowstorm.

All that afternoon the desert fall-out swamped the ships.

All that afternoon Kaptein Denny stood, short and brown and frozen-faced, alone with his thoughts, watching the foam-lashed sea.

Sunsets on the Sperrgebiet are usually spectacular affairs because of the dust in the air, but ours didn't stand a chance of penetrating the dark clouds rolling out to sea from the desert. The sun went down in a faint bleary blur and the gale thundered on hot and dirtily. The fog, too, was heavier and earlier than usual because of the hot-cold clash of the air and sea. It became a profitless business continuing the look-out for *U-160*. We couldn't have sighted her unless and until she was right under our noses.

Kaptein Denny's silence and tension were catching and Jutta and I were infected. We went below and I occupied myself with stripping and cleaning the sub-machine-gun. I also greased and checked some running gear that I thought might be useful when – and if – *U-160* showed up. I also tested Denny's blow-pipe cutter which he'd brought for the U-boat's hatch.

Jutta and I had a snack supper below. I was pouring myself a brandy to anchor it when Jutta said suddenly.

'If he's mad, and the U-boat doesn't come, what's he going to do to us?'

I nodded towards the sub-machine-gun I'd put handy on a locker.

'That gun's living with me from now on. Closer than my shirt.'

She went on speculatively, 'It all sounds so normal when he explains it and then when you're alone and come to think about it . . . it's quite some title: Master of the Equinoxes, Lord of the Solstice.'

'It rings, all right.'

'So do delusions of grandeur.' Then she came to me. 'I'm afraid, Struan, afraid for us. Deep down I'm full of doubts.'

I kissed her but her nerves and muscles were as taut as *Gaok*'s rigging in the gale.

'The waiting's sending me crazy.'

I hitched up the automatic. 'Let's got up on deck.'

I held her and blew out the lamp. The cabin didn't go dark. It was lighted silver – faintly, uncannily – from outside and Jutta's face was that spectral colour I'd seen in the channel.

She put her face against mine. 'I'd think it was part of the nightmare if I didn't know the real cause.'

We went on deck. The night had a parched and eerie splendour. The sea's shimmering fire threw up a backwash of luminosity against the overhead sand curtain and made little mobile footlights to light the cutters' hulls. Albatross Rock stood out more clearly than before as each wave that broke drenched it in liquid fire. On the bridge above us Kaptein Denny's statue-still figure and stubby head resembled a silver totem pole.

I was fiddling to get the automatic comfortable and hold Jutta at the same time, so my eyes weren't on the sea.

'Look!' Jutta's intake of breath matched the wind speed.

If it had been moving I would have said it was a torpedo whose buoyant flask was leaking air. A silver stream cascaded to the surface from under the water like a scuba swimmer coasting along blowing bubbles.

An upheaval of disturbed incandescence followed. It resolved itself into the outline of a ship.

'*Jesus*!'

Like a ghost in the grip of some primordial time machine, *U-160* rose up out of the sea.

CHAPTER FIFTEEN

'Trip that brake pawl! Let fly the anchor! Get rid of it, man, get rid of it!'

I couldn't make out Denny's face in the dark of the wheelhouse above, but I could feel his scowl.

'Now! Now! Now!'

We'd teamed the two cutters together beforehand for a snap start but we didn't anticipate that the starting chocks would have to be whipped away like this. Slipping cables is tearaway tactics. We had both boats' anchors out, from *Gaok* in the lead and *Ichabo*, streamed astern on a light hawser. You don't expect in this time and age that a U-boat will surface only a few cables' lengths away and bear down as if it meant business.

Kaptein Denny came racing down the bridge ladder.

'She'll foul *Ichabo* . . .'

There was no sign in his face that he'd registered what I was saying.

'Cut her loose!' he roared. 'Cut her loose!'

He went on past me to the engine-room. I smacked the pawl free. The rattle of cables going overside cut through the night like a small-arms fusillade. It was nothing, though, compared with the bark of the diesel starting up. Hush-kits are for jets but I'd have given a thousand pounds at that moment for a special model for fishing cutters. It sounded as if it could be heard all the way to Possession.

'You know the plan – move, man, move!'

Kaptein Denny was on his way back to the wheel. In a moment I felt *Gaok*'s screw bite and hold her against the current.

'She's – beautiful!' In the hurry I'd forgotten Jutta.

The unreal light from the luminescent fire showed the deadly, low-silhouette, black shape frozen in her last agony. Marine growths were strung from her jumping-wire – the thick cable designed to slice through undersea objects like mine moorings – which runs from bow to stern via the con-ning-tower. The water sparkled as it fell back into the sea.

There were rough lumps of barnacles everywhere. The casing was barely awash. Something – round like a buoy – hung from the jumping-wire immediately for'ard of the bridge.

'Maybe she is beautiful,' I answered. It wasn't time to gawp. 'But what we have to give that hulk now is the kiss of life – or whatever you do for drowned subs.'

'Come on! This is the time! Go! Get going!' Kaptein Denny shouted again.

I got into position to cast *Ichabo* loose. Denny allowed *Gaok* to fall back to meet her so that I could jump before the current carried her away. Whatever the sight of *U-160* had done to him it hadn't affected his seamanship.

'Jump!'

I jumped. Jutta stayed behind in *Gaok* as we'd arranged previously.

'All set there?'

'Aye,' I called back to Denny. 'Let's smack it about.'

He broke the joint plan of action before we started, though. Before I'd time to fire *Ichabo*'s engine he was off alone in the direction of the U-boat. He threw a spotlight on her when he got close. Then *Ichabo*'s engine started banging away.

Where was *Sang A*?

I headed for *U-160*.

When I came alongside *Gaok* I saw by her spotlight what the object was that was bobbing and swinging from the jumping-wire like a jack-rabbit pendulum every time a wave lifted the sub.

I cut *Ichabo*'s engine and leapt aboard *Gaok*. Denny and Jutta were together in the wheelhouse staring at the U-boat.

'Mine! That's a mine!'

I could almost reach out and touch it but nothing would have made me do so. It hung by a whisker. A U-boat's jumping-wire is a single thick cable for about half its length, then divides into two, V-shaped, somewhere above the level of the gun. The V is secured to either side of the conning-tower by sets of double shackles. One leg of the V had snapped. The other was carrying the mine's full weight. The mine's own mooring cable had snarled about the jumping-wire. The main obstacle which prevented its crashing to the deck was a flanged bit of rusty metal (probably in its own sea-bed anchor) which was wedged in one of the shackles.

'I saw it there the first time,' replied Kaptein Denny coolly.

'She tangled with one of her own mines which she'd laid in the channel. But one of the wires has snapped since I saw it last time.'

For all the concern he showed, he might have been quietly discussing some rigging technicality instead of half a ton of explosive liable to go off at the drop of a hat. Of a wire, rather.

'And the other's going to part at any moment! Especially now it hasn't the sea's lift to take the strain off it! Come on, man! Help me do something about it – quick!'

He made no move.

'Take a look at the way that thing's hanging – see?' I went on. 'It's upside down. Those spikes sticking out below are detonating horns. They're pointing downwards. If that cable snaps the mine will drop slap on the deck – Christ!'

I'd been so carried away, my eyes fixed on the swinging mine, that I hadn't paid any attention to the deck. Now I forgot even the mine.

'If we're looking for a spectacular when the next big sea shakes that mine loose, we've got it,' I said slowly. I couldn't say it fast because my mouth was too dry. 'Do you see what I see?'

'Schlebusch was an ace,' replied Kaptein Denny. 'He needed plenty of torpedoes.'

'Nine!' I managed to say. '*Nine* extra torpedoes lashed on deck! She's a bloody floating hardware store!'

The spare torpedoes, which Schlebusch would have re-loaded through special hatches on the casing, were stowed directly beneath the suspended mine with their firing heads pointing forward to give good streamlining underwater.

'I know that nowadays amatol is considered an old-fashioned explosive,' I said. 'A kilo or two of a modern type is enough to blow up a building. But, by God, there's enough here to sink the *Queen Elizabeth, Ark Royal* and *Enterprise* all rolled into one!'

A swell washed against the waterlogged hull and a ripple of phosphorescent fire spread along it.

'Put me aboard,' I said. 'This is a one-man operation. I'll fix it. Then get clear, in case I fluff things.'

'No!' exclaimed Jutta. 'No, Struan! No!'

'Do as I say. Every second's vital. I'll want some spare

cable to reinforce what's left up there and then make the mine fast . . .'

'There's some below,' replied Kaptein Denny quickly. '*Goak*'s staying. You'll want her spotlight to see what you're doing. We're all in this together.'

'Stay if you like: amatol's easy. It doesn't matter whether you're five or five hundred feet from the explosion centre of a load like this.'

Jutta's face was a mask of misery. 'Please – no old hulk is worth it!'

There wasn't time to listen to her side of the story. I'd set myself in motion to do a job and I'd narrowed down my thinking to that, to the exclusion of all else. Perhaps time-bomb defusers work that way. My muscles hadn't got over their initial shock, though; it seemed as if they were being operated by remote control.

I ducked below for some cable, lengths of securing line and wire-cutters. When I got back on deck Kaptein Denny was easing *Gaok* alongside the U-boat, millimetre by millimetre. There was a steel-clad reason, hanging by a thread, why he should.

Then I was climbing over the side.

'Wait!' Jutta called, 'I'll hold your things. I'll pass them to you while you work.'

If the mine slipped I wouldn't be able to reach her in the last few seconds; without her there my hands would be steadier.

'No.'

She didn't argue but I could feel her eyes on my back as I dropped down on to the barnacled casing. There was an unmistakable musty, wet, deep-sea smell coming off the conning-tower and I found a steel ladder up to it. It was clamped on the starboard side (where *Gaok* was) and led first to a light anti-aircraft gun platform, drilled full of holes for draining, abaft the bridge. This was surrounded by a rusty metal 'pulpit rail'. It could well have been one of *Gousblom*'s turrets which had fallen on her, because the structure was wrecked and the stanchions and rails were all crushed. The rear entrance to the conning-tower bridge – a U-shaped en-closure with the open end of the U facing astern – was blocked with twisted metal and also the remains of the periscope housing. It was just possible to edge in.

I did so, and started in on the mine. The jumping-wire to starboard was gone but the one to port was intact. I got a light line round the top of the mine and stopped it swinging: one of the detonating horns was arcing within eighteen inches of the bridge.

Easy now, easy does it, I told myself. Up to now I'd been working largely by reflex, but with the slight change of the odds in my favour I began to react consciously. You can't do anything about the main jumping-wire for'ard of the gun before it divides for the 'V', because it's out of reach, but it doesn't look too bad. Keep that infernal spotlight out of my eyes! I'd brace and lash tight my new strop on the broken section by running a loop through the nearest shackle, then secure it to something firm on the bridge. The steel pipe of the captain's jump-stool would serve. It was strong enough to take the strain.

I was sweating heavily and bracing myself against the bridge coaming and leaning forward to slip one end of the wire through the shackle to make the repair. Easy now, easy! I hope to God *Sang A* doesn't come and catch us with our pants down and a fart weighing half a ton in the pipeline waiting to hit the deck. Not the deck. At twelve feet it didn't need a computer to work out the exact spot where the mine would land. On those nine torpedoes. Would they still explode after all this time? It didn't matter really; the mine would. You're always reading about old war-time mines going up. Over a hundred thousand of them still unswept up around Britain . . . Pull yourself together. You're shaking like a soak with the *ritteltits* – hysterical DTs. The whole bloody Sperrgebiet will shake too if this little lot goes up.

I couldn't manage to complete the loop of my emergency strop. I was about six inches too far away from the shackle. I could do so, however, if I hung on the jumping wire. Add my two hundred pounds' weight to that already dicey cable. So near and yet so far. Shit on all of them who'd put me in this spot. Shit on you, you bastard Denny, Denzo, or whatever you call yourself. Stuff all the Denzos. All the long line of them in eight hundred years. And Tsushima. And Yamamoto. There's Jutta to think of now. I'm damned if this iron udder is going to bang its tits on any deck full of torpedoes.

I grabbed the jumping-wire on sudden impulse, heaved forward with my weight on it, twisted the loop tight, and then dropped back into the conning-tower and made the cable fast.

I'd flayed the skin off my fingers and palms: I descended the conning-tower ladder like a man in a dream and crunched back across the shells and marine growths to *Gaok*. The world started to come slowly back into focus and I became conscious of the gale again. Out there on the exposed casing it felt as if the whole world would disappear in one great blowing cloud. The U-boat's buoyancy had a curious dead feel and walking across her deck like that made one want to grope uncertainly with one's feet, like an astronaut on a spacewalk.

'Safe-conduct's fixed.' I told Denny when I got aboard *Gaok*.

'Struan . . . darling . . .!' The rest of Jutta's welcome was blocked in her throat.

'Now's our time!' replied Kaptein Denny. Not a mention of the thing which hung there – safe now.

I was still suffering from a carry-over of tension but I brushed it aside. 'Right!' I said. 'Let's get on with the job. But look how she's down at the head.'

You didn't need good night vision, in the almost moonlight conditions, to make an assessment that *U-160* would never be classed A1 at Lloyd's. The seas surged across the deck, which was half awash most of its length and fully awash in the bows. Even the railings and stanchions for'ard of the main torpedo loading hatch were half under water. If it hadn't been for what she carried inside I would have dismissed her as a load of old iron only fit to cover with a blanket, and call the padre. The luminescence made a bright border about a foot wide amidships round the casing, where it rode clear of the water; but in the bows, where the seas were shredded, it was like flame rippling on a burning log.

Kaptein Denny said, 'Tonight's the night. It's been this way too many times before. This is the last attempt. Now let's get that rope cradled under her.'

That had been the plan. It was simple – as a plan. It called for a double length of four-inch manila hawser attached to both cutters' bow and stern winches, and looped under *U-160*'s hull. We'd first let go enough slack to let the hawsers sink deeper than the U-boat, then close on her from both flanks, astern; stop when we came abreast the conning-tower, and then winch the cradle in tight. The cutters would act as lifting pontoons while we got busy on the main hatch with the cutting torch.

The theory was fine; the practice different. It was as if we were cowpunchers riding herd and trying to rope the most bloody-minded maverick that ever cut loose on the plains of Texas. The Ancient Mariner's undersea spirit couldn't have jinked, yawed and shoved that sodden hull in more random, chaotic and unpredictable directions than the upwell cell current did. Perhaps that was why she'd escaped being piled up on the reefs in all the years before.

The operation was also continually hamstrung by Denny's refusal to move more than a few hundred feet from the U-boat, for fear of losing her from under his spotlight. This meant I was at the perimeter in *Ichabo*, dragging two heavy lopsided cables while *Gaok* and *U-160* remained close to the operations centre. This made it almost impossible for the cables to reach deep enough to encircle the hull. Once when we nearly succeeded it was spoilt by the cradle snagging on something – possibly a propeller or hydroplane belonging to the U-boat – and before we could do anything about it she gave one of her sudden yaws and we had to go hard astern to prevent the boats being crushed. We lost her and started all over again.

This went on for about an hour. And it seemed like sending out a new invitation to *Sang A* to join the party, every time we gunned our engines full ahead or full astern – on average once every five minutes – and swung the spotlight to every point of the compass to keep it homed on the conning-tower.

When I heard through the murk the heavy crash of breakers coming from close at hand, I'd had enough. We were in the middle of yet another manoeuvre – which meant I was doing the manoeuvring while *Gaok* hugged *U-160*. I didn't cast off my end of the cradle, but cut my engine and set the winches going. This had the effect of dragging *Ichabo* bodily broadside across the gap separating the two boats. *U-160* got in the way like an unwanted third at a *tête-à-tête*, but I couldn't help that: This time *Gaok* did the manoeuvring.

I jumped aboard her and told Kaptein Denny. 'This is for

the birds. Every one of the hundred million birds in the islands.'

'Go on.'

'I hear breakers. Lots of breakers. I'd say it was Penguins Turning.'

'It is Penguins Turning.'

'I'm glad someone knows where we are because I don't. And if it's the *skietrots,* we've come less than a mile in a straight line since we began. Straight being the operative word.'

'So what? Distance isn't important. What is important . . .'

'Distance is time and time is *Sang A,*' I retorted. 'Any time is *Sang A* time and I don't fancy going on with this caper round Penguins Turning. Especially in the whirlpool behind it.'

'Are you saying you intend to throw in the towel?'

'The only towel I want is one to dry myself with when I come up on the other side of *U-160.*'

'Meaning?' asked Kaptein Denny. From his tone, I was glad for my own sake that I was still thinking positively about *U-160.*

I started to pull off my shirt. 'I'm diving and taking a light line down under the U-boat's hull. Bring *Gaok* round on her starboard beam but stop her screw, for God's sake, as soon as you can. I don't want my head cut in half by my own side as I surface.'

'If she jinks while you're diving?'

I'd got down to my underpants. 'I'll take my chance. We've lost an hour already. It's a lot of time when a gale, a salinity level and a bunch of *kamikazes* are treading on your heels.'

Jutta's face was closed and strained. I couldn't find the right words to say to her. I felt she would gladly have traded in *U-160* for anything else on the seven seas.

I returned to *Ichabo* and awaited my moment. Both cutters were lying slightly astern of the U-boat on her port quarter, and I was accordingly awkwardly placed for a dive. But we judged, both Denny and I, that her next swing would be in my direction; so he'd broken away in anticipation of it, with his damned spotlight full on the conning-tower while *Ichabo* lay dead in the water. I'd been sweating in my clothes but now as I stood poised I noticed that the fiery breath of the gale which I'd got used to wasn't fiery any more. Maybe it was because I was nearer the cold water. Maybe it was because I was down to my skin . . . maybe.

The U-boat veered. This was the moment I'd been waiting for. I went up on´ my toes and took the deepest breath I could. There wasn't time to realize that there was less dust in the air than before. I repeated the lung-filled exercise as the casing came sluggishly my way. Two. Three.

I dived.

The shock of the icy water nearly caused me to burp out all my nicely accumulated oxygen. It was cold, cold, cold. I went down, down, down. How deep was a U-boat's keep — about sixteen feet. Then I knew I was under her because the phosphorescence dimmed when her black shadow came between me and the surface. I turned on my back: I wished I hadn't. The hulk was trailing weed, rust and underwater filth. I was too deep, so I bubbled out a little air, turned right side up and stroked strongly forward. Either I misjudged, or the U-boat didn't complete the turn she'd started, because when I kicked myself surfacewards my back scraped painfully against the rough barnacles and at the same time my head cracked against a projection. I ducked automatically and threw out my hands to fend it off. I'd emptied my lungs as I gave that final kick. My fingers encountered something smooth and round, with an object (it felt like a small propeller) sticking out of its snub nose. It wasn't a deadly sting ray but I let go quicker than if it had been, kicked as hard as I could, bumped my back again, and shot to the surface. I grabbed hold of the U-boat's half-awash rail and gasped in lungfuls of air. They were as much from fear as from need.

Gaok wasn't quite in position yet but was coming up towards me, searching the water with her spotlight.

I yanked myself up on to the streaming deck.

'Full astern!' I yelled. 'Back! Keep away! Don't come here! There's a half-fired torpedo sticking out of a tube!'

Gaok went astern but it wasn't a panic manoeuvre. In a couple of minutes Kaptein Denny had the cutter fast in her proper position. I threw round a stanchion a hitch of the line which had been tied to my waist, and stumbled and sloshed my way to her. The plating was wet and cold and slippery under my feet. It wasn't only the cold which made me shake when I jumped aboard *Gaok*.

'What next? The whole bloody sub's loaded – above and under water! It could be one of the old contact-type torpedoes, driven by compressed air, which the U-boat aces liked for night attacks.'

Jutta said in a small voice, as if trying to quiet her own fears, 'It's more likely to be an electric or acoust. – pedo. Its batteries must be stoned dead. It's probably harmless.'

'I'm not particularly sold on the idea of making a practical test to see what sort of torpedo it is,' I replied. 'Just keep *Gaok* from bumping it, will you, Kaptein Denny?'

'Aye.'

'You're going back then, Struan?' asked Jutta.

'Of course. There's a job to finish.'

'I'll get you some brandy.'

It tasted good and I went and stood knee-deep in the sea, getting the hawsers fixed. Most of the time I worked by feel in the cold water. Several times big waves came and then I hung on waist-deep to the rail. If the waves were doing this to me, what were they doing against the fangs of Penguins Turning? That thought made me finish the job about as quickly as if all the hardware lying around was primed and ready to go off. I could hear the *skietrots* coming closer all the time. What worried me too was the easier give of the sea under the U-boat. It meant the upwell cell was changing.

My aching arms were quivering so with the strain that I slopped the brandy when I got back to Gaok's wheelhouse.

'Fine!' Denny exclaimed. 'Nice work.'

'Let's keep the medals in deep freeze until we get clear of Penguins Turning. I haven't a clue which way we're heading.'

'We're making a northing with some east in it.'

'I'll take your word for it; but meanwhile a couple of things won't have escaped your notice. The sea's easier; the wind's going.' I pointed to the towel I'd been rubbing my shoulders with. 'See all this dirt? It's from the fog. The fog brings down the dirt and the dirt brings down the fog. Not to put too fine a point on it, it's starting to clear. Our protective curtain's disintegrating.'

'That means *Sang A*,' said Jutta.

'Plus radar. Plus twenty pairs of *kamikaze* eyes itching for a glimpse of two fishing cutters.'

'Depends where she is,' replied Kaptein Denny.

'Maybe she's searching for us out to sea. Maybe not. You'd also have noted, if you'd been down under the hull, that the silver fire is going – fast. That means the salinity will change. Less dense; less lift. Less for *U-160*. Less U-boat above water.'

'You're overstating the dangers. We've got half the night still ahead of us . . .'

'Look!'

It was the *skietrots*. Its white chest with the breakers creaming over it was the giveaway because the main black part of it blended with the night. But you could hear it all right.

'That rope cradle okay?'

'Aye,' I told him.

'Watch your moment. We'll put both boats full ahead on *U-160*'s next swing. That plus the current should take her clear.'

'If this wreck picks up her skirts and flies it'll be the only time a skirt won't mean sex to me.'

I hurried across *U-160*'s deck to *Ichabo*, opened her diesel to full bore and waited to throw in the clutch. *U-160* was pushing the dying wind, but not the current. Her underwater surface – all eleven hundred tons of it – was solidly in its grip and being swept along.

The three vessels, tied together, came round in a wide, lazy, swinging circle. When *U-160*'s nose pointed off-centre from the white target of Penguins Turning, Kaptein Denny shouted, 'Full ahead! We'll manage it! Give her everything!'

I thought so, too – at first. Another point in our favour was that Penguins Turning was slightly farther away than I'd calculated, because the visibility was lengthening all the time and I'd judged the distance by previous cut-off standards.

The cables took the strain of the thrusting boats and *U-160* began to forge ahead the way we wanted. Two knots. Three. Four. I thought we'd make it. Then it was like steering a lead coffin with a poltergeist inside. The current took charge and dragged the U-boat and the two cutters round as if there weren't diesel-powered sheepdogs hanging on to both its flanks. She span – slowly, deliberately, menacingly – in her own way and in her own time. I gave *Ichabo* full starboard helm and I was sure Kaptein Denny was doing the same. But it was impossible to apply a correction factor.

With an extra long arm I could have touched Penguins Turning.

'Let her have her head, for the love of God!' I shouted. 'Let her go! Let her go!'

U-160 had managed it so many times on her own in the past, maybe she'd manage it this time without our fouling up whatever delicate underwater forces were in play.

U-160 managed it. Just.

At her nearest point, I wasn't sure which was the end of her bow with the white water breaking, or which was Penguins Turning with white water breaking. An eddy seemed to take over at the last moment. Then suddenly we were past and swirling, churning, spinning in the whirlpool in the lee of the *skietrots,* among the races and overfalls and blinders and spray.

We left *U-160* to make her own way. There wasn't anything else we could do. She – and we – went on swinging and turning like that: on and on, round and round. After the first few turns I began to get accustomed to the movement and pulled myself together enough to make an estimate whether we were making progress over the ground or staying in one place while we swung. We *were* progressing. But the drift was so imperceptible that it took fully half an hour to win clear of the merry-go-round and begin to follow roughly the northward line of the coast towards Possession.

CHAPTER SIXTEEN

It didn't need a crystal ball to see that the upwell cell was breaking up. The gale was down to a mere stiff breeze and was changing direction. It wasn't hot any more because it was veering away from the desert seawards. By virtue of the fog's condensation, the muck was coming out of the sky like muddy rain and forming a coating over everything – decks, rigging, railings and *U-160's* conning-tower, which appeared rustier still because of it. The silver had completely disappeared from the sea.

I crossed to *Gaok* as soon as we had settled on a steadier course.

'We've something like four hours until sunrise,' I said to Kaptein Denny and Jutta. 'We're the nut in the cracker's jaws. One jaw is time, the other is *Sang A*. If we're going to achieve anything with the cutting equipment, now's the time.'

'We'll start in right away,' Denny replied.

It wasn't as simple as that. In the first place a thick skin of barnacles overlay the steel plating of the hatch on *U-160's* bridge. At first try Kaptein Denny used the cutting blowpipe on them, but the result was a loathsome fish-fry smell which choked us, in the confined space, without getting at the metal. So we set about smashing off the shellfish with hammers. Jutta also took a hand, but it was a reluctant, silent hand. We had to use the spotlight to see what we were doing. To me it had assumed the proportion of the biggest advertising sign in Piccadilly Circus.

Finally we cleared a patch and Kaptein Denny slipped on his anti-glare visor and attacked the steel itself with the torch. Without eyeshields, Jutta and I were forced to turn our backs on the brilliant blue-white flame but we couldn't miss the showers of sparks which went everywhere. If *Sang A* was around and hadn't spotted that Brock's Benefit, all I could think was that every man jack of them was on another trip.

The length of time Kaptein Denny went on made me wonder whether his enthusiasm had taken him right down into the U-boat's control-room.

'Through yet?' I asked.

He cut the flame. His eyes had a curious expression as though only part of him were there at all.

The incision wasn't through; it hadn't begun. Four inches of toughened steel scarcely showed a mark.

I made a quick calculating survey. Not only was the hatch itself secure but the frame surrounding it was distorted and sealed by rust. I experienced some of the frustration he himself must have known the first time, when he'd boarded *U-160* all those years before and realized there was nothing he could do to get inside her. The situation didn't seem to have changed much. I knew in my heart that it was a dockyard job, but I wouldn't admit we were licked.

Both Kaptein Denny and Jutta were regarding me as though I had a solution ready: I hadn't. Jutta's eyes were very big and there were dark circles under them. The furrows in Denny's face were deeper.

'We're wasting our time with that thing,' I said. 'We'll use up all our gas without making a hole big enough to get your finger into. What we really need is an explosive bolt fired through the pressure hull at the end of an air line. Then the hull should be pumped full of compressed air to give it buoyancy. The next requirement is a couple of powerful derricks to get rid of the mine and torpedoes – plus a skilled demolition squad. After that, relays of men with special gear to slice her open.'

Kaptein Denny looked stockier and grimmer on hearing my evaluation of the situation. When he looked at me, some sort of change was in process behind his eyes. His voice held a threat.

'Is that what you suggest?'

'Give me a chance to think.'

'Think then, because I want you to understand one thing very plainly: *U-160* is never going to fall into *Sang A*'s hands.'

With or without *U-160,* we looked like being the losers. I wasn't going to say that to him, though. My mind fumbled with the problem. Explosives. Mine. Torpedoes. There was an embarrassment of riches in that direction. Embarrassing enough to blow a hole in the sea-bed . . .

The word sea-bed sparked a solution. The idea tumbled out rough-cut and unformed, because I hadn't had time to think it out.

'I've got it – we'll blow her open. We'll use the salvage bomb I filched from *Sang A* to do it with.'

'Excellent!' Denny replied. The strange unseeing look went from his eyes. 'Excellent! That's it! That's what we'll do! Where's the bomb?'

'Still in the dinghy.'

'Struan – listen!' exclaimed Jutta, who had flinched at my suggestion. 'It won't work! A small bomb like that won't accomplish what a salvo of depth charges failed to do! That hatch is fast. If you use the bomb anywhere else on the hull she'll come apart at the seams and go down like a stone.'

'Jutta's right,' said Kaptein Denny unexpectedly. 'That doesn't mean to say the idea's basically unsound.' He indicated the mine. 'That could go up in sympathy with the bomb if we detonated it on the conning-tower. The torpedoes, likewise.'

For the second time a word gave me the clue to a solution. This time it was torpedo.

'I see a way!' I said quickly. 'We'll draw that half-fired torpedo out of its tube – we can manage it in shallower water with a dragline attached to one of the cutters! All that will then stand between us and the interior of the sub will be the torpedo-tube door. The salvage bomb will take care of that!'

'And send her to the bottom in the process,' objected Jutta. 'It won't work . . .'

'It *will*,' retorted Denny. 'We'll make it work. We'll beach her, that's what we'll do. We'll put her ashore on her side at the Bridge of Magpies – it's the only place hereabouts. We'll dump the mine in the channel. We can do that once she's ashore by using *Gaok*'s mainboom as a derrick . . .'

It sounded good to me – not to Jutta.

'You both talk as if you expect the night is never going to end!' she exclaimed. 'What about *Sang A* while you're busy beaching her and blowing her open? What about . . .?'

But Denny went on, as if he hadn't heard her, 'We've time! We'll tow her! We'll use the up-channel current in our favour!'

'How far is the Bridge of Magpies, do you reckon?' I asked.

Jutta stood back, resentful and mistrustful.

'Seven-eight miles,' he replied.

'We've come less than two in the past three hours. We've got to do better than that.'

'We will. We must.'

It was a desperate last-chance throw; and we both knew it. We both knew, too, that we were discounting the signs in the sea and the wind. The writing was on the wall that the salinity lift had dropped – and *U-160*'s buoyancy with it: the casing aft the conning-tower, which had been a good foot above the water when we'd first come aboard, was now occasionally awash. For'ard, it was almost continuously so. Our race against the sea and *Sang A* was likely to turn out a very close-run thing.

'I'd like to have Jutta with me in *Ichabo* now,' I said.

'Right,' he replied. 'We'll work up speed gradually. We can manage six knots if we try.'

Maybe we could have done so if it hadn't been for that misfired torpedo, which we couldn't draw until the water shallowed. We safely crashed the two-and three-knot barrier on a north-easterly course towards the channel mouth and the Bridge of Magpies, when suddenly *U-160* yawed, and wheeled at right angles. We fought her with both cutters' engines until we brought her to a halt. Lights. Engines. Shouts. Time. Time. Time.

Where was *Sang A*?

'She's sinking slowly by the head,' I called across to Kaptein Denny in *Gaok*, on the opposite side of the U-boat. 'We've got to do something to stabilize her and offset the torpedo's drag.'

When I looked at the sodden hulk I began to have secret doubts: the odds were mounting against us. The U-boat was riding – if her dead action could so be described – so low that most of the time now the deck was flooded. Attached to the dead-weight by the hawser cradle, the cutters, too, were beginning to wallow.

'No time!' answered Denny. 'It's still too deep here. Try again!'

We got going and worked up a little speed, crabbing through the water; then with a sudden swirl we swung broadside on and the U-boat and cutters became unmanageable again. It takes twenty minutes and two-and-a-half miles for a supertanker to come to a halt. It didn't take us two-and-a-half miles, but it did take twenty minutes. It also needed another ten to bring the U-boat on to a rough course again towards the Bridge of Magpies.

For the next few hours we threw the book at *U-160* — short and long bursts ahead and astern, jointly and independently, full and half rudder or simply no rudder at all. Nothing helped, really. We may have gained half-a-mile, a distance the current would have carried us, anyway. The only difference in the later stages was that the acute swinging gave way to a long sweeping eddy-like motion as we cavorted up the coast into the mouth of the channel at its southern entrance.

Jutta stood with me in *Ichabo's* wheelhouse and watched the first light of dawn tarnish the eastern edge of the sky. *Ichabo* was to port (the seaward side) and *Gaok* to starboard (landwards). Sperrgebiet dawns are something all of their own. They're not grey but sand-coloured and you first see a long shape loom out of the blackness; and it takes on the form of the top of a dune while night still hangs around the base. The light comes quickly, too: the fact that we began to make out the long lines of the dunes ashore was ominous. They should have been hidden in dense fog at that hour, but the disintegrating upwell cell had thrown everything out of kilter.

Jutta asked in a small, thin voice, 'How far to go still, Struan?'

'It depends on how much mileage is left in the sub.'

There didn't seem to be much. It was a marvel, really, that she was still with us. The sea, which had moderated to a swell, swept clean across the casing now, though the stack of torpedoes was still above water. The deeper she sank the more the current took hold of her — and of us. We were in one of the relatively quiet phases, when *U-160* was heading the way we wanted and the cutters were just nudging her along. The wind was only a fresh breeze now, but it had changed direction completely and settled in the south-west, its true quarter.

There was a kind of basic despair about Jutta when she surveyed the scene, as if she couldn't break out of a trap of inner darkness.

She asked suddenly, 'Struan — what if he's mad? Really mad?'

I glanced across at *Gaok*. Kaptein Denny stood like a statue at the wheel.

It was both a question and a call for reassurance.

She added, 'Master of the Equinoxes, Lord of the Solstice – it sounds like something out of a phoney old-time operetta.'

'He isn't a phoney. Nothing could have sounded more way-out before than his story of *U-160* returning. Yet she did.' I gestured. 'You couldn't have more concrete proof – we're not lashed fast to a dream, Jutta.'

'I know, I know. But I can't go along with the rest of it, Struan. Maybe he suffers from some kind of delusion – paranoia, schizophrenia, or whatever they call his particular brand of mania.'

'We'll prove his genuineness, one way or another, pretty soon, when we blow the sub open and see what's inside her.'

'What happens then?' Her attitude implied, 'if', not 'when'.

'After we've got the Book of Tsu, I'll take it from there.'

She looked so cast down that I put one arm round her and drew her close to me.

'Look, there's our target.'

Ahead, wisps of fog clung to the Bridge of Magpies. It appeared more brown than black in the muted light.

'It's not far – only about a mile to go. Fog lifting. Clear day. Empty horizon. Moderate sea. Not a thing in sight.'

'I want you to know that, whatever happens in the next few hours, I love you more than any words of mine can say.'

'And I you, Jutta.'

But her body against mine was hard and unresponsive and tension-shot. She went on. Her voice was higher pitched, vibrated with nerves.

'Where *is Sang A*, Struan? Where? What if she's tracking us at this very moment with her radar, now that the sand-storm's over; just waiting to pounce when it suits her, watching us . . .'

'Steady,' I said. 'Steady. There's not a sign of her. We'll win out yet.'

'It's all too quiet! Everything's cooking up underneath! I feel it, Struan! Isn't there anything you can do? The wait-ing's sending me crazy!'

'Ahoy there!'

It was Kaptein Denny from the sub's conning-tower. I

was surprised to see him there. I reckoned he must have left *Gaok*'s bridge, unnoticed, while we'd been occupied.

'Come up here, will you? Both of you. And bring the bomb along too.'

'Right,' I called. 'I'll fetch it from the dinghy.' To Jutta I said quietly, 'I wonder what he's got in mind – we shouldn't need the bomb until we beach her.'

She didn't answer, but cast an anxious glance round the widening horizon.

I collected the bomb and we sloshed across the wet deck and up the rusty ladder to the U-boat's bridge, stepping over the rubber cables which led to the cutting torch. After that long effort previously, we'd changed cylinders and connected up to full ones in *Ichabo*. We'd switched them from one boat to the other, to obtain a better weight distribution.

Kaptein Denny was seated on the Captain's jump-stool, to which I'd secured the emergency wire which held the mine. The brass nozzle of the blowpipe cutter was hooked on to the coaming which encircled the bridge at chest-level. I was surprised to see *Sang A*'s sub-machine-gun on the floor.

I looked up to question Denny about it – I was more curious than apprehensive – and immediately I was aware of a great change in him. What had previously disquieted me about his eyes, when we'd been deadlocked over the problem of opening up *U-160*, had now become a reality: they were slightly hooded with tiredness but clear and intense, with a kind of exultation. He had a smile of welcome for Jutta. He might already have found the Book of Tsu rather than be facing a day of peril and difficulties.

'What do you want the bomb for at this stage?' I asked.

He replied with a question. 'How secure is that mine?'

'If it lasted last night it'll last today. The sawing effect of the sea's gone, as you can observe for yourself.'

'What I mean is, if your emergency cable broke suddenly, would the original cable still hold?'

'Probably. It took my weight for a short while when I fixed it.'

I noticed then that he had his Taisho pistol in his belt, along with an odd-shaped knife with a flat handle I hadn't seen before.

'Put the bomb down,' he went on.

I did so.

'Would you agree with me that we're heading north?'

'North – sure. But why . . .'

I didn't complete my question because something crossed his face which sent an adrenalin-charge of fear and doubt racing through me.

'Good,' he said. 'Good. In Japan the dead always face north, both ships and men.'

He got to his feet and pointed ahead, changing the subject rapidly before our apprehension had time to crystallize.

'Look!'

The top of the Bridge of Magpies was catching the first sun. The soaring arch wasn't composed of rock but of feathers – hundreds of thousands of dun-coloured little birds that had been blown out of the desert by the gale and had found shelter on the arch's seaward side.

'They aren't real magpies, of course, but little desert birds they give that name to.' He was speaking rapidly, as if time were running out on him and he had something important to say before it did. 'It was like that the day you were born, Miss Jutta. There's an old Hottentot superstition. Once a year, they believe, on the day after the great gale, the Girl walks across the Bridge of Magpies and joins the Lover . . .'

I glanced at Jutta, who stood taut and poised, a mixture of pity and growing horror in her eyes. Outwardly she was composed but I knew she was very close to the edge. She'd been right about his sanity. The unconnected prattle and mercurial leaps from subject to subject meant only one thing.

His next words to me confirmed it.

'I'd like you to cut the old mine cable with the blow-pipe. Leave the new one you used for the repair. Here, where I can reach it.'

He reseated himself on the jump-stool and plucked at the wire. I noticed that he put his foot on the sub-machine-gun.

'Kaptein Denny . . .' There was a rising note in Jutta's voice.

'The dead always face north, both ships – and men, Miss Jutta. We're now facing north.' The final clincher on the fact that he was out of his mind came when he added, 'I'm going to drop that mine on the stack of torpedoes and blow up *U-160.*'

Kamikaze. That's a good word for what's happening, I thought, my eyes fixed on Kaptein Denny's seamed, exalted face. That's the way the *kamikaze,* or divine wind spirit, worked in the Jap fliers who plunged their bomb-laden planes to self-destruction through the Yanks' withering ack-ack fire and on to their carriers' decks. *Kamikaze –* Sperrgebiet-style. Divine wind spirit gone bad. The thing's eaten into his mind all the years and now he's at the end of the line. I wonder what the C-in-C will say when he gets to hear of it? He won't know what happened, of course, because there won't be any survivors.

Kaptein Denny wasn't reacting to my scrutiny. His face was remote. In his last moments he was remembering things and places we'd had no part of. The external world – our world – meant nothing to him.

'You can't . . .!' exclaimed Jutta.

'Why?' I demanded peremptorily. I had to get past that mental state of his. 'Why?'

I did get past: 'There!' he pointed.

There was no mistaking *Sang A*'s whalebacked snout and low hull. She was rounding the southern end of Possession, past the tiny horseshoe-shaped curve called Black Prince Cove, and heading into the channel. At us. He must have spotted her out to sea before he crossed to *U-160* from *Gaok.*

Jutta and I stood rooted. Then from behind us there was a smothered noise from Kaptein Denny. We swung round. He'd pulled up his jersey and jabbed that odd knife into himself. He covered up the wound right away but we'd seen the rush of blood. Jutta's face screwed up.

He said in the same quiet and compelling way he'd had when he told us about being Master of the Equinoxes'

'What I must do now I must do alone. This is *hara-kiri.* I must admit that the method of dropping a mine on a load of torpedoes is rather unique. Crude, but effective. The first ceremonial cut in the stomach is called *seppuku.*' The pain lunged at him and he caught his breath. 'There won't be time for the rest of the procedure.' He tried to smile. 'Traditionalists even have a warrior's meal of dry chestnuts and cold *sake* beforehand. How close is *Sang A*?'

'Out of range, but she's got a heavy machine-gun mounted for'ard . . .'

'I know.'

Jutta and I also knew now that he was as sane as we were.

Only his eyes looked a little tired and his face was sallower and finer-drawn – from the blood he was losing, probably.

'I said, "the Girl goes to join the Lover". Now go.'

We didn't take it in for a few moments that he was giving us our lives. Then Jutta broke the spell. She went towards him – to kiss him I think – but he waved her back gently. 'Sorry, you mustn't touch a dead man, Miss Jutta. After *seppuku* I'm dead.'

She knelt on the rusty plating and he sat on the jump-stool with his right leg stretched out in front of him to ease the pain. He took the Taisho from his belt, slipped a shell out of it, scratched some words on the blade of the knife, and gave it to Jutta.

'*Mei fa tzu – it is fate*,' he quoted.

'What do you want me to do?' I asked hoarsely.

'First cut away the old mine cable.'

I put a match to the blowpipe. It was only a matter of seconds before the section of rusty cable snapped under the flame and thumped against the conning-tower. The new piece I'd fitted still held the mine suspended.

'Good,' he said. He handed me his pistol. 'Now I want you to take *Gaok* – have her afterwards for yourself – and fire four shots as a signal. When *Sang A*'s close *enough*, do you understand?'

'I understand, Kaptein Denny.'

'I won't be able to get up and judge the range,' he went on. 'You'll be my eyes. I want the signal distinct because *Sang A* will be firing too. One-two. One-two. Then I'll know. Where's *Sang A* now?'

There was a burst of machine-gun fire from the black ship. I ducked involuntarily.

'Out of range. That'll be Kenryo trying his hand.'

'That machine-gun of theirs can't train completely for'ard because of the whaleback,' he said. '*Sang A* will have to sheer slightly to one side when she comes closer, to bring it to bear. She'll lose ground by doing so.'

I shot an anxious glance at the approaching ship.

'Anything more?'

'No. You weren't a headman, of course?'

'No. Navy.'

'Give my regrets to your chief.'

'I'll do that.'

Jutta said in a strangled whisper, 'Master of the Equinoxes!'

He said, 'Kaptein Denny was a long, long act. It's good to be myself again. Now run for your seventh life!'

Jutta clung tight to me and I half-led, half-carried her down the ladder off the bridge. There was another spatter of fire from *Sang A* when they saw us but they were still too far away to do us any harm.

I slipped the rope cradle which held *Gaok* to *U-160* and gunned the engine. *Gaok* pulled away from the U-boat.

Sang A was pushing hard, and the water was white under her bows. She sheered to one side in order to bring the heavy machine-gun to bear, as Kaptein Denny said she would have to, enabling *Gaok* to gain some valuable distance. There was a staccato ra-tat-tat but the volley fell short. Twenty yards short. Extreme range.

Sang A pulled back on to her course: *Gaok* was working up to full speed but the black ship wasn't interested in us — yet.

Then she veered again and the next burst spanged off the conning-tower. They're in range now. Judge it, I told myself, judge it and don't panic because a few yards will make all the difference between life and death when the moment comes. *Gaok*'s life and death. Ours.

The machine-gun cut off abruptly. They'd got wise to that mine. Then came several isloated, lighter shots. Sniper. That's Kenryo's gun. He's trying to pick off Kaptein Denny. He'll be all right if he doesn't show himself from behind the protection of the conning-tower.

I daren't wait any longer! *Sang A*'s coming on like an express. Two or three other automatics joined in with Kenryo's.

Now.

I stepped out on deck with Jutta. I raised the Taisho and fired into the air.

One-two. One-two.

I crushed Jutta to me.

'There!' she whispered.

Above *U-160*'s conning-tower the blue-white flame of the blow-torch was brighter than the daylight and there was a little cascade of sparks where Kaptein Denny attacked the wire at the point where it looped over the bridge coaming. *Sang A* was close to her, well within the explosion area, and firing non-stop.

Then the sparks flared up.

I pulled Jutta to the deck with me.

Gaok's steel rail rolled up like fencing as the blast from the explosion hit her. She leapt and bottomed again with a keel-shaking crash. Water, bits of glass, metal, rope and planks rained on us. We lay there until they had stopped.

Then we picked ourselves up, and I held her, and we looked. Her heart was hammering away against my chest. The sea was empty. There was no sign, through the yellow haze of the shock-wave, of either *U-160* or *Sang A*. The surface of the water, where they had been such a short while before, was littered with steaming, blackened fragments and unidentifiable pieces of ship, sizzling as they sank. Landwards the mushroom of the explosion towered above the Bridge of Magpies. It wasn't smoke. It was a million birds.

We stood silent, trying to comprehend the swift totality of the catastrophe. The silence was as total as if our eardrums had burst. The only thing that stirred was the yellow haze over the water.

It was because I was watching the movement of those wisps, rising like a ghost from a body, that I spotted another movement out at sea, above the low promontory where Black Prince Cove was situated. It, too, was wraith-like – a tall lattice mast with radar scanner and aerials, swinging slightly with the roll of ship to which it belonged.

I stared at the disembodied thing above the point of land, as if I'd never been a Navy man and had never seen a frigate's top-hamper before.

'Jutta! The frigate! She's here!'

Like a film image growing out of the island's extremity, the bow of the frigate emerged, then the low lean midships section, and finally the stern with its boil of white thrown up by engines going full speed ahead.

Jutta said, 'Kaptein Denny must have got off your message after all.'

'No, Jutta. He assured me he had not. There's some other explanation.'

The sound of engine-room bells came across the water. The *Fairest Cape* went full astern when she sighted us, and altered course to avoid the stained patch of debris on the sea's surface. She skirted it and came slowly towards *Gaok*.

White-clad figures were at her rail and on her bridge, gawping unashamedly. All you could say for *Gaok* was that she was still afloat.

The frigate lost way and stopped. They threw us a line.

'Come on up,' said a voice from her deck. 'Have you any casualties?'

'No casualties.'

Jutta went first up the rope ladder and I followed. When I got level with the warship's rail there was a shrilling of bo'sun's pipes. For one impossible moment I thought they were for me. But no navy extends an ex-captain an admiral's honours. They were for the C-in-C. He came along the deck towards us and I found myself wanting to jump to attention at the sight of so much brass, until I remembered my stained, torn headman's rig.

The little admiral held out his hand to me. He barely spared Jutta a glance.

'Glad to see you, Struan. What was the big bang?'

'A mine and an old sub full of torpedoes.'

He gave me a shrewd, penetrating glance and the other extreme of his vision took in the dirty patch of sea. Reaction began to hit me. All I wanted was a drink. Maybe two.

'Rough?'

'Pretty rough.'

'I was hanging around out of sight below the horizon. I couldn't get here in time when things started to get hot. The sandstorm put paid to using the ship's helicopter, of course. In addition we didn't want to scare *Sang A away* – I'd also had fake radio signals sent off to bluff her into thinking that the frigate was hundreds of miles away.'

'They worked, all right.'

Resentment – and a strange wave of feeling for Kaptein Denny – swept over me at the thought that almost within reach had been the help we'd so desperately needed to pull off our plan. The little bastard all in white and gold braid had used me as a bait while he sat at the ringside watching the final drama take place on a radar screen, safe out of harm's way of mines, torpedoes and *Sang A*'s guns . . .

'I don't need a nursemaid – then or now,' I snapped.

He grinned, and I hated him the more for it. 'It seems you've got yourself one. You haven't introduced me.'

'Jutta Walsh,' I said. 'She's part of the story.'

He shook her hand and then swung on his heels, linking his arms in both of ours and leading us along the deck between the crew. I wasn't sure who was more astonished, they or us.

'And it's a long story – from both sides,' he added. 'I think we all could use a drink.'

I'd downed my second pink gin, sitting with the admiral and Jutta in a big private cabin, by the time I'd given him an outline of the events which led up to the last fatal explosion. Because it was nearest in time and so vivid still, I started with it, relating events backwards. When I told him about the Book of Tsu and its naval significance he stirred unhappily in his chair, but he let me finish.

Then he asked, 'When did you get wise to *Sang A*?'

'I found out she had a machine-gun mounted for'ard . . .'

'Ah!' he exclaimed. 'That machine-gun! That's what gave her away to us, too . . .'

'Us?'

'Weeks ago, when you were still enjoying the delights of Santorin, one of our long-range maritime reconnaissance planes located *Sang A* about three hundred miles south of the Cape. We caught her with her pants down. They were exercising with that gun. We photographed her. It confirmed our earlier suspicions.'

'Earlier? What d'ye mean?'

'*Sang A* first came to the Navy's notice when she arrived at Mauritius about two months ago. An agent of ours there reported her – we keep an eye on all the Red Navy's comings and goings now that they use Mauritius as a base for the Indian Ocean. It was a routine report which *wasn't* routine. *Sang A* was at that stage sailing in company with a Soviet *Amur*-class naval repair ship, the *PM 129*, and a modified *Akademik Kurchatov*-class oceanographic ship. At first glance she appeared to be a salvage vessel which the Reds were using in conjunction with the other two. What intrigued Silvermine, however, was that such an old-fashioned type of vessel should be in use with all the modern stuff Russia has nowadays. That ancient funnel and whaleback. At that stage *Sang A* was no more than a tantalizing suspicion. We decided to watch her.

'She sailed from Mauritius – alone. We thought we'd lost her until one of our planes found her again at extreme range between the Cape and Marion Island. The fact that she was so far away from normal shipping routes chalked up another black mark against her. She was photographed and shadowed. The pictures showed she was doing eighteen knots – not bad for the type of old crate she pretended to be. They also revealed something else – part of her underwater lines, as she rolled in the rough seas of the Roaring Forties. We decided that her hull was a modified *Kashin*-class destroyer with all that junk on top as a bluff.'

I refilled my glass. 'It would have helped me if you'd told me some of this.'

'By hindsight yes, by foresight no. What did Silvermine really know? We have suspicious ships passing the Cape all the time. The other day we had an entire Red squadron, complete with the new *Kresta II*-class guided missile cruiser *Marshal Voroshilov*. Our long-range planes shadowed them, too.'

'What made *Sang A* any different?' I demanded.

'I'll tell you. We kept tabs on her as she approached the Cape, both by means of long-range flights and Silvermine's own top-secret electronic detecting apparatus. Then, as I said before, a plane spotted her gun in action. But it was when she used her radio that she gave herself away.'

'What did she say?'

'It's not what she said but the way she said it.'

'I don't get you.'

'We'd been monitoring her signals, of course. They'd ostensibly been directed to the *Basjkiriya*, the ocean research vessel she accompanied to Mauritius, which was then working in the southern Indian Ocean. Incidentally, the *Basjkiriya* was much too near the Kerguelen Islands (where the French intend building a naval base) for anyone's liking. *Sang A*'s signals were in code, naturally, but we had a pretty fair idea of what they were all about.' He chuckled ironically at some inner amusement. 'Weather. Sea. And so on. Another bluff.'

'How'd you know they were?'

'Since your day we've built up at Silvermine an Intelligence service which we modestly think is as good as the Yanks used to have during the war at Pearl Harbour. In the code-busting game you never get more than ten to fifteen per cent of any signal straight; the rest is a lot of inspired deduction from isolated word groups. You also learn to know the "fist" of your opponent – every radio operator has his own way of transmitting. It's an individual as fingerprints. And my men recognized the "fist" of *Sang A*'s operator. He'd been Admiral Gorshkov's – head of the Soviet Navy – own choice for a new type of super-cruiser called the *Kara*. To be in *Kara* he would have to have been tops. We'd spotted the *Kara* on her maiden shakedown voyage south of the Cape.

'All this was mighty interesting, but it still didn't tell us what *Sang A* was up to or where she was bound for. Then, by chance, I myself came in on the code-busting. *Sang A* got off a long message – most of it was lost on us – but my team picked up the words *U-160*. It meant nothing to them. It meant everything to me. After that I was prepared to put my head on a block that her destination was the Bridge of Magpies.'

Jutta said, in a distant voice, as if she were still frozen inside by the disaster she'd witnessed, 'It's history repeating itself.'

The C-in-C gave her a considering glance and went on.

'That's when I decided that you were the man for the job. The lost city was a blind, of course . . .'

I found myself another drink and said dryly, 'I had come to that conclusion myself. '

'You wouldn't have been the man I thought you were if you hadn't.'

He went on, brushing aside the interruption, 'If the Bridge of Magpies hadn't been *Sang A*'s destination, no harm would have been done: Koch would have kept stringing you along. You nearly blew us sky-high when you recognized the picture of the fresco. It *was* Santorin's, of course. Koch touched it up a little. He is quite genuinely a midden-hunter, although he's on Silvermine's Intelligence muster.'

'Was,' I corrected. He stared at me and his face darkened. 'If you take your binoculars you can see his grave next to a burnt-out Land-Rover ashore.'

I told him about it and how Kenryo's gang had killed him and Breekbout.

When I'd finished he said very quietly, 'I'd like to have been able to shake Kaptein Denny by the hand, for what he did at the end.'

After that he also got himself another drink and went to

the porthole and stared out for a long time. Then he swung round on Jutta and said in a matter-of-fact tone:

'You're the only piece of the jigsaw which doesn't fit. You're not a relic of a vanished civilization.'

I rushed to her defence and he gave me an amused man-to-man look.

'I'd like it better in her own words.'

'My father . . .' she began; and told him of her search and researches. As she went along I watched his attitude change. Until now it had been brisk and business-like – with a shade of appreciation – over *Sang A*. Now it softened, if a face hewn by war, sea and command could be said to soften. He went and sat on the arm of a chair next to her and swirled his drink round and round, his eyes fixed on the spinning liquid as if it were a crystal ball which was mesmerizing him by conjuring up the past. He never looked up until she had finished.

She added, 'I missed my chance to speak to you about it when I didn't get to Luderitz. But my own business has been completely lost sight of in these other terrible things that have happened. If it's worth anything now, my file's still open.'

The C-in-C stood up and looked down at her with a curious, unexpected compassion. She met his eyes, startled and questioning. He held out both his hands to her and she raised herself to her feet.

'I think I have a final notation for your file,' he said. He put his arm round her shoulders. 'Come. This is for you alone. It may be something of a shock . . .'

He opened the door and led her out on to the deck and as he did so the sun came out and shone on her bright hair.

Fontana Books

Fontana is best known as one of the leading paperback publishers of popular fiction and non-fiction. It also includes an outstanding, and expanding, section of books on history, natural history, religion and social sciences.

Most of the fiction authors need no introduction. They include Agatha Christie, Hammond Innes, Alistair MacLean, Catherine Gaskin, Victoria Holt and Lucy Walker. Desmond Bagley and Maureen Peters are among the relative newcomers.

The non-fiction list features a superb collection of animal books by such favourites as Gerald Durrell and Joy Adamson.

All Fontana books are available at your bookshop or news-agent; or can be ordered direct. Just fill in the form below and list the titles you want.

- -

FONTANA BOOKS, Cash Sales Department, G.P.O. Box 29, Douglas, Isle of Man, British Isles. Please send purchase price plus 6p per book. Customers outside the U.K. send purchase price plus 7p per book. Cheque, postal or money order. No currency.

NAME (Block letters)

_____

ADDRESS

_____

_____

_____

Geoffrey Jenkins

Geoffrey Jenkins writes of adventure on land and at sea in some of the most exciting thrillers ever written. 'Geoffrey Jenkins has the touch that creates villains and heroes – and even icy heroines – with a few vivid words.' *Liverpool Post* 'A style which combines the best of Nevil Shute and Ian Fleming.' *Books and Bookmen*

A Grue of Ice

Hunter-Killer

The River of Diamonds

Scend of the Sea

A Twist of Sand

The Watering Place of Good Peace

 Fontana Books